PRAISE FOR THESE BESTSELLING AUTHORS

EVELYN ROGERS

"Evelyn Rogers has proven herself to be
the Queen of Gothic Romance."
—*Huntress Reviews*

"Evelyn Rogers has helped revitalize the gothic romance
genre; she takes the classic gothic elements and
turns them into something new and contemporary."
—*Writers Write*

KATHLEEN O'BRIEN

"Ms. O'Brien is a master at crafting stories
that speak to the souls of her readers."
—Diana Tidlund, *WritersUnlimited.com*

"Kathleen O'Brien is a master at her craft,
creating superb, entertaining fiction peopled with
charming, realistic characters. Each of her stories is
wonderfully unique, artfully done and speaks to my
heart in a way that makes me remember the tale
long after the last page is turned. If you're looking for
a fabulous read, reach for a Kathleen O'Brien book.
You can't go wrong."
—Catherine Anderson, *New York Times* bestselling author

DEBRA WEBB

"Debra Webb delivers page-turning, gripping suspense
and edgy dark characters to keep readers hanging on."
—*Romantic Times*

"With her in-depth characterization and
her captivating storyline, Ms. Webb proves why
she is an auto-buy for this reader."
—*WritersUnlimited.com*

W9-CGZ-501

EVELYN ROGERS

was born in Alabama but reared in Texas. Before becoming a full-time writer, Evelyn was a schoolteacher, a librarian and courtroom reporter. She is the author of thirty-one full-length novels and eight novellas, and has written both historical and contemporary romances. But it is gothic romances, that intriguing mixture of love and suspense, that have captured her heart. Evelyn lives in San Antonio and devotes her time outside writing to family and travel.

KATHLEEN O'BRIEN

Three-time finalist for the Romance Writers of America's RITA® Award, Kathleen is the author of more than twenty novels for Harlequin Books. After a short career as a television critic and feature writer, Kathleen traded in journalism for fiction—and the chance to be a stay-at-home mother. A native Floridian, she and her husband live just outside Orlando, only a few miles from their two grown children.

DEBRA WEBB

was born in Scottsboro, Alabama, to parents who taught her that anything is possible if you want it badly enough. She began writing at age nine. Eventually she met and married the man of her dreams. When her husband joined the military, the couple moved to Berlin, Germany, and Debra became a secretary in the commanding general's office. By 1985 they were back in the States, and living in a small town in Tennessee. With the support of her daughters, Debra took up writing again. In 1998 her dream of writing for Harlequin came true with the publication of her first novel.

Evelyn ROGERS

Kathleen O'BRIEN

Debra WEBB

MYSTERIES of LOST ANGEL INN

HARLEQUIN®

TORONTO • NEW YORK • LONDON
AMSTERDAM • PARIS • SYDNEY • HAMBURG
STOCKHOLM • ATHENS • TOKYO • MILAN • MADRID
PRAGUE • WARSAW • BUDAPEST • AUCKLAND

ISBN 0-373-83625-2

MYSTERIES OF LOST ANGEL INN

Copyright © 2004 by Harlequin Books S.A.

The publisher acknowledges the copyright holders of the individual works as follows:

A FACE IN THE WINDOW
Copyright © 2004 by Evelyn Rogers

THE EDGE OF MEMORY
Copyright © 2004 by Kathleen O'Brien

SHADOWS OF THE PAST
Copyright © 2004 by Debra Webb

www.eHarlequin.com

Printed in U.S.A.

CONTENTS

A FACE IN THE WINDOW   9
Evelyn Rogers

THE EDGE OF MEMORY   115
Kathleen O'Brien

SHADOWS OF THE PAST   231
Debra Webb

A FACE IN THE WINDOW

Evelyn Rogers

CHAPTER ONE

HIGH ABOVE the circular drive, evening mist swirled between the twin turrets of the Lost Angel Inn. Like an unsettled ghost, Ellie thought with a shiver. Directly below, welded onto the face of the inn, a bronze angel stood guard, as if holding back any evil the ghost might inflict on anyone who dared enter.

A sense of dread held Ellie in place beside her car.

"Not much inspiration for a rekindled romance," she whispered, breaking the momentary spell.

When she was tense, she talked to herself, or to her late mother. She'd been doing a lot of both lately. Right now she was questioning what she was doing at this isolated island inn off the northern shore of Maine. The man who'd invited her was pleasant enough, sophisticated, handsome, but he did not arouse her to anything more than friendship.

"So who does?" she asked, and answered with a lonely, "No one."

Twenty-eight, a successful designer of Web sites,

she wasn't sure she was capable of being aroused. On this vacation weekend, she hoped to find out.

"Miz Gresham?"

Ellie shook herself from her maundering and watched as a gray-haired, angular man came down the front steps of the inn. He had a sunken, sullen face, and was dressed in loose jeans and a work shirt beneath a worn tweed coat. He could have been anywhere from fifty to seventy.

"Miz Livvy says I was to help you in," he said in a no-nonsense Maine accent.

Ellie clicked open the trunk of her car, but before she could retrieve her suitcase, the man had it gripped in his bony hand and was headed back the way he had come.

"What about the car?" she asked after him.

"Leave the keys. I'll get it."

Ellie glanced around her, but saw only more mist drifting across the crest of the hill where the inn had been built more than a hundred years before. Once a private home, and later abandoned after an old scandal, it had been converted by its newest owner into a bed-and-breakfast. For this—the opening weekend—guests would be asked to solve a murder mystery.

From somewhere in the distance a foghorn blared mournfully. Ellie's eyes shifted to the dark ivy-covered front of the inn, but she thought of the ghost. The inn was supposedly haunted by the spirit of a nineteenth-century chambermaid who had come to an unfortunate end. Through the years the islanders had reported the sound of weeping coming from the attic that separated the turrets.

Instead of keeping the legend a secret, the new owner had played it up in the publicity announcing the mystery weekend. Truth or fiction? she had asked. Whatever the facts might be, Ellie decided, Lost Angel Inn was a perfect setting for a murder.

She stretched her travel-weary muscles, then hurried up the stairs, holding her jacket close to ward off the damp June chill. A wide covered porch stretched across the front of the inn, but before she could give it more than a glance, the front door opened and a woman stepped out.

"Miss Gresham, I've been waiting for you," the woman said, a smile on her pretty face. "The ferry from the mainland is usually dependable, but in weather like this you never know."

Ellie's artist's eye took in the woman with one quick study: above-average height, slender, long brown hair tucked behind her ears, matching brown eyes reflecting the smile for only an instant before a shadow passed across them, as if smiling was something she did not do very often. She wore a black sweater over an ankle-length paisley skirt and heavy, sensible shoes.

Ellie took the extended hand and felt an immediate warmth, a connection she had experienced with only her closest friends. The feeling was pleasant and decidedly welcome.

"You must be Olivia Hamilton," she said.

"Please call me Livvy. I hope all my guests will be on a first-name basis, but if that makes you uncomfortable…"

"Not in the least. I'm Ellie."

Livvy stepped aside and gestured for her to enter. "You're the first to get here, and we're still pulling things together. The inn was closed for so long there's been a lot of work to do—" She broke off. "Please forgive me. If you let me, I'll launch into a description of all the renovations going on."

"I'd love to hear about them."

"But not now. You must be exhausted after your long drive from Boston."

"It wasn't so bad. I broke the trip into several days."

Livvy backed away and Ellie stepped inside a paneled entryway with a polished wooden floor, hall tree, side table holding a large bouquet of spring flowers, more angels in a painting on the wall and a sparkling chandelier hanging from the high ceiling.

Overall, the effect was warm and welcoming, everything warmly greeting though Ellie detected a mustiness beneath the scent of fresh paint. A dining room opened to her left and, to her right, a parlor. But her eye fell to the winding staircase at the back of the entryway. It led upward into darkness.

As if sensing Ellie's unease, Livvy moved with a pronounced limp to the base of the stairs and switched on an upstairs light. "Joseph has taken your bag up to your room."

"I can find the way by myself."

"Don't worry. I manage the stairs just fine. The limp came from an accident of long ago. I hardly notice it now."

Maybe not, Ellie thought, but the fact of it obviously still bothered the inn's proprietor. The memory showed in her eyes, a shadow that belied her words. Ellie sympathized.

As she led the way up the stairs, Livvy described the layout of the inn. Originally it had been L-shaped, but one of the many previous owners had added another wing and a second turret, changing the configuration to a U.

The renovations had been completed in the western wing, where the weekend guests would stay; to the east, in the wing closest to the ocean, there was still much work to be done.

"The young man who's in charge of the work is out searching for period furniture, trying to scour up whatever he can find, especially pieces that were originally in the inn. Chris is a wonder. I don't know what I'd do without him."

As they reached the hallway, Livvy turned to the left, then hesitated.

"You're at the end of the wing in one of my favorite rooms, snug and quiet. I thought I would give the room across the hall to Mr. Davidson. If that's all right. I can change the plan easily enough. He doesn't arrive until tomorrow."

Was it all right? Ellie hadn't seen Curtis Davidson in more than a year, although they had corresponded, the letters warmer on his part than on hers. His call, his invitation for the vacation weekend, was not totally unexpected, nor was it unwelcome. It had come at a time in her life when she wanted to get away.

"No," she said. "Don't change the arrangements. Across the hall will be fine."

Ellie tried to feel the assurance of her words, but by the time Livvy left her to rest before dinner, she began to wonder whether she had made a mistake. With the time for her to meet Curtis drawing closer, her doubts about him and her own ability to handle a relationship with him increased.

Their friendship had been more platonic than physical. Throughout the months of their sporadic dating, she hadn't wanted more than an occasional kiss, and he hadn't pushed the issue. She credited his academic lifestyle—he was dean of a private college—for the absence of passion.

He had even talked once of a more permanent partnership between them—*partnership* being his choice of word—but he had spoken in a thoughtful, almost pensive way that had hardly touched her heart.

What *had* surprised her was how passionate he had sounded over the phone, wanting to see her again to find out if the months apart had intensified the feelings between them. He hadn't spelled out his immediate desire, but he hadn't needed to. He wanted intimacy. He wanted sex. Maybe he even wanted a commitment from her. The only issue remaining was how she felt.

Ellie hadn't been repelled by the suggestion, but she hadn't whooped with joy, either. Mostly she felt tense, uncertain, unsure of where her life was going. In the past few years she'd struggled with the breakup of her parents' marriage and her mother's long illness. She'd been unable to shake the sense of loneliness that had overtaken her. She had men in her life, most of them friends. But no one she wanted to be serious about.

And that had always included Curtis.

He'd never been her dream man, her Mr. Right, someone who could stir her passions, yet was gentle and fun-loving. But maybe nice, safe, steady Curtis was exactly what she needed. She was here to find out. Nothing wrong with that, she'd told herself more than once on the long drive.

Yet, alone in her room, surrounded by furniture from the late Victorian period, including a high four-poster with tufted step stool at the side, she could not settle her unease.

"I'm being silly. I'm too old for girlish doubts."

She could almost hear her mother's answer. *No one is ever that old, Ellie.*

Her lips curved into a sad smile. Three months had passed since she'd lost her mother, but she still felt Joyce Gresham's presence and suspected she always would. With her father and his new trophy wife living in Florida, she needed that presence to give her a sense of belonging somewhere.

She unpacked quickly, changing from her jeans and denim jacket into a pair of comfortable slacks and a sweater, preparing to go down for the evening meal. She wasn't hungry, but Livvy had seemed proud of the food her cook had prepared and Ellie didn't want to disappoint her.

Not wanting to disappoint anyone was one of her flaws.

When she was dressed, she switched off the bed-side lamp, but stopped suddenly when she heard a sound coming from somewhere she couldn't deter-mine; a soft sound that sent a chill down her back.

Standing in the dark, she realized it was the sound of weeping. It drifted into the room from outside, more mournful than the foghorn had been, lasting for only a few seconds before fading, raising prickles along the surface of her skin.

Here was the legendary weeping she'd read about in Livvy's pamphlet. On paper the weeping had seemed enticing. In reality, if the listener believed the publicity, it was terrifying.

Suddenly a scream broke the now-eerie silence. Frightened, Ellie cried out and flew to the side win-dow of the small room. Opening the draperies, she looked out on a world of swirling mist. The wind had risen and she saw the outline of tree branches danc-ing in the gloom.

The air cleared momentarily to reveal the inn's un-opened wing that ran parallel to hers. A light flick-ered in the room directly across the courtyard and she recognized the cloaked figure of a woman, her back to the window as someone moved close to her—a man.

The scene was amazingly clear, no more than twenty feet away. Ellie could see the way the woman's dark hair lay against her collar, the backward tilt of her head as the man moved closer, could see his hands raised, his head bent, and thought she was witnessing a tryst between two lovers. She ought to look away. But then the raised hands came down on the woman's throat and a scream rent the air once again.

Gasping, she slapped a hand over her open mouth and watched in horror as the woman pulled at the hands, her second scream more desperate than the first. The piercing cry was stifled as the grip tightened, its echo even more terrifying than the weeping had been.

Suddenly the woman dropped from view and the man stepped to the window, peering out, as if searching for witnesses, like a villain in a Hitchcock film. Then the curtain of fog returned and Ellie could see only swirling mist and the skeletal tree.

Somewhere in the courtyard a shutter slammed against the wall of the inn, piercing the air like a gunshot, and Ellie stumbled back into the protection of her darkened room. She squeezed her eyes closed, but in her mind she pictured the face of the assailant; lean, shadowed, his hair dark and disheveled, his eyes darting into the night.

She took a slow, steadying breath. Everything had happened in no more than a few seconds. She must have been wrong. Forcing herself back to the window, she saw only darkened windows along the opposite wall, the mist, the wind-tossed tree. The shutter banged once again.

She blinked. She must have imagined the scene. The long drive, her uneasy state of mind. Too well she remembered how she'd seen a ghost in the mist hovering above the inn.

And yet...

She started to run for the door to call for help, but something held her back, something far stronger than any notion of making a fool of herself. She wasn't sure of what she had seen. It was too bizarre, too horrible to be real.

Falling into the chair close to the window, she inhaled deeply. Was she losing her mind? Were the pressures of the past months finally getting to her? She'd always had a vivid imagination. In fact, she relied on it in her design work. But the scene she had just witnessed—or thought she'd witnessed— crossed the line between imagination and delusion.

Maybe.

An answer came and she laughed to herself. A nervous laugh. This must be a start to the weekend, she told herself, the first step in the drama created for Lost Angel Inn by the famous horror writer Denton Drake. Nothing else made sense.

"Oh, my God," she whispered to herself, "I actually fell for it. Some sophisticated city woman I am."

At the window she stared at the dark room across the way. After a moment she closed the draperies, shutting out the night, and went downstairs to find Livvy setting a tureen of soup in the center of the table.

She started to tell the story, then held back. She'd wait until later, after she'd eaten, when she could talk about it calmly.

Dinner was as delicious as Livvy's Web site and brochure had promised: chowder followed by perfectly baked rosemary lamb and asparagus. After what Ellie had experienced the past half hour, she couldn't quite work up the appetite the food deserved, but under the watchful eye of her hostess, she made a valiant effort.

Over coffee and pie, deep in thought, she looked up to see Livvy staring at her.

"Is something wrong?" her hostess asked. "Is it the room? Maybe you don't care for Victoriana the way I do."

"Oh, no," Ellie hastened to say, "the room's wonderful. It's just that..." She had to tell her, she couldn't keep it to herself a second longer. "You ought to know I fell for it."

"Fell for what?"

"The setup murder. I saw it and for a moment believed it was real."

Livvy set down her coffee cup. "I don't know what you're talking about."

Ellie hesitated, suddenly chilled. "You know, the mystery weekend." Even as she spoke, she wished she had not mentioned the incident. But there was no taking back her words now. "I looked out my window and saw what looked like a man choking a woman to death. But of course that couldn't be."

As she was talking, Livvy held very still.

"Of course," she added, hurrying on, "with the wind and the fog and the shutter banging, I couldn't be exactly sure what I saw. I can only say what I *thought* I saw."

"Where did you see it?" Livvy asked in a tight voice.

"In the room opposite mine. In the eastern wing. The curtains were open and—"

Livvy stood abruptly. "I'll have to check it out."

This wasn't the reaction Ellie had expected. She'd wanted a laugh and a you-caught-us look.

Instead, Livvy was taking her seriously.

"I'll come with you," Ellie said.

Livvy didn't try to argue, and both women hurried from the dining room and up the stairs. As she opened the door to the eastern wing, the smell of dust and freshly sawn wood struck Ellie. When the hallway light came on, she could see a row of doors similar to her own hallway, three to a side, except here the carpet was tattered and needed replacing and half the doors were ajar.

But not the last one. Livvy used one of the keys to open it. Reaching inside, she snapped on an overhead light and Ellie stared into an empty room. Faded paper on the wall, faded carpet on the floor, there was no sign it had been occupied in a long while.

Relief struck her and she realized she had been holding her breath.

"I know it's silly, but I heard the scream coming from here, right after the weeping. That's why I looked outside. And then saw…something, I'm not sure what right now."

Livvy turned to face her. "The weeping," she said as if the one word answered everything. "You read about it, didn't you?" She sounded relieved.

Ellie nodded. "It dates back to when the mansion was first built. The first owner was stabbed and all suspicion fell to a chambermaid."

"She was convicted and hanged."

"But she swore her innocence and called down a curse on the house." In Ellie's mind she could hear the weeping, as pitiful as before, and she shuddered. "The locals say she still cries for absolution."

Too well Ellie remembered the details of the story, about the handsome and charismatic young senator who had built the house for his bride shortly after the Civil War. He'd brought her here on their wedding night. After he'd been stabbed, after the chambermaid's curse, his widow had suffered a miscarriage and hanged herself, dying just as her husband's killer had done.

Through the next century the curse had become more specific: every twenty years—to commemorate the age of the chambermaid when she died—someone would meet an untimely end. Some of the islanders swore by the legend. They pointed to the accidental or suspicious deaths in or near the house that had occurred in the appropriate years. The staunchest believers, relating the stories that had been passed down to them over time, attributed seven deaths to that curse.

Others scoffed. But the legend remained.

And this was the twentieth year since the last death, when a beautiful young widow had suffered a fatal fall from the cliff close to the inn. An accident, authorities had ruled, and nothing had been proven otherwise. But the publicity had been enough to close the place, until tonight.

"There's been much unhappiness here," Livvy said, as if she could read Ellie's mind. "I hoped to change all that."

"I'm sure you will."

Ellie wasn't sure she believed her own words. She was brushing off the incident, chiding herself for taking it too seriously, but the heaviness in her heart would not go away.

What if she really had witnessed a murder?

Impossible. Things like that didn't happen in her ordinary world.

As they walked down the long hallway, Livvy pushed open the door to each of the rooms, but instead of a woman's body or a lurking killer, there was only more dust, more work to be done. It was apparent no one had been in them for a while.

When they returned to the hall connecting the wings, Livvy shrugged, her expression calmer.

"I guess you were right. It must have been the wind or the fog. This is the kind of place that works on the imagination. That's one of the reasons I bought it."

Bidding her hostess a good evening, Ellie went to her room, where she spent a restless night.

The next morning a pretty young woman, who introduced herself as Beverly, delivered a tray of coffee, fruit and hot muffins. As Ellie ate, she looked out her window to beautiful sunshine. The window to the room across the way was wide open, its interior as empty as it had been in last night's search.

Even the tree, rising from the center of the court-yard, had ceased its wild dancing and Ellie could see the early leaves on the branches she had thought skeletal.

She couldn't have witnessed a murder. True, she'd been jumpy since the death of her mother, at loose ends, not her usual no-nonsense self. But she hadn't been delusional. She recognized that her mother didn't really answer when Ellie spoke to her.

Fresh air was what she needed, maybe a hike into town. Tugging on jeans and a sweatshirt, she hurried out of her room.

Downstairs she heard voices in the dining room and went to investigate, hoping that Livvy would give her directions for her walk. She found the owner of the inn talking to a man she took to be a second guest. He stood with his back to Ellie, a tall man with dark hair that brushed against the collar of his shirt, a leather jacket worn over jeans, everything casual, but obviously expensive. Interesting, she thought, and felt a rare, small flutter inside.

Livvy stood in front of him. When she spied Ellie, she smiled. Any worry from last night's events had vanished, or at least been carefully hidden beneath a patina of graciousness.

"Ellie, I'd like you to meet another of our guests, Jeff Cunningham. Jeff, this is Eleanor Gresham."

The man turned, smiling, as Livvy went on. "If you don't mind, I'll leave you two to get acquainted. I need to find Joseph."

She departed quickly through the back door of the dining room, and Ellie gave her attention to this second guest. At first she was aware only of the strong, handsome features, the interest in his incredibly blue eyes, the electricity that passed between them as they stood alone together.

Then reality took hold and she took an involuntary step backward. Swaying, she waited for the sudden dizziness to pass.

Jeff was certainly darkly handsome and very appealing, but he was also the man she had seen in the window.

The man who had strangled a woman to death.

CHAPTER TWO

"Is SOMETHING WRONG?" Jeff Cunningham's eyes turned dark and assessing, and his smile died. "You look like you've seen a ghost."

Not a ghost, a killer.

"You," was the only word Ellie could manage. She fought the urge to rub her eyes, to make certain the face she was staring at was the same face she'd seen last night.

But she didn't have to rub her eyes. She already knew.

He cocked an eyebrow. "You want to tell me what's going on? I may not sweep women off their feet, but I usually don't terrify them."

She wiped her palms against her jeans. "You're not really terrifying me. It's just that I thought I saw you last night."

Light, keep it light. But he must have heard the tremor in her voice.

"I'm sure I would remember seeing you. Was it on the mainland?"

"No, here at the inn."

"I rode the ferry over this morning."

"No," she said, unable to stop herself. "You were here last night, standing in the room across from mine. You were with a woman."

"We must have been doing something very bad."

"As a matter of fact, I could've sworn you were choking her."

Even as Ellie said the words, she knew how absurd they sounded. Wanting to take them back, she tried to pass them off with a smile. While he was smiling in return, she saw a glint in his eye that wasn't especially comforting.

Why shouldn't he be a little upset? She'd just called him a killer.

"Last night, you say."

"After ten." The more Ellie talked, the more ridiculous the accusation sounded, but she couldn't stop. "You were in the room opposite mine, at the end of the unopened wing. The lights were on and the curtain open. Everything was quite visible."

Or so it had seemed at the time.

"You'd think I would remember something like that," he said, and she was distracted by his infectious grin. They might have been talking about a movie they'd both enjoyed.

Except for the glint that did not quite go away.

"Livvy insisted on investigating," she added.

"And found?"

Here was where she began to feel really foolish.

"Nothing, of course. But you could've taken her body with you." The words didn't come out quite as lightly as she'd intended.

"I just said 'poof' and the two of us disappeared."

"You're making fun of me, Mr. Cunningham." Ellie's head began to pound. "Look, this is an absurd conversation. I thought what I saw was the beginning of the mystery weekend, but Livvy says no. There was a lot of fog and wind whirling about the court-yard between the two rooms. The only thing I don't understand is why I saw your face so clearly. I'm certain we've never met."

"I'd remember if we had. And please call me Jeff."

She sensed his interest in her. Not in what she was saying but in Ellie herself. It was, she had to admit, the way she had been interested in him.

He was flirting, and she found it a relief. He was, she had to admit, a very attractive man. But she didn't want him laughing at her.

"It would be a shame if word of this got out," he

added. "Some of the Mainers around here aren't particularly thrilled about the reopening of the inn."

"Why on earth not?"

"They don't like strangers coming into their world and they don't mind letting their views be known."

"I don't plan to say anything to anyone. I feel foolish enough as it is."

"Don't feel foolish. Maybe your seeing me was a kind of precognition. You knew me before we met. Sounds like destiny to me."

Ellie's heart skipped a beat, which could be the most ridiculous reaction she'd experienced yet.

Looking at him and not remembering last night was difficult. Looking at him and not touching him was difficult, too.

She stared at him for a long moment, at the sharp planes of his face, the thick brows, the deep-set eyes. And the mouth, curved in a small smile, as if he shared some kind of secret with her.

But she sensed that he wasn't totally relaxed. Nor was he completely dismissive of her story. Whoever he was, Jeff Cunningham was a complicated man.

And Ellie did not need more complications in her life.

She needed air. She needed space. With a good-bye nod, she hurried from the dining room and out the front door, down the steps, not stopping until she stood on a narrow path that wound alongside the eastern wing of the inn. She paused to take a deep breath.

What's going on here? I've never reacted to a man like this.

If her mother was listening, she had no words of explanation for her daughter, no advice, no guidance. For reasons she couldn't begin to understand, Ellie felt more alone than she'd felt in a long time.

On impulse, she began to explore the courtyard between the two wings. She circled to find a lovely, manicured stretch of green with freshly planted beds, picnic tables and chairs, an old dry fountain that had not yet been restored, and the tall, budding tree she had seen outside her window last night.

Moving deeper into the courtyard, she spied a series of ground-level doors along each wall. One in particular caught her eye, almost hidden in the interior corner under the eastern wing. Something moved her toward it, almost as if she were being propelled against her will. She quickened her step in its direction, looking around to see if anyone was watching, feeling inexplicably guilty, as if she were doing something wrong.

But that didn't keep her from opening the door

and slipping inside. Then through a second door, she found herself in a narrow hallway with doors at each end. Curiosity drove her forward. The furthest door opened into a small, cluttered office she took to be Livvy's center of operations. The other door revealed a large empty kitchen.

But it wasn't the office or kitchen that got her attention. It was the corner staircase winding upward into darkness. She'd seen no sign of such a staircase when she'd gone upstairs last night.

Estimating the width of the inn and the width of the hall, she decided the steps led to the towering turrets and the attic where the legendary weeping supposedly originated.

Here was an exit for the man she'd seen in the window.

For a moment fear returned, and she hurried out to sunlight, back to the path at the side of the inn, lecturing herself not to panic, not to run. She had enough worries in her life without letting her imagination create more.

STANDING QUIETLY in the dining room, contemplating this sudden turn in events, Jeff Cunningham ran a hand through his hair. Ellie Gresham was trouble. He hadn't expected someone like her to show up. She was appealing, he had to admit. Pretty, fine-featured with bouncy, honey-colored hair and eyes as big as golden coins.

But those eyes saw far too much, and their owner didn't hesitate to talk about what she'd seen. Or thought she'd seen. She was most definitely mistaken, but being wrong didn't keep her from talking about it.

"Is something the matter, Jeff?" Livvy spoke from the kitchen doorway. "When I was upstairs I heard raised voices from down here." And then, as she looked around, "Where did Ellie go?"

Jeff shrugged, his mind working fast as he turned to face her. "Your first guest at the inn has a vivid imagination."

Livvy sighed and her eyes rounded with worry. "She told you about last night."

"She told me a pretty wild story."

"She thinks it was staged as the beginning of the mystery weekend."

"But it wasn't."

"No," Livvy said gravely, "it wasn't."

He could hear the question in her voice, the need for reassurance. He gave it to her.

"I didn't sneak upstairs and choke a woman to death. Whatever she saw, or thinks she saw, it wasn't that."

"Of course not. But if she keeps talking about it, she could cause trouble. I dread to think what Chief

Fraley would think if he heard her story. She's passing it off as a fantasy, but he might not agree."

"Let me deal with this. I'll try for some damage control."

Livvy's eyes were warm and moist as she smiled her thanks. "This is the second time you've come to my rescue."

"Hey, if it takes a third, I'm your man."

"I'd better get busy with lunch. More guests should be arriving soon on the morning ferry."

Jeff watched her leave, thinking her limp was more pronounced today than the last time they'd talked. He shifted his eyes toward the front door. Yes, Ellie was trouble. He'd best forget her face and her eyes and the fit of her jeans, and treat her with all seriousness.

He had his own plan, his own agenda, and he could not let Eleanor Gresham get in his way.

CHAPTER THREE

TAKING A DEEP, settling breath, Ellie hurried down the path that wound through the landscaped hilltop, past shrubs and boulders, the level packed dirt changing to a sandy walkway. At last she passed through a thick, dark stand of trees that rose like a wall against a stretch of thick grass, arriving at the flat, rocky surface that marked land's end.

A small, weathered sign swayed in the wind close to the edge.

Danger. Keep Away.

Ignoring the warning, she moved toward the sign and stared at the wooden staircase that zigzagged down the face of the cliff to a small beach. Huge boulders surrounded the strip of sand, protecting it from the crashing waves.

Hastily she stepped back. The staircase, its wooden steps gray with age and decay, looked as if it hadn't been used in years.

With the wind whipping her hair, she stood and

stared at the endless ocean, a rolling gray-blue that stretched beneath a remarkably clear sky all the way to the horizon.

She looked again at the waves crashing against the jagged rocks of the rugged Maine shore, nature's beauty mixed with jarring violence. When she thought of the woman who had fallen to her death on those rocks twenty years before, her heart pounded painfully.

Closing her eyes for a moment, she willed herself to calmness, but she took another cautious step away from the edge.

Feeling better, she studied the rest of the scenic wonder that was Lost Angel Island. Farther around the coastline to the left, she could see the town of Cliff's Cove, its buildings, houses, docks nestled along a bend in the land, taming the violence that lay a short distance away. She directed her vision carefully until everything within her line of sight, from the soaring birds to the church steeple rising from the town center to the boats in the bay, looked peaceful, the tranquillity of this lovely island undisturbed.

Again she closed her eyes, breathing in the brisk salty air, seeking that same tranquillity in her heart and mind. The effort ended with the sound of footsteps behind her. She turned to see Jeff Cunningham approach.

Instinctively she moved farther away from the cliff's edge. He stopped a dozen feet from her, tall and lean, hands at his sides, the expression on his sharply hewn face too intense to be friendly or comforting. Still, despite all the warnings she gave herself, she felt a jolt of attraction.

"I'm sorry," he said, "you left so quickly, and I wanted to be sure you were not taking all this seriously."

All this? What was he talking about? Last night, him, what?

For a moment, with the wind ruffling his dark hair, he looked almost boyish. But he wasn't a boy. He was a complicated man.

He gestured toward a bench she hadn't noticed before. The bench was carefully placed against the stand of trees so that anyone sitting there could stare at the distant horizon. The view of sunrise must be spectacular.

"Let's sit and talk awhile. Get to know one another. You have to admit, Miss Gresham, we got off to an unusual start."

"Ellie."

It was easy—too easy—to be friendly toward this man. Despite the warning voice in her head, Ellie found herself going to the bench, where she sat and leaned back, keeping her eyes on the expanse of water, wishing they weren't quite so alone. Listening for a spiritual word of advice, she heard only the whisper of the wind.

You're on your own, the whisper seemed to say.

She was not comforted.

When he sat beside her, their bodies, their clothing, did not touch, but she was acutely aware of his presence, aware of how he studied her before turning his attention to the sea.

She took a quick glance at him. His profile was sharp, his cheeks hollowed, his skin shadowed by the hint of bristles. Nothing about him was soft or gentle. For some reason she thought of the waves crashing below.

"Let's start again. Where are you from, Ellie Gresham?"

The question was far more benign than his looks, and his voice was wonderfully deep and rich.

"Boston," she said, clasping her hands in her lap. What harm could a little conversation do? She wasn't going to get involved with him. Precognition indeed.

"That's a long way from Lost Angel Island," he said. "Did you fly up?"

"I drove up the coast, taking my time getting here."

"It's a long way to drive for a weekend vacation."

She started to tell him about Curtis Davidson, about his invitation and the chance for a renewed relationship, but something held her back. Her reluctance was something else she would have to analyze later. For now, she felt as if Curtis did not exist. She also didn't feel the least bit guilty about forgetting him.

"I needed to get away for a while," she said, studying a bank of clouds that had begun to move in from the horizon. And then, another response she had not planned, "I lost my mother to cancer a few months ago."

He nodded, as if he understood the pain, the sense of desolation, of rootlessness that had taken hold of her since that loss.

"So what do you do in Boston?"

"I design Web sites."

"How does one get into work like that?"

"Mostly you teach yourself, which is what I did."

She went on to explain how her degree in graphic arts helped, how she'd started by working for a Boston advertising firm before setting up her own small business. She also told him about jogging along the Charles River three times a week, her interest in local theater, the Boston Museum of Art, a jazz club near her apartment.

She kept the discussion light. She talked about her pastimes, her special interests, her daily routines. She did not mention her dreams, her fears, the longings that haunted her in the middle of the night.

And she certainly did not talk of her conversations with her mother. Joyce Gresham's continued presence in her life was her secret. Ellie was suddenly aware that the front she presented—the calm, self-assured woman talking about herself to an interested man—was very different from the private insecure person who was struggling to make sense of her world.

By the time she fell silent, Jeff Cunningham could have written a biography of her life without getting to her heart and soul.

"Any love interests?" he asked.

"Too personal," she said, and meant it. "What about you?"

He hesitated, but his expression gave no hint of his thoughts, only that they were not easy to explain.

"I'm gainfully employed—"

"That's not very specific."

"I'm a contract worker."

"A builder?"

He thought a minute. "Of sorts, and a designer. I live in a small town in upstate New York, I've never married but haven't ruled out the possibility in the future. And I've never harmed anyone in my life."

Not yet.

Ellie could almost hear him saying the words, and she was plunged back into the nightmare she'd experienced briefly last night. Was he deliberately trying to confuse her? If so, he was doing a good job.

He seemed so reasonable, and everything around them so normal. The sun bright on the water, the sounds of cawing birds and the rustle of the trees that clung to the rock near land's end, even the thunder she heard in the distance wasn't at all like last night. As long as she didn't think about those crashing waves.

Or remember the image of his face in the window.

Ellie sighed. There she was, taking it seriously again.

"Did you hear weeping?" he asked, and she thought he must be reading her mind. "That's what most people claim to hear," he added.

Yes.

"I heard a scream," she said, letting his specific question go unanswered. "Or what sounded like a scream. The wind was making quite a racket at the time."

"And you're a woman with an imagination. You'd have to be, considering your profession."

Oh, yes, she had an imagination. Hadn't she been thinking what touching him would feel like?

She changed the subject. "Do you know Livvy personally? Have you been here before?"

"Why do you ask?"

"Because you mentioned ugly stories coming

out of the inn could cause trouble for her with the townspeople. How would you know that without inside information?"

He stared at her for a long unnerving moment, then shrugged. "The truth is simple and rather boring. I know small, insular towns. The inn will bring strangers. The old-timers around here don't like that."

He smiled at her. It was a very nice smile and it softened the lines of his face.

"Like you," he added, "I'm a guest for the weekend." He glanced out to sea, at the distant darkening clouds. "This is a perfect place for a mystery to unfold. The old legend about the widow who killed herself, the servant hung after slaying her master, the sudden death every twenty years. Do you know how the island got its current name?

"The story goes that when it was first settled it was called Cliff's Island, like the town of Cliff's Cove. Then a child wandered into the water searching for her drowned father and was never seen again. The island's name change was in tribute to her. Eventually the inn itself—once it became an inn years ago—changed its name accordingly."

"Lost Angel." Ellie shuddered. "How sad."

"Early death is always sad."

The bleakness in his voice prompted her to say, "You sound as if you've lost someone."

He shrugged. "I was speaking hypothetically."

Ellie didn't believe him, though she could not have said why. So what did she believe about this man? She lived such an ordinary life. Could she possibly sit beside a killer and carry on a quiet conversation? How could she talk with him, confide in him, feel herself drawn to him?

The truth was she couldn't. Therefore she had to be wrong about last night. Didn't she?

She looked down at the blunt-fingered, strong-looking hands he was resting on his thighs. An urge to take one of those hands struck her, to hold it in both of hers. She resisted the urge, not wanting him to think of her as truly delusional, believing she could comfort him in matters she didn't know anything about, matters he wanted to keep to himself.

Whatever events Livvy had planned for the weekend, for Ellie the real mystery came in the form of the man sitting next to her. Not Mr. Right. Not the gentle, fun-loving, openly sympathetic man who visited her in her dreams.

But as she sat next to him, her thigh close to his, glancing at his masculine profile, listening to his deep voice, she definitely felt a spark ignite within her. Sympathy, character, humor had nothing to do with it. His appeal was purely physical.

The realization was startling. For the first time she understood the moth's fascination with the flame.

He glanced at her and their eyes met. She was not the only one ignited. Her glance fell to his mouth. A nice mouth. A great mouth; firm, thin but not too thin. She was about to lift a hand to touch his lower lip when she heard voices and laughter coming from the trees. Guiltily she jumped to her feet, pushing her hair from her face, hoping no one could see how her cheeks were burning.

"Hi, you two," Livvy said as she neared the bench, a half-dozen people in tow. "I was taking your fellow guests on a short tour of the grounds."

She spoke in a sprightly manner, but her eyes held a questioning look as she glanced at Jeff. He gave a brief nod, imperceptible if Ellie hadn't been looking at him. What was that all about? Suddenly she felt cold inside.

Livvy went through the introductions quickly. Elton and Grace Simpson, a middle-aged couple, both comfortably rounded and gray-haired; a younger pair in their late twenties, Bob and Lori— she didn't catch their full names—who stood close together holding hands; a flashily dressed woman in her forties, Andrea Delgado, introduced as a widow; and, trailing them all, Curtis Davidson.

"Ellie, dear," he said, stepping around the others,

taking her hand and brushing his lips against her forehead.

He was looking especially dashing this morning, his brown hair stylishly cut and combed, a beige wool jacket tailored to fit his broad shoulders handsomely, a toast-brown shirt open at the throat to reveal a strong neck. With his even features, his face carefully shaved—in contrast to the sharp, shadowed look of Jeff—he was every inch the college dean.

Except for an intensity about him that she had never seen before. It shook her for a moment, but that's all it did. She did not feel a spark.

She pulled free. "I hope you had a pleasant journey." Mundane, but under the scrutiny of everyone, it was the best she could come up with.

"Most certainly, though I was impatient to get here."

There was little doubt she was the cause of the impatience.

"Oh, my," the widow Delgado murmured with a trill, staring at Curtis through thick-lashed gray eyes, her scarlet lips pursed. "Are we having a little tryst? Forgive me, I do speak my mind."

Ellie gave her a more thorough look. High cheekbones, skillfully applied makeup, long, thick hair an unnatural black, she gave no sign of her age, except in the wrinkles at her throat.

Curtis chuckled. "Ellie and I are old friends. Make of that what you will."

"I most certainly shall," she responded, her eyes narrowing to shrewdness. She stepped close and linked her arm in his. "I do believe we're going back inside for lunch." She smoothed her hair, a useless gesture in the constant wind. "Please escort me back and tell me all about yourself. Eleanor will have you to herself soon enough."

He gave Ellie a helpless shrug and a wink that promised more than she wanted to think about. In the months since she'd last seen him, Curtis had changed.

She watched the pair lead the way toward the inn, a gust of wind pushing them forward. She started after them, listening to the chatter of the others as they questioned Livvy about the island. She came to a halt when she realized Jeff had not fallen into step.

Turning to face him, she caught a harsh look on his face and an anger that stunned her. His eyes were cold and cruel. For a moment she couldn't breathe.

"Be careful, Ellie. Be very careful over the next two days. Take this as a warning. I won't be held responsible for anything that might happen to you," he said in a dispassionate tone. Then he hesitated a moment. "Leave. Go back to Boston, or anywhere. Just get the hell out of here."

With that, he turned in the opposite direction, away from the inn, his long legs taking him along the edge of the cliff, then down the hill. Like magic, he dropped from sight, leaving her to stare after him, to listen to the echo of his words.

She felt as if he had struck her. What had happened to the congenial charmer who'd sat beside her on the bench, who'd started her thinking about things she didn't know lay in the back of her mind? He was neither congenial nor charming now. He was frightening.

Had Curtis's warm attentions effected such a change?

Maybe Jeff expected her to play one man against the other, flirting with one at a time. How absurd.

But misreading her intent should not have angered him so completely.

The thought occurred that maybe he was unstable, incapable of dealing with the obvious sexual attraction they had shared before the others had arrived. At least the attraction was obvious to her.

She burned with embarrassment and, to her surprise, her eyes misted. If that's what he'd meant, he need not worry. His precious body was safe from her lustful hands.

The trouble was, she was too emotional, too on edge. And she most certainly was not—she was *not*, she repeated to herself—a frustrated spinster letting her unfulfilled urges push her into seeing things that weren't there. Such an absurdity was for head doctors and fiction writers to contemplate.

Pulling her jacket close, she hurried toward the inn while she wondered what she was going to do about Curtis. A friendly Curtis she could deal with, but not the intense man he was today.

Some carefree vacation this was turning out to be.

And the mystery part of the weekend, the planned mystery, had not yet begun.

CHAPTER FOUR

ACCOMMODATIONS AT THE INN included breakfast and dinner, with lunch optional for an additional fee. On this first full day of operation, however, Livvy offered her guests a noontime meal laid out in the dining room, after which she would direct them to a boat excursion leaving from the town dock.

"If," she said, "the storm holds off. Sometimes it does."

Wonderful, everyone agreed when they returned to the inn. Only Ellie didn't respond. And of course, Jeff, who hadn't put in an appearance.

Throughout the meal, Ellie sat on the edge of her chair, unable to relax, unable to eat more than a bite. Where was he? What had he meant?

He was up to something, something that boded ill for someone. Her? That made no sense, but she was the only guest he knew. Livvy? He'd seemed very protective of the inn's new owner. Was he a true friend? Was he her lover?

Ellie pushed the thought from her mind.

Leave.

The harsh word echoed in her mind, but it remained as illogical as it had when he'd flung it at her.

He'd meant to frighten her. And he had.

Dimly, she was aware of the conversation around her. The Simpsons would soon be celebrating their thirtieth anniversary. Bob and Lori, whom she took to be lovers, did not seem nearly as contented as the older couple. But that was no more than an impression, and she gave the couple little thought.

Except for when the maid, Beverly, brought a tray of food from the kitchen and lingered for what seemed an excessive amount of time beside Bob, placing the bowls just right on the table in front of him, as if her pay depended upon this part of her job. As for Bob, he smiled sweetly at her, especially whenever her breast brushed against his arm.

The widow Delgado, seated across from Ellie and Curtis, noticed, too, and she and Ellie shared a brief, knowing glance. If Lori saw anything, she gave no sign.

The widow shifted in her chair, obviously bored by the talk, until Curtis let it slip—his words—that he was a college dean in the western part of the state, the author of a couple of philosophy of education books, a bachelor and long-time friend of Ellie's.

A friend she'd only occasionally heard from since his move to Maine, she might have pointed out. He didn't bother to explain that part of their relationship.

Ellie watched the beaded sweater stretched across Andrea Delgado's ample bosom rise and fall with each breath. The light from the chandelier reflected off the silver surface of each bead. The sight hypnotized Ellie, almost made her quit worrying, quit trying to understand what she had wandered into in this seemingly placid place.

"Ellie."

She looked at Curtis, who was leaning close. He was frowning. He must have said her name more than once.

"Are you all right?" he asked.

Suddenly she was aware of the silence around the table.

"I'm afraid I've come down with a headache," she said, and it wasn't a lie. She smiled at Livvy, who was standing at the head of the table. "I think I'll skip the boat ride and take a rest this afternoon." Her eyes relayed what she didn't say. *I didn't sleep well last night.*

"Of course," Livvy said. "I'll have a cup of tea brought up to you."

"Please don't bother."

Ellie pushed from the table and, with a nod to the

gathering, hurried from the dining room and toward the stairway. Curtis was at her heels. When she reached out for the banister, he grabbed her hand. She tried but could not pull free.

"Get whatever rest you need," he said, all sympathy. "I don't have to go on that boat, either. I can stay here and make sure you're all right."

She shook her head and immediately regretted it when tiny hammers pounded at her temples.

"No, please don't. I'm sure after a little sleep I'll be fine."

He chuckled. "I hope so. We've got so much to talk about. I can't tell you how much I've been looking forward to this weekend."

Then he pulled her close and kissed her, the deed accomplished so quickly she didn't have time to maneuver out of reach, his lips moist and soft and not in the least arousing.

"I should have done more of that before," he said warmly. "Being away from you showed me how wrong I was to break off our relationship."

But he hadn't broken it off. Neither of them had done anything so definite. And he had kept up their correspondence without a great deal of encouragement from her.

She'd met him in Boston while he was on a leave of absence from his position in Maine. "A sabbatical rest," he had said, from the demands of his work. He hadn't spelled out what those demands were, and she hadn't asked. When it came time for him to return home, they'd shared a last dinner and a hug goodbye, with a few hints of regret at what might have been.

This time when she tugged at her hand, he let her go and, without looking back, she hurried upstairs. Curtis was being kind, thoughtful, affectionate. So why couldn't she think of him romantically instead of thinking about a dark and angry man ordering her to get the hell away?

WEARING PANTIES AND BRA, Ellie slipped under the covers. But the instant her head touched the pillow, the storm struck and she spent the next few hours tossing, turning, trying to read, listening to the rain strike the window, listening to the roar of the wind.

Listening, too, she confessed, for the sound of weeping. But she heard nothing but the storm.

After what seemed an eternity, it was time to get dressed for dinner. She took a quick shower in the small adjoining bathroom, set her jeans aside and slipped into the nicest dress she had brought, a scoop-necked, sleeveless green silk sheath, just far enough above her knees to show off her legs. To

counter the evening chill, she draped a fringed multicolored shawl across her shoulders.

She hesitated for a second about putting on her stiletto heels. Then she slipped into them. She wasn't
planning a nighttime hike, she told herself. And
dressing up—for whom, she did not ask herself—
made her feel better after everything that had taken
place.

Before leaving to go downstairs, she stared from
her room at the darkened window across the way.
The storm had passed and the first stars of evening
were beginning to appear. Everything was quiet.
Everything, even the courtyard tree, was still.

Take care, Ellie.

The murmur of her mother's voice quickened her
heart. The clarity, the seriousness of tone, stunned her.

"Take care about what?" she whispered.

*Take care of yourself. And pay special attention
to Jeff.*

Ellie clutched the shawl close. "Why? What's
going on?"

But the whisper did not return and she was left
staring into the night, questioning herself and everything about Lost Angel Inn, wondering if she
wouldn't be smarter to crawl back into bed and pull
the covers over her head and wait until morning to—
as Jeff had put it—get the hell out of here.

But she didn't feel especially smart and so she locked her room and headed downstairs.

The other guests had already gathered for cocktails in the long, wide parlor. She could feel the tension the instant she walked into the room. It rose like an invisible wall to confront her. No one was looking directly at anyone else, no one was talking, no one even stirred.

Except, unfortunately, for Curtis, who appeared openly and disturbingly pleased as he strode toward her, all smiles and compliments when he took her hand and asked her what she would like to drink.

A woman could ask for nothing more from her man. The trouble was that Curtis wasn't her man. She might be exploring the possibility, but right now the possibility of a future with him was fading fast.

As for the way she was dressed, she simply wanted to look her best.

She could almost hear her mother laugh.

"White wine," she said, and as he went to the ornately carved dark-wood bar that Livvy had set up at the side of the room, she made a quick survey of the other guests. She didn't have to look for Jeff. She'd spotted him immediately standing by the fireplace at the far end of the parlor.

He'd changed into chinos and a V-necked pale blue sweater. Even from a distance, she could see the flash of warmth in his absurdly blue eyes. He must know the sweater brought out his coloring. What he didn't know—what she *hoped* he didn't know—was how his appearance gave her a kick in her midsection. A good kick, if there was such a thing. A powerful, lusty kick.

She truly was losing her mind.

Proof came in the quick way the warmth of his expression turned to disapproval.

So be it. She lowered the shawl, exposing the low line of silk over her breasts. Taking the glass from Curtis, she drank it down, then held it out for a refill.

"Feeling better?" he asked with a smile.

"Much."

She spoke the truth. She'd eaten only a little at lunch and the alcohol hit her with a punch. She wasn't much of a drinker, but this was just what she needed—a brief respite from reality, an admiring man, people around her, a feeling of recklessness that, if she kept a little control of herself, could not lead her astray.

"Good," he said, leaning close and speaking softly into her ear. "We've had a rather difficult time of it down here. With the storm, we were thrown into each other's company rather soon. A few hours with strangers playing parlor games. It was a bit of a strain."

"Oh, dear," she said, looking around the room, taking in everyone but Jeff.

"I've had some experience with group psychology. It seems to me no one likes anyone else. Except for you and me, of course. That goes without saying."

Ellie's spirits sank lower, but she was saved from responding when the maid entered with a tray of hors d'oeuvres. Ellie declined, keeping to the wine, then watched idly as Beverly took a position behind Bob and Lori, looking around the room but obviously listening to what the couple was whispering about.

At least, Ellie thought, the two were keeping their disagreements to themselves.

"Ladies and gentleman," Livvy said from the doorway, "please take a seat. First, let me assure you the weatherman promises to cooperate tomorrow and for those who would care to go on the boat excursion, arrangements can be made. Next, I need to explain how the mystery is going to work."

Their hostess was wearing a floor-length black wool skirt and a tucked-in sweater the color of old gold. She looked lovely, Ellie thought, but the smile on her face did not hide the tension around her eyes. This weekend could ensure success for her bed-and-breakfast, or doom it to failure. Ellie's heart went out to her, along with her admiration for tackling such a challenge all on her own.

What could have made the woman leave California, gather her resources and buy the old inn? Ellie couldn't ignore the feeling that something more than the accident that had left her with her limp had brought Livvy to Lost Angel Island. Was it her connection to Jeff Cunningham?

Was he her friend or her lover? Of course, Livvy's relationship with him was absolutely none of Ellie's concern.

But she had seen him in that window. She couldn't be wrong. Funny how the wine had cleared her head enough to allow her to see the truth.

She caught Curtis staring at her.

"Good wine," she said, lifting her glass. Indulging in subterfuge wasn't all that hard, she was finding.

Knowing Jeff watched her, she let Curtis lead her to a love seat. She sat and crossed her legs, not bothering to tug at her skirt, which was hiked to midthigh.

Jeff remained by the hearth as Livvy began to speak.

"As you know, the famous writer, Denton Drake, has been kind enough to create a mystery scenario for this opening weekend."

"Isn't he that horror writer?" Mrs. Simpson asked, then shuddered. "Please tell us he hasn't come up with anything as gruesome as his books."

"Don't worry, Grace. I promise you're safe," Livvy said, still smiling.

I hope, Ellie thought.

"But I must warn you," Livvy went on, "that not all the people here at Lost Angel Inn are the way they are presenting themselves."

Eyes immediately began to dart around the room. Everyone's eyes but Jeff's. He kept them trained on Ellie.

Livvy waited until she had everyone's attention once again before continuing.

"Get to know one another so that when one of you turns up dead—" she nodded at the nervous laughter "—you can begin to figure out the culprit. This isn't a contest so you can work on the solution alone, in pairs or as a group, however you choose." She smiled. "I've never done this before, but we have a great script and I think this will be a lot of fun."

Ellie wasn't sure she sounded convinced, and she vowed to do what she could to make the mystery a success.

"So will we meet this Drake?" Elton Simpson asked.

"I'm sorry," Livvy said. "He's quite reclusive. I'm not sure where he lives in Maine. We've communicated by e-mail. But rest assured the mystery will be a challenge without being threatening.

Beginning tonight, look for clues not only identifying the villain but also his or her victim."

"Oh," Grace Simpson said with a trill, "this is exciting."

Ellie wasn't sure *exciting* was the right word. She glanced at Jeff. The harshness, the disapproval, on his face was gone, and he was, as he had been once before, all innocence, looking past her to the others, taking a survey, playing the game as Livvy had suggested.

Unstable, she thought. He had to be, considering the way he kept changing moods.

But that didn't keep a persistent butterfly from fluttering in her stomach. She finished her wine and looked away, wishing Curtis wasn't sitting quite so close.

"I'll leave you all now and see about dinner," Livvy said. "Clara has prepared something very special for us. I hope you'll be pleased."

In her absence, no one spoke for a moment.

"What kind of clues are we supposed to look for?" Grace Simpson asked the room at large.

"They probably won't be too subtle," Lori said.

"You wouldn't catch them if they were," Bob muttered loud enough for all to hear.

Lori didn't pretend to misunderstand. "Are you saying I'm stupid? I've about had it with your cracks."

So much for the hand-holding, loving couple who'd arrived hours ago, Ellie thought. Apparently they'd given up the pretense that all was well between them. Beverly must have got an earful standing so close behind them.

"We have to be very careful how we use words, don't we?" Grace said to no one in particular. "Comments can so easily be misunderstood."

A peacemaker, Ellie thought. Her mother had been like that, wanting everything to be pleasant, hardly saying an ill word about anyone, not even the young woman who had taken her husband away.

Andrea Delgado stood, tossed back her mane of black hair and headed for the bar.

"I find actions always speak louder than words," she said. "Trite, I'm afraid, but true."

She was wearing tight black pants and another beaded sweater, this one black with gold trim and scooped lower over the bosom than Ellie's green silk. After fixing herself a shot of Scotch over ice, she returned to her chair and settled back comfortably, obviously used to the kind of attention she was getting.

"On the other hand," she said, "maybe we should try words. We can tell a little about ourselves, then decide individually who's lying."

A moment of silence ensued.

"I can start," Grace said, and no one looked surprised.

"No, I will," Andrea snapped. "After all, it was my idea."

Taking a sip of Scotch, she raised her thick black brows and looked around the room, her gaze lingering on each of the four men, passing over the women almost as if they weren't there.

"I've buried three husbands, live handsomely on my inheritance in Bar Harbor, and I'm not planning on taking a fourth to my bed. Not for wedded bliss, that is." She laughed throatily. "Other kinds are negotiable. When I read about this mystery weekend thing, I decided it sounded interesting. I do like to try new experiences."

New men, she might as well have said.

Her declaration stopped conversation, but not for long.

"Goodness," Grace exhorted. "I don't know how to top that."

But she wasn't deterred for long, promptly launching into a long story about her childhood on a Midwestern farm, her marriage, the move to Pennsylvania, then to Maine, the children, grandchildren, more details than anyone cared to hear, even her husband, who bore the patient, pained look of someone used to such lengthy discourses.

When Grace was finished, the young couple stirred.

"I don't think that's what Livvy had in mind," Lori said sharply, and Ellie began to take a dislike for her.

"If you know so much, demonstrate," Bob said as he got up to freshen his drink.

The couple were dressed casually, he in an open-throated brown shirt and slacks, she in a short, loose-fitting yellow cotton dress and flat sandals.

"Well, I'm twenty-five, single but not unattached—" she flicked a challenging glance at Bob "—and I'm an administrative assistant at an Augusta law firm near the capitol."

"I'm the law firm," Bob said.

"Like hell," Lori said softly but loud enough for Ellie to hear.

Bob flushed with anger. "I'm a junior partner, that is."

Ellie noted that he did not say he was single, nor whether he was unattached. Lori's narrowed eyes showed she'd noted the same.

"Is it true what they say about lawyers?" Andrea asked.

Grace bit. "What do they say?"

"That you can tell one by his briefs."

Grace took a moment to think it over, then giggled. Bob shook his head. Lori smirked, but her response was for Curtis.

"Do they say anything about college deans? Something about how they make the grade? Do they grade on the curve? Surely there's something. A clever man like you would know."

Her flirting was more unexpected than it was discreet. Was that a glint of appreciation in Curtis's eye? If so, it didn't last long.

He patted Ellie's free hand. She eased it away and curled it in her lap.

Instead of being discouraged, he put his arm around her. "I've made no secret why I'm here." He smiled at her. "Want to tell everyone why you're here?"

She slipped from his embrace and stood. "Time for more wine," she said, and this time she poured it for herself. Everyone was waiting for her to say something. Especially Curtis. From the smug look on his face, she wondered if he was expecting a toast in his honor.

He didn't get it. Instead she told about her work in Boston and the need for a vacation, without saying exactly what had brought on the need.

"When Curtis sent me the information on Lost Angel Inn, I thought it would be a wonderful place to get away for a while."

Curtis obviously didn't like what he'd heard. From the anger flashing in his eyes, she knew he didn't like it at all. But she wasn't about to lie.

An awkward silence ensued, broken by Andrea Delgado's sharp laugh.

"We find the strangest things about one another, don't we?" She glanced toward the fireplace. "Jeff, it's your turn."

Before he could answer, Livvy arrived to announce dinner and they all went into the dining room. Conversation was civil for a while, small talk, the weather, a possible trip into town before the big murder the following evening.

And then the argument started. Ellie wasn't quite sure how it began, but it centered around something Bob or Lori had said. They were hissing at one another. Grace was trying to break in with a peacemaking comment and her husband Elton was whispering to her to stay out of it. Suddenly Bob was pushing away from the table and throwing down his napkin.

"Please excuse me," he said to everyone. "I'm going to call it a night."

He no sooner had left the room when Andrea stood and stretched.

"I'm exhausted. Inactivity always tires me more than anything."

She practically ran from the room.

"Guess where Bob's spending the night," Lori said. "I think I'm going to have another drink." She looked around the table, her eyes lingering on Curtis. "Anyone want to join me, feel free to come on over."

Then she was gone on her hasty return trip to the parlor.

Suddenly, Ellie could take the tension no longer.

"Excuse me for a few minutes," she said, pushing back from the table, hoping Curtis thought she was going to the rest room. Feeling Jeff's intent eyes on her, she hurried from the dining room, but instead of going toward the stairs, she went out the front door, finding the path that wound through the grounds of the inn.

Someone had artfully placed soft lights in the shrubbery and beds lining the walk, and she had no trouble finding her way. A rising moon and a canopy of stars helped. Taking a deep breath of the cool night air, she held her shawl tight around her shoulders and made her way quickly to the trees, stopping half a dozen yards from the Danger sign at the edge of the cliff.

She stood for a moment staring at the moonlight on the water, thinking how peaceful the scene appeared, thinking, too, how deceiving appearances could be.

She was also thinking she definitely shouldn't have worn stiletto heels.

Then, strangely, the ground began to shift beneath those heels and she heard a rumble behind her. She turned in time to see something big and dark roaring out of the trees in her direction, moving fast, giving her no time to move out of its path.

CHAPTER FIVE

SUDDENLY, ELLIE FELT herself being swept into a pair of arms that came from out of the dark, solid and sure and unrelenting as they jerked her to safety. No more than a second passed before a giant boulder tumbled toward the cliff's edge, thundering by so close she felt the rush on her bare legs.

In an instant the boulder was gone, crushing everything in its way before shooting into space, falling silently to the waiting rocks and water below. She scarcely heard the crash over her racing heart.

Trembling, she clung to her rescuer, too frightened to cry, to speak.

Soothing words finally penetrated her skittering thoughts. She pressed her hands against a broad, strong chest and felt a heartbeat thundering in time with her own.

Gradually the supporting arms loosened their hold on her and she looked up into Jeff's dark eyes. In the moonlight she could see his fury, but as they looked at one another, the fury blazed into an emotion far hotter, a passion that would have scared her even more if she hadn't felt the heat inside of her. Heat that had nothing to do with fear.

He cupped her face. "You're all right," he whispered huskily.

"I'm all right."

She wasn't sure she spoke the truth. She didn't know what *all right* meant anymore.

She would have told him so, but he brought his lips to hers and she let her answering kiss tell him what words could not say.

What they were doing made no sense, but she couldn't stop, couldn't pull away. Emotions she had never experienced swirled through her. She couldn't think, couldn't begin to reason. The brush with death had rendered all thought unimportant, leaving only feeling, as if this were the right and only way to rejoice in life, and this the only man with whom to share that joy. He made her forget everything but him.

He broke the kiss, but kept his lips maddeningly close to hers.

"I followed you," he whispered.

"If you hadn't—"

Her voice broke, her mind unable to think the unthinkable. For a moment terror returned, bubbling inside her, threatening to explode.

"I saw it," he said, brushing at her hair. "It came out of nowhere. I didn't think I could get to you in time."

She pushed away just far enough to look into his eyes. "But you did."

She heard the wonder in her voice and a thick communicating need for another kiss. His lips moved toward hers once again. A not-too-subtle cough sounded behind them and they slowly parted.

She backed away and saw Curtis standing on the path, his stance rigid, his eyes blazing, even in the moonlight, and for a moment he resembled a wild animal that had lost its prey.

She brushed the thought from her mind. She wasn't thinking clearly. He was angry because he'd found her in another man's arms, that was all. With more reluctance than she would have imagined possible, she put space between herself and Jeff, then had to hold on to his arm for support when she found her stiletto heels mired in the muddy ground close to the path.

"I'm not dressed for this," she said, trying to speak lightly but unable to suppress the quaver in her voice. She was still terrified, and she wondered if her heart would ever slow to a normal beat.

She made it to the path, then gave her attention to Jeff. The pale moonlight was kind to him, soft-

ening the planes of his face. In that moment he was
the most beautiful man she had ever seen.

But it was more than his physical appearance. He
had saved her life. For a moment, as she watched
him watching her, she felt a warmth burgeoning inside, strong enough, sweet enough to ease her fright.

Then she looked away, embarrassed that he might
see in her eyes something she didn't understand herself. She focused on the edge of the cliff, and on the
Danger sign now more ominous than ever.

"What happened? I'm not sure I know."

"I'm not sure I do, either. I was walking along
when I saw something crashing through the trees."

"The rock, right?" she asked. "I got only a
glimpse." But it was a glimpse that would stay in her
mind forever.

Jeff nodded. "Then I saw you."

Ellie could feel the burn of tears, a silly reaction
now that the danger was past.

"The rain must have washed the dirt from under it,"
Curtis said, walking closer. He took Ellie's hand and
pulled her toward him. "Livvy ought to be more careful. Let's go back and let her know what's happened."

Ellie felt trapped. She wanted to pull free, but his
grip was strong and she didn't want to make a scene.

"Please don't say anything. At least don't tell her
my part in it."

Already she'd called attention to herself as a pur-
veyor of doom. And there was nothing Livvy could
do about something that was obviously an accident.

Curtis took another view. "My God, Ellie," he
said sharply, "you could have been killed."

"But I wasn't. The only things harmed are my
shoes."

Curtis's expression turned to a smirk. "Women.
Worried about your shoes."

Ellie wanted to kick him or to at least wipe her
heels against his pristine trouser leg. In her ire she
was able to pull free.

"There seems little purpose in staying down here.
I'm fine. A hot bath is what I need right now. And a
good night's sleep."

She spoke the last words to Curtis.

Don't come knocking at my door.

Even he should get the implication. But before he
could speak, she hurried on.

"I can get back on my own. Don't worry about es-
corting me."

She glanced from man to man, including them
both in her pronouncement, but she knew she lied.
She would have enjoyed walking back to the inn
with Jeff, to her room, to whatever else the night held
for them both.

But looking at him now, she could not read his expression. She would have liked a smile, a nod, something to let her know he was thinking about the kiss they had shared. But he wasn't looking at her. He was looking at Curtis.

She didn't understand him. She didn't know what he wanted from her. Or what she wanted from him.

But she was a big girl. She'd been on her own for a long time, including the months she'd spent nursing her mother. Pulling her shawl tight around her shoulders, she took a long look at the surrounding dark. She did not look at the men.

"If I don't see Livvy," she said, "I'm sure one of you will tell her what happened. Please let her know I'm not complaining, and I'm perfectly all right."

She made the walk back to the inn quickly, saw Lori sitting in the parlor with the Simpsons, but Livvy was not in sight, and she hurried upstairs for the hot bath and the soft, warm bed that she needed more than she cared to admit.

After the bath, using the tufted step stool, she climbed onto the high bed and pulled the covers to her shoulders.

Then she began to tremble, a delayed reaction, she told herself, to what could have been a fatal accident. Curling into a tight ball, she heard the earth rumble beneath her, saw the dark object rolling toward her like a messenger of death, gathering speed, coming at her with explosive speed.

Her heart pounded and she cried out softly, until she felt Jeff's arms. Suddenly she was flying through the air, free from the demands of gravity, with Jeff holding her tight, keeping her safe.

This was madness, everything in her imagination an exaggeration of reality, a distortion of a sudden and terrifying event.

But a small, barely audible inner voice counseled that not everything she was remembering was wrong. When Jeff Cunningham kissed her, she had been transported in several ways...from danger, most certainly, but also into a frantic vortex of passion. Strong words—*vortex, passion*—fantasy words, but they were not exaggerations. Nothing resembling the power of his kiss had ever happened to her before. He made her blood boil.

It had to be the near-death experience that made her so receptive to him. She could allow herself no other belief. Jeff wasn't Mr. Right, he wasn't funny, kind, considerate...

Ingrate, the voice said. *He saved your life.*

And hadn't the ability to arouse her passionately been one of her requisites? The one she wondered if any man could meet?

Jeff did. In spades.

Yet she knew she'd seen him last night. Could it be only twenty-four hours since she'd looked out her window and watched in growing horror a scene right out of a movie?

She'd lived a lifetime in the past night and day.

Listening to the wind keening outside her window and the scrape of tree branches against the side of the inn, she waited for the sound of weeping, the anguished cry of a long-dead woman unable to find eternal peace.

But the weeping did not come, not this second night. She heard only the wind and the creaks of the old house settling down for the night, and at last she fell into a deep sleep.

She didn't waken until she heard a soft knock at her door. Easing from the bed, she pulled on robe and slippers and opened the door to see Livvy standing in the hallway, a tray of muffins, coffee and fruit in her hands.

Livvy's face was lined with worry and there were dark circles under her eyes. Still, she managed a smile.

"This is the second morning in a row I've had breakfast up here," Ellie said, stepping aside to let her enter.

"It's my pleasure. It's so late, I was worried about you."

Ellie brushed her hair from her face and stepped aside. "I'm fine. Please come in. What time is it?"

"Close to nine."

"It can't be. I never sleep this late."

"You must have needed the rest. After last night." Livvy's voice was heavy with regret and apology.

"Curtis told you."

"Yes. Jeff came in later. He'd been searching for the place where the boulder had come from. I can't imagine such a thing happening. Joseph is out now making sure nothing else like that can happen. I've put the gardener to work on it, too. If there's any way I can make up for it, I promise you I'll do it."

"It was a freakish thing," Ellie assured her, taking the tray and setting it on the table close to the window. "And there was no harm done."

Livvy bit at her lower lip. "Still, it shouldn't have happened. It's almost like—"

"Please don't say like an omen." Ellie opened the curtain to let sunshine stream into the room. "Look, it's a beautiful day. If you're choosing evidence of what the future holds, choose that."

Livvy smiled, but there were tears blurring her eyes. Ellie hurried over to give her a hug.

"I mean it. Thanks for breakfast. You must have a dozen things to do. I'll get dressed and be down before long. And I'm going to have a great day. I will accept nothing less."

"I owe you," Livvy said.

"You've already paid in full. Those muffins smell delicious."

"They're Clara's doing. The best thing I did was hire her as cook."

"You've done hundreds of good things, Livvy. This room, the renovations to the inn. Remember, I saw the other wing and know what these rooms looked like before you and Christopher, the miracle worker of yours, got to them."

She had meant the words as a compliment, but they served only to stir up the memory of everything that had occurred last night.

An uneasy silence settled between them, then Livvy smiled.

"Dress for a boat ride. I was able to arrange one for this morning about ten. It will be cold out on the water, so bundle up."

"Is everyone going?" Ellie tried to make the question sound casual, but she caught the understanding look in Livvy's eyes.

"Everyone. Curtis, Jeff, everyone."

She mentioned the two names as though Ellie could have her choice of either man.

Jeff won hands down. Sort of. If only he weren't

so changeable. At least Curtis was predictable. She always knew how he felt, even if his feelings were not what she wished.

With a sigh, she fell to her breakfast. Today, she told herself, she would be out in broad daylight with others close around. Nothing bad could happen to her today.

She waited for the voice of her mother to contradict her, but all she heard was the sound of a bird singing in a branch of the tree. A good sign, she told herself, even after the singing stopped and the bird took wing, taking the music and a little of the day's beauty with him.

CHAPTER SIX

EVERYBODY BUT THE squabbling Bob and Lori met on the front porch for the walk down to Cliff's Cove and the dock where the boat awaited. Livvy accompanied them to complete the arrangements with the captain.

The town was busy on Saturday morning; shoppers, joggers, bicyclists moving up and down the main street that fronted the bay. More than a few paused to stare at the visitors. Livvy nodded and smiled when she caught someone's eye, but no one came over to wish her a good morning.

"I need to get back to the inn," she said when the arrangements were completed. "I need to check a few things with the housekeeper. I want to make certain everything's all right."

She spoke with her usual efficiency, but Ellie could see in her carriage and drawn features she was trying to keep from breaking down.

With a wave to her guests, Livvy began to retrace her steps along the waterfront street.

"Hold up there a minute," Ellie heard someone call out gruffly. She turned toward the speaker, a florid-faced portly man in a policeman's uniform, his polished badge shining in the sunlight.

Ellie watched as he ambled over to her, making Livvy wait while he took his time. Ellie walked toward her, ready to back her up in whatever complaint the law might throw at her.

She didn't have to wait long.

"I heard someone almost got killed at your place last night," the chief growled.

"Chief Fraley," Livvy said, paling, "who told you that?"

"You ought to know that nothing goes on around here without my hearing about it."

Fraley grinned, full of himself, Ellie thought.

"It wasn't much of anything. A loose rock," she said. "And I'm the one who should know, since I was standing near the cliff as it rolled by." She smiled. "If that's the worst thing that happened on the island last night, you've got a peaceful little town to watch over."

She looked behind her at the weathered docks extending into the water, at the variety of boats anchoring down the sides, at the clear blue sky, the birds, the few unfurled sails flapping in the breeze.

"A lovely town," she added. "I'm so glad I had a

chance to see it." She almost batted her eyes, but figured that would be overkill.

The chief eyed her with suspicion. "I heard it was more than a rock."

"I'm sure you did," Livvy said. "You know how stories build around here. Who told you this one?"

"That's none of your business, Mrs. Hamilton. You ought to know by now I keep on top of things. I'm watching you," he warned, his eyes taking in both her and Ellie, then moving on to the guests standing on the dock. "Make sure nothing else goes wrong up there or I'm closing you down."

"You can't do that," Livvy cried, losing her composure.

"Something wrong?" Jeff asked as he joined the gathering.

"Nothing you can fix," Fraley snapped. Then back to Livvy. "Remember what I said. I told you nothing good would come from opening that old place again."

With that he turned and crossed the street, headed back toward the two-story white building with City Hall written above the front double doors.

"What an unpleasant man," Ellie said.

"He thinks he's doing his duty," Livvy said, but she couldn't hide the worry in her voice. "Somehow I got off on the wrong foot with him. As far as he's concerned, I should never have reopened the place. I haven't done anything right since I got here."

Then she brightened, as if she realized she was presenting the wrong picture to her guests.

"Some people are never satisfied," she said.

But conviction was not in her voice.

Ellie knew why. Something was wrong at Lost Angel Inn. Something was terribly wrong. She'd known it that first night, before she'd walked through the front door, and she'd felt it ever since. Her heart went out to this woman who was trying with everything she possessed to see her dream fulfilled.

Ellie spared a quick glance at Jeff. He was looking at Livvy in a way that said he shared her thoughts. He, too, knew something was wrong, something as threatening as it was mysterious.

Maybe that something was Jeff Cunningham. She'd thought it before; maybe she should think it again.

Before she could consider the possibility further, Curtis appeared at her side. He was dressed in white slacks and jacket, with a captain's hat worn low on his forehead, the perfect costume for a boat ride. Everything he wore seemed like that: clothes chosen for their effect on others, not because of comfort or fit.

Ellie found herself wondering if he was all he appeared, a respectable college dean hoping to form an attachment with a former acquaintance. A silly thought, but it nagged at her.

Then she glanced at Jeff. His expression as Curtis approached stunned her. She had never seen such undisguised hate in the eyes of anyone. It came at her in waves, like heat, and she felt grateful that it was not directed at her.

In a flash, the hate was gone, replaced by the bland expression Jeff frequently wore the way Curtis wore his carefully chosen wardrobe, but the change had come too late. She'd seen the emotion on his face.

For her, whatever joy had been in the day before the police chief's warning evaporated into the salty air.

She rubbed at her arms, chilled despite the sweater she had on. When Curtis took her arm, she shared a brief glance with Jeff. His expression hardened before he looked away.

Her stomach knotted. She shouldn't let him get to her this way. Why couldn't she forget that moment on the cliff when he'd looked down at her, so full of concern until he was sure she was all right?

And then the kiss. Why couldn't she forget that, too?

She would, eventually.

"Let's have that boat ride," she said with a forced

smile, pulling free of Curtis's hold but falling into step beside him as she hurried toward the dock, thinking that if things went as badly they had been going, the craft on which they would be sailing would spring a leak and sink into the bay.

She was wrong about the sinking, but not about the way things were going. As they cruised on the choppy waters, standing along the railing, staring out at the curved shoreline, Grace Simpson was struck with seasickness and had to retreat into the small cabin, her husband helping her, carrying the bucket provided by the captain.

The cabin walls were mostly windows, and there was no avoiding Grace's condition. When one of the captain's men brought out the sack lunches Livvy had prepared, no one had much of an appetite.

And no matter what Ellie did, Curtis stuck to her like the salt spray on her skin, despite Andrea's obvious attempts to attract his attention.

Jeff was no help. He stood at the stern of the boat, watching the wake as if it were the most fascinating thing he'd ever seen.

All in all the outing, like her entire weekend so far, was not a rousing success. Danger, the sign had read at the edge of the cliff. It was in the wrong place. It should have been on the front porch of the inn.

And wasn't that a terrible thing to think about Olivia Hamilton's dream?

By the time the boat docked and the small group of vacationers had made their way back up the hill, Ellie was in a foul mood indeed.

She felt close to despair. A man had finally made her realize what really could happen between a man and a woman, then he'd turned cold, almost hostile, as though he hadn't meant to arouse her. Now he seemed to wish she would simply go away and not bother him anymore. The same man might be guilty of murder, except that she was possibly hallucinating that whole incident.

And the man she was supposed to welcome into her embrace, if only as an experiment to test her emotional capabilities, made her skin crawl whenever he came close.

As they walked up the front steps, Ellie was already thinking about how she could let Curtis know once and for all his company and his attentions were not welcome—she was, after all, paying for her own accommodations. Suddenly a scream rent the air. This time she wasn't the only one who heard it.

"My God," Grace Simpson cried, "what was that?"

"I'll find out," her husband Elton said. "You stay here."

"No," she said stubbornly, holding on to him. "You stay here, too. We don't know what it is."

Livvy appeared in the door, a wan smile on her face.

"We've had our murder," she said. "Beverly just found Lori Webster's body."

Grace swooned.

"Don't worry, honeybunch," Elton said, struggling to hold her up. "This is part of the mystery."

"Yes," Livvy said, "it most certainly is." Her smile strengthened. "Let's go inside and look for clues."

Ellie held back. "Where is she?"

Livvy could barely meet her eyes. "In the eastern wing."

"The last inside room," Ellie said, not bothering to put the words as a question. Livvy nodded.

"How did she die?" Jeff asked.

"She was strangled."

Ellie looked at Jeff, but he wasn't looking at her. He was watching Curtis.

"I'm certain we can figure it out," Curtis said.

"I'm certain we can," Jeff said. "Some of us already have."

He was talking about something else. Ellie was sure of it. But what?

"Bob did it," Andrea announced, flouncing up

the steps and settling her slim behind on the porch railing. She was wearing navy slacks and sweater, the latter decorated with studs in the design of an anchor. Another costume, Ellie thought.

"How do you know he did?" Grace said. "Just because he wasn't with us…oh, I see what you mean. Who else could it have been? I mean, none of us was around."

"It appears to have happened before we left," Livvy said. "But come on in. You're supposed to figure it out for yourselves."

One by one they went inside and trooped upstairs, none of them particularly eager to see a dead body, even if it was a pretend death.

Ellie stood at the doorway to the room where the woman calling herself Lori Webster lay, one arm stretched over her head, the other resting at her side. She looked horribly real in her make-believe death, legs twisted to one side, her blouse pulled askew over the band of her trousers, revealing an expanse of pale skin at her waist. Only the slight rise and fall of her breasts gave evidence she was still alive.

Ellie stood in the doorway, feeling as if an invisible wall had dropped in front of her. She couldn't go in. The memory of her mother's lingering death, her own near-death, the strangulation she'd already witnessed…it was all too much.

There was evil in that room. She knew it, and so did someone else. But who? And why had it come to Lost Angel Inn? She couldn't bring herself to believe in the chambermaid's curse. Yet it was proving the easiest explanation for the darkness she felt around her, even in this well-lighted room.

She barely heard the Simpsons and Andrea talking, speculating, Grace tittering more than she was actually reasoning things out, Andrea making pronouncements about how the culprit was obvious, even if the murder had taken place early in the morning.

Enough. She could barely breathe.

But this new, emotional Ellie was no more eager to cause a scene than the old one. So without saying a word to anyone, she backed away from the door, planning to head for her room.

She backed into a hard body and turned around to look into Jeff's cold blue eyes. She swallowed a cry, but she didn't move. He seemed to want to touch her, but dropped his hands.

"Going somewhere?" he asked.

"I don't find this game any fun."

"Maybe it's not supposed to be."

"That doesn't make any sense."

"What else does? I told you to leave. You should have listened to me."

"You send mixed messages. I don't know which one to believe."

She felt an unexpected urge to cry and closed her eyes to blink back the tears. When she looked at him again, the coldness in his expression had disappeared, replaced by something hotter, more explosive, something akin to desire. Which didn't make any sense at all. She couldn't breathe, couldn't think. The world had gone mad, and she along with it.

She turned to see Curtis watching the two of them. In his eyes, a distant look, as if he was looking at them but seeing something, or someone, far, far away.

Without another word to either man, she fled down the hallway, not stopping until she was standing in front of her door in the opposite wing.

When she was inside with the door locked behind her, she slid to the floor and sat hugging her knees to her chest. She still had to get through dinner, and then the long nighttime hours before she could do the one thing Jeff really wanted her to do.

Leave!

No weeping, no whispers from her mother indicated whether Ellie would be doing the right thing.

Right or wrong, it was the smart thing. And it was long past time she started acting smart.

CHAPTER SEVEN

"ISN'T THIS FUN?"

Grace put the question to the guests gathered around the dining table, sounding as if she couldn't quite bring herself to believe her own words.

"Hilarious," Andrea answered flatly, her eyes trained on Curtis.

No one else responded. Ellie concentrated on her soup.

"Come now," Curtis said, full of good cheer. "We just have to stay in the spirit of the thing. A murder has been committed. Who did it? We thought at first Bob Cooper was responsible, but Livvy assures us he checked out early. He'd already left the inn when she was killed."

"When she was strangled," Jeff said.

"Yes, of course," Curtis said. "If you want to be specific."

"Strangulation calls for very strong hands. I don't think a woman could do it. That leaves only Elton, me and you, if, as Livvy says, Bob was long gone by the time the murder took place."

An uncomfortable silence settled on the group, broken by Grace's laugh.

"Elton?" she asked with a trill. "You really suspect Elton? He can't stand to put a mousetrap in the barn."

"That's what cats are for," her husband said. "We sure got plenty of those danged animals hanging around. Let 'em earn their keep."

"What a relief it is that in this twentieth year since the last death, the old curse seems to be satisfied with a pretend death," Curtis said.

"Yes," Jeff said. "A relief. But I wonder whether it echoes the real world, a beautiful young woman breaks off with the man she's supposed to love, then turns up dead. She must have become involved with someone dangerous, someone lethal."

Curtis cocked a brow. "Unless the murder was committed by a stranger, a random death that happens so often in our modern world."

The two men looked at each other, as if no one else around the table existed. An uncomfortable silence settled between them, broken by Livvy's cough.

"Of course this one's not random. That's the point of the mystery weekend," Livvy said, but the words came out barely above a whisper.

Ellie wondered whether Livvy was regretting her decision to stage a murder in a house haunted with mystery and frightening legends.

But it wasn't the game that was the problem. Another force seemed to be at work here. Ellie was more convinced than ever that despite the pretty floral wallpaper, the polished floors, the myriad angels decorating the rooms, something was terribly wrong.

She set her folded napkin beside her place. "If you'll excuse me…"

Without meeting anyone's eye, she hurried from the room. Behind her she heard Grace say, "I hope the poor dear's all right. She's looking very pale."

Ellie didn't hang around to hear if anyone agreed. She needed fresh air. Without bothering to get a wrap, she hurried out the front door and down the steps, then into an enveloping fog that was drifting over the island from the ocean. It blurred the driveway, the landscaping, even the lights along the winding path.

Tonight, instead of sexy silk and stiletto heels, she was wearing slacks, a loose-fitting sweater and sensible shoes. When she'd made her appearance at dinner, Curtis hadn't looked nearly as appreciative as he had the previous night.

And Jeff had hardly looked at her at all.

So her outfit wasn't pleasing to them. Tough. It was perfect for a nighttime stroll.

Walking in a world of gray, she kept on, moving slowly, following the path she could still see at her feet, taking one slow step at a time until she had made her way to the side of the inn.

"Ellie."

She jumped. "Jeff, I didn't hear you."

He was at her elbow. She could barely make out his features in the fog.

"You shouldn't be out here," he said. "It's not safe."

"I shouldn't be here period. Isn't that what you mean?"

He didn't answer for a moment. She couldn't hear him breathe. But he loomed tall and strong beside her and she felt as if they were the only people in the world.

He touched her hair; that was all it took. She was in his arms and he was kissing her again, his mouth covering hers, his tongue thrust between her lips. She grabbed his arms and answered the kiss, making it long and deep and as intimate as such a kiss could be. He made her dizzy, he made her want him, he made her love him, if only for the moment. It didn't matter who or what he was.

He broke the kiss, then with a low groan kissed her again, his arms tight around her, pulling her hard against him, trapping her hands against his chest. She wanted to crawl inside his skin.

When he suddenly thrust her away, his hands cruelly gripping her arms, she swayed toward him, then held still, willing herself looking at him coolly, though she still burned inside.

"I know," she said. "You don't have to tell me again. I shouldn't be here. I must be a terrible inconvenience."

He loosened his hold on her, but his eyes kept her in place. "You're a torment."

"What every woman wants to hear."

"Ellie—" He ran a hand through his hair. "Damn."

"You seem at a loss for words."

"You don't know how ironic that is."

"I don't understand."

He shook his head. "Damn it, of course you don't. You don't deserve what's happening to you."

She laughed. "I might agree with you if I could figure out what's going on."

She was giving him a chance to explain. He didn't take it.

"I'm not leaving you out here alone. If I have to throw you over my shoulder and carry you inside, I will."

"That sounds like a hoot. For Livvy's sake, I'll take a pass."

Leaving him standing on the path, she hurried

back to the inn. In the foyer she glanced at the people still in the dining room. No one looked her way and she moved quietly up the stairs, stopping on the second-floor landing, but she was too tense to go to her room.

The door at the end of the landing must lead to the back stairway, the one she'd only partially explored. Without questioning the wisdom of what she was doing—why should she start now?—she eased through the door, then closed it behind her. Groping for a light switch, she found it and turned it on. The wall fixture illuminated steps that wound upward to what she supposed was the eastern turret and the attic. Time to find out for sure.

As she climbed farther from the light, the curved walls began to close in on her and she felt a bubble of panic rise in her throat. When she came to a small landing and a second door, she turned the knob and was relieved to feel the door opening outward. Its creak was like a scream in the night, but she pushed on and stepped onto a walk connecting the two turrets.

Misjudging the width of the walk, she stepped out too far. Only a high railing kept her from hurtling over the side, and she swallowed a cry.

She took a couple of deep breaths. Calmer, she realized that on her arrival that first night, this was where she had seen the fog swirling, its movement reminding her of a restless ghost. But there was no ghost here, only the silhouettes of two turrets piercing the black sky and a distant foghorn with its mournful cry.

Standing at the railing, she looked out at the darkness and listened to the crashing of the waves against the rocky shore.

And she thought about all that had happened, unable to make sense of anything, not what she'd seen or imagined or been threatened by. Jeff didn't make sense. Curtis didn't make sense. Nothing made sense. How could she have thought for even a second that she might be falling in love? She was sex-starved, that was the problem. She'd come a long way to find that out.

And if her inner voice protested her conclusion, she decided to pay no attention to it. Facts were facts. Jeff would never know how easily he could have climbed into her bed.

It was a depressing thought. All it would take to complete her mood was the sound of weeping, or warning whispers from her mother, but she heard only the sound of her own breathing and the beating of her heart. She had no idea how much time passed—a minute? an hour?—but when the door creaked open behind her, she jumped and whirled around, her back to the railing, the panic returning as she swallowed a cry.

In the dim light she was able to make out Curtis's face and she breathed a sigh of relief. Irritation, too, but mostly relief.

"Ah, at last I've found you," he said, coming to stand close to her.

Too close. She took a backward step.

"Why are you looking for me?"

"You ought to know that, Ellie. I've made no secret of how I feel about you."

"You kept it to yourself in Boston."

"I was a fool in Boston. I didn't realize it until I got back to the college and saw the years stretching out in front me, years without you."

"Look, Curtis," she said, rubbing at the throb in her temple, "you're a nice man, but we simply don't suit one another."

No sooner were the words out than she felt a change in him, a coldness that came on in an instant, and she began to be afraid.

"That's what the others said."

"The others?"

"We don't suit." He said the words mockingly. "Can't you women come up with a better line than that?"

Slowly she began to inch her way along the railing, toward the door.

"You're a wonderful friend. Smart. Educated,"

she said. "You're handsome, too. I'm proud to be seen with you. But that's all. I'm sorry. I wish there could be more."

All the while she spoke, she kept moving.

"Sorry?" Again he mocked her, his voice cruel. "If you're not now, you're going to be."

"What a tease you are, Curtis," she said, playing the fool, and then she lunged toward the door. He caught her by the wrist and twisted her arm until she cried out in pain.

"I'm going to strangle you, you know. Just the way I did the others."

He spoke flatly, as if he was discussing the weather. Her heart stopped. She had never faced insanity before, but she faced it now. She could see it in his eyes.

"I'm sorry there were others, Curtis," she said in a gentle voice, the way she might talk to a child. "Maybe you could tell me about them. Then I would understand how you feel."

"You're not at all like Jennifer. When I told her what I was going to do, she started screaming."

"You had to quiet her, didn't you?"

"Missy didn't scream. She tried to run."

"But you're fast, aren't you?"

"I keep in shape."

"I can tell."

Keep him talking. Keep moving. Both were hard to do when she was frozen with fear.

Then he smiled. She hadn't believed she could be more afraid, but the smile pushed her close to panic.

"I know. I won't strangle you. You've done some strange things since you got here, claiming to have seen a murder... Oh, don't look surprised, I know about that. There was your mother's death, the divorce, your father's remarriage. So much has upset you."

He was rambling, thinking out loud, but Ellie could see he couldn't stop.

"And then you came here and the mysteries of this place fed your depression. I've seen it. Andrea commented on it. She's waiting for me, did you know that? In her room. I have a bottle of wine I'm going to take to her. She thinks I'm getting it now."

"The police will know the truth, Curtis."

"Will they? I've already investigated Fraley. He's a fool, looking for ways to close this place. You heard him yourself this morning. He'll say the walk was slippery, you fell, an accident. Or was it? Did you take your own life? The possibility will exist. When your body is found, I'll be locked in her embrace. Isn't that the way it's described? 'Locked in her embrace.' The perfect alibi."

He spoke with the logic and the calm of the insane. She let out a loud scream which startled him into loosening his grip on her arm. But as she darted past him toward the door, he caught her by the waist and shoved her back against the rail, one hand clamped across her mouth, choking off her cries.

"Fight me, Eleanor. I like it when a woman fights."

But he held her so tightly she couldn't move, and her fists landed limply against his chest. Exploding with panic, she scraped her nails across his cheek and drew blood.

He roared and lifted her off her feet, ready to topple her off the walk. She heard the door behind him slam open and felt him being jerked backward, his hold on her broken. Jeff! Suddenly freed, she swayed for a moment against the railing, then fell to the walkway and watched in helpless horror as the two men grappled. They fell against the railing and it creaked in protest.

She tried to help, but there was nowhere she could reach, no weapon to use. In the swirling mist the figures seemed too much alike. And then a solid blow was landed. She scrambled backward as Curtis fell to the walkway and lay still.

For a moment neither she nor Jeff moved, then she rose and threw herself at him, buried her face in his chest, held tight and willed herself to realize that both of them were safe from harm.

"It's okay, Ellie," he said, stroking her hair, her back, then holding her close.

"I knew you'd be here."

"No, you didn't."

"Okay, I didn't." To her amazement she was able to laugh. "But I should have."

"You've got that right."

Just as she began to breathe without gasping, Curtis was up, shoving them both aside and darting through the open door. Jeff threw himself after him. She heard a scuffle, then a cry. By the time she made it to the landing, Jeff stood alone, peering down the curved stairwell.

Curtis lay at the bottom, one leg abnormally twisted. He held it and moaned.

"I don't think he'll be going anywhere," Jeff said. "We better go down and call the police. I'm sure you've figured out by now I've got some explaining to do. But not before this."

He kissed her, softly, sweetly, then kissed her eyes before taking her arm and helping her down the stairs.

CHAPTER EIGHT

"YOU SCREWED everything up."

Ellie stared at Jeff in dismay. "What do you mean? By almost getting killed?"

"Yeah." He grinned, and her heart melted. She would forgive anything under the power of that grin.

"I'll try not to do that again."

He took her hand in his. "Good."

They were sitting on the love seat in the parlor. The police were gone—Chief Fraley and his far more competent deputy—after taking statements from everyone, including the cook Clara. Under police guard, Curtis had been taken by ambulance to a local emergency center to get his leg attended to.

Blustering and waving his arms as he stomped around the inn, Fraley tried to pin Curtis's injury on Livvy, but even Grace Simpson roared in protest and he backed down.

Much of Jeff's testimony had been given in private. Ellie was ready to hear the highlights, as long as he didn't stop holding her hand.

"You already know the murder mystery was a setup, right?"

"I gathered it from the little I heard you tell the police. And Livvy filled me in more. She said it was conceived by this Denton Drake, after she contacted him at his Web site."

"After she contacted me."

Ellie stared at him a moment. At last the truth dawned and everything fell into place, like tumblers in an opening lock. "You're Denton Drake," she said.

Another grin, this one lopsided, and her heart raced.

"Livvy thought I was Drake's liaison," he said. "Even she didn't know we were one and the same." He hesitated. "Does it bother you that I'm this famous, wealthy writer?"

"Oh, yeah, it's a real problem." Then she grinned at him. "Does it bother you that I've never read any of your books?"

"That's something that can be changed." A shadow passed over his face. "Some things can't. It's way past time I told you everything. There was this woman, a girl really, when we first met."

"Jennifer or Missy? Curtis mentioned them both."

"Jennifer. We were close when we were in college—hell, you know what I mean. We were lovers.

But things didn't work out. I had this dream of becoming a famous writer, a typical English major, and she promised to wait until I could establish myself, at least earn a modest living, before we got married. We both thought it was the smart thing to do."

"But she changed her mind."

"Yeah, she changed her mind. I got an assistant editor job in New York at a small publishing house. The pay wasn't much, and as for writing, I couldn't give the stuff away. So she saw a long wait ahead of her."

"Your own publisher turned you down?"

"They only acquired nonfiction. I could edit it, but I couldn't write it. Jen wasn't out of school yet, and she moved north to another college, getting far away from me, she said, making a new start. Curtis was dean. Within a year she was dead."

Ellie squeezed his hand. "How terrible. The poor girl."

"We'd kept in touch. I went up there with letters she'd written about this older man she was dating, about how he frightened her sometimes, and in the last letter she said she was going to break off their relationship."

"You showed these letters to the police?"

"I did. But they had already decided someone

had broken into her apartment, found her home, robbed and killed her. As you can imagine, this killer burglar was never found."

"You talked to Curtis?"

"No. He had taken a sabbatical. They'd allowed him to leave the state." His voice was bitter. "Then last fall when I read about another student at the college being killed in the same way, by a burglar who got away, I knew I had to do something, push the bastard a little, find out if I could make him crack."

"But by now you were a big success."

"After Jen died, I threw myself into my work. But everything I wrote kept turning darker and darker until it got so bleak it actually sold. Horror pays, I found out. But I was obsessed with keeping my identity secret. What I wrote didn't seem a part of me. And I didn't write it for fame. Fortune, yes, I'll admit that, but I've always been a private man."

"So how did you and Livvy get together?"

"She e-mailed my Denton Drake Web site about a mystery weekend. She said she knew a famous writer like myself couldn't possibly be interested in providing her with a mystery, but my name attached to the publicity about her opening weekend could very well make the inn a success."

"You were interested."

"You can't imagine how much. I got my publicity department to work on her Web site and brochure, sent the brochure to Davidson, saying his presence would be considered a real coup for the inn's management. He would add panache, I told him. Men like him respond to words like panache. And, of course, his travel costs and lodging would be comped."

"And he called me, asking if I could join him."

"When you showed up, I was furious. Everything had been set up. Lori and Bob, a couple of actors, and Beverly the maid—I had them all in place."

"And Joseph? Was he your guy, too?"

"Nope, strictly local. And the gossip monger for Cliff's Cove, apparently. Livvy has already sent him packing. Lori was my star. She was supposed to strike up a flirtation with Curtis to make Bob jealous, get him alone, then dump him the way Jen and the student Missy had done. Lori is a black belt. He couldn't have taken her down easily."

"But he didn't take her bait."

"You were cuter."

"Somehow I'm not flattered."

"And you made me furious. What the hell were you here for? Curtis wasn't supposed to bring anyone with him."

"He didn't. I paid my way. We had a casual relationship a year back. He wanted to…well, you can imagine what he wanted to do, and I thought a few days away would be a great distraction. If I found myself caring for him, okay. If not, that was okay, too. As soon as I saw him, I knew he wasn't the man for me."

"Want to know what I thought when I saw you?"

"You were furious."

"I also knew you were the woman for me."

He said it simply, as if it were natural for a man to declare himself in such an offhand way. But Ellie almost fell off the love seat.

She couldn't look at him. It took her a moment to speak.

"You hid it well enough."

"Not too well. I'm a shy guy. I don't normally kiss women the way I kissed you."

"That's a relief."

"Which means you liked it?"

He moved in close. She pushed him away.

"Just a minute. You knew I was in danger. What took you so long to get up to the widow's walk?"

"I thought you were in your room. After cussing myself out for a half hour, I went there to tell you the whole thing, but when you didn't answer my knock, I went crazy. No one had seen you, and Curtis was missing, too. Then guess what? I heard weeping. It brought me up those stairs to the walk."

"But I didn't hear it."

"No one else did, either. I think I was being guided."

Ellie's skin tingled and she couldn't speak for a minute. "The weeping drew me to the window that first night. That's when I saw you."

"Yes, you did. Lori and I were acting out how the murder might take place, if he didn't actually attack her. Things like how we would play it and how she should fall."

"You had me thinking I was crazy."

"Livvy wanted to throttle me for being seen. I owe her a bundle, and believe me, I'll see that she gets help in keeping the inn open, even though she plans to drop the mystery weekends. But I owe you more."

"You told me it was precognition that caused me to recognize you. That we were destined to meet."

"I wasn't completely wrong."

His voice was thick, husky, the words filled with warmth. Before she could find her own words to respond, he stood and pulled her to her feet.

"Can we move this confession to a more private place?"

She made him wait a minute for her answer. "My room."

"Exactly what I had in mind."

They went out to the darkened foyer and she led the way up the stairs, walked ahead of him to her room, wishing she'd had a chance to comb her hair, freshen her makeup, perhaps even put on the green silk dress. But having almost lost her, Jeff was staying close. And, really, that was all right with her.

She opened her room to him, locked the door, then leaned back against it, watching as he turned to face her.

"You must be a very clever man, dreaming up all those twisted plots. What do you do with this scenario?"

"First I'd say I think I'm falling in love with you."

Oh. She swallowed, then managed to say, "Too soon and too vague."

"Whatever. I've decided to tell the truth from now on. I *know* I'm falling in love with you."

"You don't know me."

"I plan to, in a very short while. If you know what I mean."

"I know what you mean." She took a deep breath. "It's warm in here."

"You're overdressed."

"That's easy to fix."

She pulled the sweater over her head and tossed it aside. Okay, she was dressed pretty casually for this first time, but she did have on her fanciest black underwear. Push-up bra and bikini panties. She stripped down to show him.

Then, with him standing there, his eyes taking in everything as if his life depended on what he was seeing, she was hit by belated shyness and hurried full-speed to the bed, planning to dive under the covers.

He caught her by the wrist and pulled her hard against him.

"If you don't want to do this, you don't have to, Ellie. But the authorities will be coming over from the mainland tomorrow and I don't know when we'll have a chance to be alone again. So, since we have to get through this night somehow, I was hoping we could get through it together. In a way that doesn't have us thinking too much."

She stared at his lips. "I'm thinking lots of things."

"You said this was my scenario."

"I changed my mind. But you can have input from time to time."

He laughed. The sound was glorious. When they kissed—and they did for a long, long time—she knew she had found her destiny.

Especially when she heard her mother whisper, *Good job, my darling. Now it's time for me to leave.*

Ellie smiled to herself, not feeling in the least bereft or lost. Turning to Jeff, she knew she would never feel lonely again.

THE EDGE OF MEMORY

Kathleen O'Brien

CHAPTER ONE

"I TOLD YOU we should have waited until morning. This island is horrible at night. Ridiculous to put a hotel in such a godforsaken spot in the first place."

Emily Carlyle glanced over at her aunt. Was that fear she heard in Dorothy Murphy's voice? At fifty-six, Dorothy was fierce and forceful and intimidated by nothing. Emily, who had been orphaned at the age of eight and left in Dorothy's care, used to be terrified by Dorothy's stern manner. But eventually she'd come to rely on it as the one steady spot in an ever-tilting universe.

So where was all that ferocity now?

"It's okay, Dorrie," Emily said, reverting to her childhood nickname for her aunt. "I can see the road just fine. We're almost there."

Dorothy clamped her teeth onto her bottom lip, staring out into the darkness, her whole body stiff, as if she expected the fog to form a human shape and glide toward them, prying at their car windows with translucent silver fingers.

"Horrible," Dorothy repeated. But her normally gruff voice was little more than a whisper, not even as loud as the growling black surf fifty feet below them. The abnormal timidity unsettled Emily more than the fog ever could. Had she been wrong to let Dorothy come with her on this sad pilgrimage?

But Dorothy had been insistent. Emily didn't really see how she could have stopped her.

Emily turned back to her driving, concentrating on keeping her tires centered as they climbed the winding path. She took the last hairpin turn slowly and suddenly there it was. *Lost Angel Inn.* It loomed above them, its complicated roofline black and spiky against the gray fog, like the silhouette of a crouching beast.

She heard her aunt's sharp intake of breath and she couldn't really blame her. The hundred-and-forty-year-old Victorian inn, with its thrusting turrets at each end, was so shrouded in fog that the mansion seemed to float in mid-air.

"It's not too late to turn back," her aunt blurted with a physical jerk. "Even now. There's one more ferry. We could go back to the mainland. Come back in the daylight, if you must come at all."

Emily loosened her fingers, which had tightened on the steering wheel. "Don't be silly," she said mildly. "We're already here. And, honestly, Dorrie, just because it's dark doesn't mean—"

She didn't finish. Surely, Dorothy knew as well as

Emily that true evil didn't need Hollywood props, didn't arrive with a soundtrack of ominous organ music. It didn't require fog or storm or midnight.

They'd known that truth for twenty years, ever since Emily's mother had been murdered, here at Lost Angel Inn, at high noon on a gorgeous summer Sunday.

The sky that afternoon had been clear and golden, the bright sun set in its tip like a diamond in a crown. Just moments before her mother's death, she and Emily had been sitting on a yellow-checked picnic blanket, sharing a peach, giggling as the juice dribbled down their chins. Below them, the blue ocean had glistened with winking fairy lights. In the distance, the gardener was running his mower and a sweet wind had blown soft blades of new-cut grass against Emily's sunburned cheeks.

Emily had been only eight, but she'd never forgotten that day—never forgotten how all that love and beauty and peace had not, in the end, been enough to protect them. While Emily had played just a few yards away, someone had pushed Melissa Carlyle over the cliff edge. Melissa had died bathed in sunlight, facedown on the sun-warmed rocks.

So, no, Emily wasn't afraid of the dark. She was only afraid of going through the rest of her life without ever knowing what had really happened to her mother. The state police had believed the killer to be Melissa's married lover, though they hadn't been able to prove it. The locals had insisted it was the Lost Angel curse, claiming another victim, as it was destined to do every twenty years.

Only Emily herself could have known for sure. Only eight-year-old Emily could possibly have seen the murderer. But the memory, if there was a memory, remained locked in her paralyzed subconscious, surfacing only in an occasional confusing dream of falling, falling and weeping.

And an illogical sense of guilt.

Which was why, as soon as she'd heard that the Lost Angel Inn had been reopened, she had known she had to come. Her aunt had argued against it vehemently, but Emily had been determined. She had to try. She had to see if she could set the memory— and perhaps herself—free.

"Why don't you check us in?" Emily pulled the car to a stop beside the front portico, where the blind eyes of a bronze angel watched their arrival.

All of a sudden Emily remembered that tragic, drooping angel. She'd been afraid of it back when she was a child, but now she saw it as a lovely work of art.

As she recalled, the angel theme was repeated many times in the old mansion—large ones in statuary and paintings, and smaller, startling ones carved into lintels and mantels and pillars and the arms of heavy chairs. It was undoubtedly the builder's homage to the Lost Angel Island history.

According to legend, the island had got its name when, in the 1700s, a golden-haired, three-year-old girl had gotten lost here. The child had wandered off, looking for her father, who had drowned. Though the frantic searchers found the father's body, of the child they recovered only a small cotton bonnet caught in the rocky shallows. Everyone presumed the child drowned in the same waters that had taken the lives of so many sailors and fishermen, foolhardy adolescents and heartbroken lovers.

A tragic story. But though the angel echoes everywhere might strike a modern visitor like Emily as slightly macabre, it must have delighted the death-obsessed Victorians.

Emily suddenly realized her aunt was still hesitating, her fingers wrapped around the door handle.

"I could go with you," Dorothy said. "To park the car. We could walk back together to register."

Emily shook her head. "No, you go on in," she said. "I'll be fine."

Still her aunt didn't move. Emily waited patiently, touched by this rare sign of vulnerability. She felt a rush of gratitude for all the years of strength, and she was glad that, for once, she could let her aunt lean on her. If she'd thought Dorothy would allow it, she would have reached out and hugged her.

Finally, Dorothy set her jaw and opened the car

door. The fog rushed in, wrapping itself around Emily's calves, cool and clammy.

"It's just a bunch of superstitious baloney, you know," Dorothy said suddenly, her voice a little too loud. "There's no such thing as a curse."

Emily smiled. "I know."

Dorothy nodded several times, as if to confirm her own words. Emily wondered who she was trying to convince.

"Right." Taking one deep breath, Dorothy launched her long, mannish body out of the car. She adjusted her navy skirt, turned and, as she poked her head in for her purse, gave Emily an emphatic glare. "And there are *no ghosts*."

With that proclamation, she disappeared, not waiting for Emily's answer.

Which probably was just as well.

No ghosts?

Emily wasn't so sure about that.

WHEN CHRISTOPHER MAXWELL had told his poker buddies the other night that a piece of furniture was much easier to handle than a woman, he obviously hadn't been talking about *this* piece of furniture.

He braced his knees against the base of his truck and began to carefully lever the mahogany *secrétaire* that, in spite of its ornate, spindly legs, weighed a damn ton, down onto the hand truck.

Halfway there, the *secrétaire* shifted and he scraped a knuckle against the lift gate, catching her. *Hell.* He sucked the blood off irritably and went back to wrestling with the hunk of wood. Pretty as she was, right now he'd trade her for the meanest woman in Cliff's Cove. At least women didn't give you ten busted toes and a hernia.

He should have waited to deliver this until tomorrow, when he could actually see what he was doing. But he was eager to show the *secrétaire* to Livvy, who didn't even know yet that he'd won it at the auction. It was one of the original furnishings, from back in the mid-1800s when the mansion was a senator's wedding gift to his trophy bride. Back when things were built to last, and did. Lasted a lot longer than the senator, who had been found dead in his bed the morning after his glamorous wedding, stabbed in the heart by a crazy chambermaid.

See? It was always women, just like Christopher had told his friends at the poker game. They might as well stop matchmaking. He'd been in love once, engaged once—not the same woman—and up to his ears in romantic quicksand more often than he could count.

It just never worked. He didn't care enough, when you got right down to it, to make it work.

"Know what's wrong with you?" His best friend, Mark, who had been pretty drunk that night had asked. He'd pointed his beer at Christopher over the poker table, sloshing foam on the chips, which had sent a rumble of irritation through the other players. "You're froze up. Just like the mechanic says when you take the car in. Yeah. Froze up. That's what."

Mark took a long swig, wiped his mouth and stared into the beer like a Gypsy looking into tea leaves. "Yeah," he repeated finally. "I say it's because of your dad."

The silence that fell over the table was almost comical. Nobody but Mark would have dared to utter those words, and even Mark wouldn't have if he'd been sober. Christopher's father, an artist who had ruined his life by marrying a cold, eternally dissatisfied woman, had made the mistake, in his middle years, of stealing a few blissful encounters with a vibrant young beauty, a visitor to the island. When the woman ended up murdered, the police had suspected Martin Maxwell—even the chief of police, who had been Martin's best friend.

They still suspected him, twenty years later.

Though Martin himself had always been fairly philosophical about his ordeal, Christopher, who had been fifteen at the time of the murder, burned with the injustice of it every time he thought about it. His gentle, witty, brilliant, long-suffering father—a *murderer?* Martin Maxwell wasn't a subject Christopher allowed anyone to bandy about over cards.

But anyone could see Mark was plastered, and

Christopher was too mellow, after three beers of his own, to make a thing about it. Besides, it didn't seem fair to jump all over a guy for telling the truth.

"Right. I'm froze up. But see, the thing is, I like it. That last woman you guys suckered me into asking out—that Kelly Whatshername—she still calls my place six times a day. Give me a good five-foot length of oak any day. Feels good, smells good and just sits patiently in the corner till you're ready to grab hold of it and go to work."

The other men laughed, relieved that their beloved weekly game wasn't going to turn sour. Christopher tossed a chip into the center pile. "So what's it going to be, buddy? Pass out or ante up?"

The *secrétaire* wobbled again, bringing him back to the present problem. Somehow he straightened it on the hand truck, wrapped the elastic cord as tightly as he could and began to roll it across the thick grass toward the house. He was going to have to go in through the front—the kitchen door was too narrow and he refused to scuff the corners of this handsome piece. He'd paid top dollar for it.

The fog parted in front of him like a thick gray curtain, but only a foot at a time, so he had to trust his intimate knowledge of the grounds. Livvy wouldn't appreciate it if he crushed her flower beds.

Suddenly, without warning, the parting fog revealed a human form. A woman, dressed in black, only inches away from the leading edge of the huge desk. He was on top of her before his conscious mind could register the danger.

He stopped abruptly, which was risky—the *secrétaire* was too precariously balanced—but what else could he do? He thrust an arm out to try to steady the heavy, rocking hunk of mahogany, but it was hopeless. It had an awkward shape—too much leeway inside the elastic cord. Within two seconds, it had shifted, tilted. Begun to fall.

The woman must have heard his curse, because at the last second she turned her head. He caught a quick glimpse of a pale face, brown hair trailing with wisps of fog. He couldn't identify her—he was too busy trying to avert disaster—but he could see the swirling mist as she tried to dart away.

Damn it. Luck was against them. She guessed wrong, jerking back. Right into the path of the falling *secrétaire*. It seemed to catch her on the side of her head—Christopher felt the hitch in momentum as wood connected with skull. She cried out softly. Then, somehow, they were tangled together on the ground, though the *secrétaire,* thankfully, had fallen to the side and not on top of her.

The fog made ghosts of them all. Kneeling, Christopher felt around and found her arm. He ran his hands lightly across soft skin until he reached her head. She was moving, trying to sit up, making small, confused sounds. Conscious, he thought. *Thank God.*

But when he touched her temple, the hair was sticky and warm.

"Wait…don't try to stand up." He put his hand behind her back, bracing her in a sitting position. "Let me help you get inside."

"I think I'm all right," she said, putting her hand to her temple. It must be throbbing like hell, he thought.

She pulled her fingers away and stared at their wet, darkened tips. "Oh," she said, as if surprised. "I'm bleeding."

"Let's get you in where there's some light." He put his other hand under her legs and lifted her. It was ridiculously simple. She weighed almost nothing, and she was still too shocked to resist.

He carried her quickly through the fog toward the inn's front porch light. He cast one quick, regretful glance back at the *secrétaire*, which he'd left face-down in the grass—how could he have been such a klutz?—but he could hardly make it out. The fog was already swarming eagerly over it, burying it from its curved legs to its topmost finial.

"I'm sorry," the woman in his arms said. "I didn't hear you. I didn't see—"

"No, it was entirely my fault." He stopped the apology quickly. "I feel terrible. I didn't realize anyone was checking in tonight and—"

But suddenly his own voice faltered. As they approached the front porch, the light was finally stronger than the fog and he got his first clear look at the woman in his arms.

His feet stumbled over one of Livvy's landscaping rocks, but somehow he kept his balance. *What the hell was going on here?*

He knew this woman. He knew her thick swath of long hair, as glossy brown as the truest mahogany. He knew her blue eyes, which weren't really blue, but as subtly multicolored as pebbles lying at the bottom of a clear tidal pool. He knew that when she smiled everyone near her smiled stupidly, too, as if they had swallowed a tickling ray of sunshine.

Yes, he knew her. He'd never forget her. The only catch was—

She had died twenty years ago.

CHAPTER TWO

AS THE MAN CARRIED HER inside, Emily registered the house in little snippets, just strobelike details absorbed through the pounding ache in her temple. A cut-glass chandelier that shone over her head like sunlight. The soft brush of real flowers against her dangling feet. The faint scent of something delicious that probably had been the dinner they'd missed.

Apparently the forbidding exterior of Lost Angel Inn was misleading. Inside, the inn was as warm and welcoming as a friendly hug.

Funny, she didn't remember it like this. She remembered deep shadows and dark corridors and heavy-booted policemen with unkind voices.

And weeping. So much weeping. Her own, her aunt's...and that strange, disembodied sobbing that had seemed, somehow, to come from the house itself.

But the last time she'd been here she'd been only eight years old and she'd just lost her mother. Her recollections were obviously jumbled, a mixture of shock and fantasy and mutated memories.

"Oh, Christopher! What on earth? What's happened?"

The worried words came from the back of the hallway. Emily lifted her head, wincing against the pain, and watched as a young brunette hurried toward them, holding a sheaf of papers in her hand. The woman, who was beautiful in a quiet way, seemed to walk with a slight limp.

"I'm afraid we've had an accident, Livvy." The man—Emily now knew his name was Christopher, at least—spoke with the same calm he'd showed from the beginning. "I was carting in the *secrétaire*, and I mowed this poor lady down. With the fog, we just didn't see each other in time. Can we go into the kitchen? We need good light. She's bleeding."

Emily couldn't help noticing the quick, alert glance that passed between Livvy and Christopher.

"The *secrétaire*?" Livvy caught her lower lip between her teeth. "You got it?"

Christopher nodded.

"Oh—" Livvy turned back to Emily, her face suddenly shadowed with contrition. "But that's not important right now. We need to see how badly you're hurt."

Emily shifted, embarrassed by all the fuss. "I'm sure I can walk," she said, though she realized her ankle was throbbing, too, and she wasn't at all confident it would hold her. "It's nothing serious, really. If you'll just let me—"

Christopher's firm hands didn't relax. Obviously he had no intention of letting her down yet—he and his friend Livvy, who Emily deduced was the Olivia Hamilton who owned the inn, were probably already fearing a lawsuit.

And if he didn't agree, there was no way she could free herself. She was suddenly aware of just how much power this man possessed. He seemed to carry her hundred and twenty pounds as if she were no heavier than a bird.

"Oh, let Chris give you a ride," Livvy said with a smile. "Just to be safe."

"Emily!" Suddenly, Dorothy burst into the foyer, too, her sensible shoes making emphatic thuds against the hardwood floor. She looked at Christopher. *"You!"* Her strong black eyebrows drove together. "What are you doing here? What have you done to her? Give her to me."

Livvy looked from Christopher to Dorothy, apparently just as mystified by the older woman's attitude as Emily was herself.

Livvy's smile seemed strained. "Do you and Ms. Murphy already know each other, Christopher?"

Dorothy made a low scoffing sound under her breath. Emily glanced at her, confused. Dorothy was sometimes brutally straightforward and she certainly didn't believe in being sugary or coy—but she was rarely as rude as this.

"Yes, Livvy, we do," Christopher said. His voice was still calm, but Emily felt a tension thrum through his arms. Held close like this against his body, she could read him like a lie detector. He was just as disturbed as Dorothy—though he hid his emotions well under that civilized tone.

"Ms. Murphy and I met the last time she stayed at Lost Angel Inn," he said. "Didn't she tell you, Livvy? When she made her reservation, did she forget to mention that she's Melissa Carlyle's sister?"

Livvy's mouth went slightly slack. "Melissa… You mean, the woman who—"

"Yes. Melissa Carlyle. The last victim of the Lost Angel curse. The woman who fell from the cliff twenty years ago."

Dorothy lifted her square chin. "She didn't fall," she said, her voice full of a venom that made Emily's blood run cold. "She was pushed."

"Dorrie—" Emily began, holding out her blood-tipped fingers, entreating her aunt to stop. They mustn't expose their personal miseries and inflict them on these people. These people had nothing to do with all that.

"My sister was *murdered*," Dorothy went on, apparently unstoppable. She turned her blue-black gaze onto Christopher. "And this man's father is the cheating bastard who killed her."

"I'M SORRY, EMILY," Dorothy said later when they were alone upstairs unpacking. "I don't know what came over me. It was just seeing you there, bleeding in that man's arms. He looks so much like his father, I just couldn't—"

"It's all right, Dorrie," Emily said for at least the third time. And it *was* all right. They had gotten through the awkward moment somehow, offering explanations to the distressed Livvy Hamilton, who indeed did own Lost Angel Inn, and apologies to the poker-faced Christopher Maxwell, who was the son of Martin Maxwell, the man the police had suspected of murdering Emily's mother.

They'd gotten through it, but it had been miserably uncomfortable. Livvy had washed and dressed the cut on Emily's temple, which had thankfully turned out to be superficial. Christopher, standing stiffly by the kitchen door, had stayed to be sure she was all right, but had left as soon as the bandage was in place.

What a mess! Emily couldn't imagine why Dorothy hadn't warned Livvy who they were before she'd made the reservations. Had she been hoping that they could remain incognito? Surely not—if she was anything, Dorothy Murphy was a realist. She must have known that someone was bound to recognize them. Everyone said how much Emily looked like her mother, though of course Melissa had been far more beautiful, more outgoing and vibrant.

Or…maybe it was just an example of Dorothy's usual intensely guarded privacy. Emily remembered how often, through the years, Dorothy had scolded her for telling people about her mother. Dorothy's insistence that they pretend the whole thing had never happened had confused the young Emily. Was it somehow shameful to be related to a person who got killed? Had they, in some indefinable way, allowed, even invited, terrible things to enter their lives?

But she couldn't sort it all out now. It was one in the morning. She was tired and she wanted to go across the hall to her own bedroom.

Dorothy was standing in front of the cheval mirror, holding one of her tailored navy-blue dresses limp in both hands, staring at herself as if she didn't recognize the woman she saw there.

Emily came over and took the dress gently from her.

"I really do understand, Dorrie," she said, slipping the dress across one of the scented hangers provided in the armoire. "It's being back here, where it all happened. It's emotionally—unsettling. We need to get a good night's sleep and start fresh tomorrow."

But when she was alone in her pretty room, with its Victorian furnishings and flowered wallpaper, Emily still couldn't sleep.

She had obviously underestimated how disturbing it would be to come back to Lost Angel Inn. She had dismissed most of her strangest memories as the phantasms of a bereaved child. When she returned as a clear-headed and rational adult, she told herself, she would see how absurd those memories were.

But now, as she lay in the four-poster with its filmy white hangings moving almost imperceptibly in the air, everything came flooding back to her.

And it all felt startlingly real.

Almost every night of the month little Emily had stayed at Lost Angel Inn, she had heard a faint weeping coming from the floor above her bedroom. She'd told her mother, who had laughed and tickled her and said, "My little girl is going to be a writer, she has such a vivid imagination." Emily had told her aunt, who had rounded on the inn owner, saying, "See what happens when you exploit such foolishness in your advertising? The child is having nightmares."

No one believed her and, finally, because the weeping sounded more sad than scary, Emily had simply gotten used to it.

The day her mother died, Emily had played outdoors too long and her face had blazed with sunburn. In the aftermath of violent death, no one had had time to worry about anything so trivial. The distracted grown-ups had put the shell-shocked little girl to bed without lotions or cool cloths to soothe her red, scalded skin. Without thinking maybe she shouldn't be alone, alone in that room she'd been sharing with her mother all these weeks.

It had been difficult to sleep. She had almost looked forward to the ghostly weeping. It would be better than hearing her aunt in the room next door, choking on harsh sobs she tried vainly to hold back.

But the weeping never came. Instead, in the black middle of the night, Emily had heard a soft singing. The voice was high and sweet, but the words had made no sense. They were in a language she'd never heard before.

In spite of her burned skin, goose bumps had prickled all over her from scalp to toe. It wasn't Dorrie. Dorrie's voice was deep and, besides, she never sang lullabies.

It wasn't her mother, either. Her mother was dead. Emily would have been happy, so happy to see her mother's ghost float into their bedroom, but even without opening her eyes Emily had known it wasn't her mother's voice.

She'd realized then that she didn't want to open her eyes. She didn't want to know who it was—she didn't care. The voice was kind and the lullaby pretty. It made her feel safe. It made her think maybe she could go to sleep after all.

When she woke up in the morning, the room was empty. The voice gone. All she could remember hearing was the sound of gulls screaming over the Atlantic and Dorrie just outside her door, telling a policeman that no, he could not ask Emily a few questions; Emily was asleep, Emily was traumatized, Emily hadn't seen anything anyhow, leave the poor child alone.

She'd never heard the voice again. As the years passed, Emily had convinced herself that the whole thing must have been a dream.

She got out of bed and walked to the window, careful to tread lightly. These old hardwood floors creaked—probably the cause of many a ghost story themselves.

The U-shaped inn had rooms that faced the interior courtyard, a pretty place of bricked paths and winding vines, and rooms that faced the ocean, which could just barely be glimpsed beyond the extensive grounds that led to the cliffs.

This time, Emily had a courtyard view. She wondered if Dorrie had asked for that specifically, so that Emily wouldn't spend all her time looking out, driving herself mad, imagining her mother walking across the grounds that last day, heading for the cliff, where she would meet her death.

Or perhaps trying to imagine who else had walked the same path, with evil in mind.

She looked down into the courtyard now. A cool breeze blew the gray swirls of fog around, giving the illusion of movement to the shapes below. In the rose garden at the back, a few night-black blooms swayed in and out of the mist as if dancing to some slow, secret music. In the corners, misshapen fog ghosts sat on the wrought-iron benches, shifting restlessly, melting away and reforming into new, ever-stranger shapes.

She had been gazing at the furthest bench for several seconds when suddenly her heart began to beat unpleasantly in her chest. That one particularly dense shape wasn't fog at all.

There really was a man sitting there.

He was so still, stiller than the fog, really. He was bending over something he held in his hands, rubbing it, or squeezing it, or...

Carving it. Suddenly the weak moonlight sparked silver against the blade of a knife. At that moment the man looked up, right at her, his knife motionless, gleaming in the one shaft of light that dared penetrate this haunted courtyard.

She backed away from the window, suddenly breathless.

There was nothing to be afraid of, she told herself. It was only Christopher Maxwell. She recognized his light hair, his broad shoulders, his strong-boned, handsome face.

But for one blinding moment, he had looked just like his father. And in that moment, looking at him, she had remembered one of the smothered details from that terrible day.

Martin Maxwell had been out there, too. Martin Maxwell had been on the cliff the day her mother died.

CHAPTER THREE

THE SUMMER SUN had already burned away most of
the fog before Emily woke up the next morning. She
went immediately to the courtyard window and
looked down on the bright scene below.

The bench Christopher Maxwell had occupied
was empty, but on the other side of the courtyard a
middle-aged couple sat sharing a breakfast that, even
from this distance, looked so good it reminded Emily
she'd had nothing to eat since lunch yesterday.

Her foot still twinged a little when she walked, but
her head had stopped throbbing; overall she felt re-
freshed, ready to meet the day. She knocked lightly
on Dorothy's door, but didn't get an answer, so she
went down the winding stairs, assuming her aunt
was already in the dining room.

The front foyer was flanked by a sunny raspberry-
papered dining room on one side and a charming blue
parlor on the other. The sideboard in the dining room
was heaped with food, but the room itself was empty.
Lost Angel Inn must have very few guests right now.

Emily was munching on a piece of toast when she heard voices coming from the parlor. It sounded like Livvy, so Emily stepped across the foyer to say good morning.

Livvy and Christopher stood together at the far end of the room, and at first they didn't see her. They were obviously absorbed, studying an elaborate Victorian desk, or *secrétaire*. Emily suspected it was the piece that had nearly run her down last night.

Livvy was sliding her fingers along the back of the desk and Christopher was kneeling in front of it, apparently trying to insert a key into each of the various drawers. As Emily entered, he reached the last lock.

"Nope," he said. He dropped his hands between his knees, obviously disappointed. "None of them."

Livvy sighed. "Darn. I was so sure this was it."

Christopher reached up and squeezed her hand. "We'll find it eventually. Lucy wouldn't have taken such pains to hide this key if it weren't important."

Livvy sighed again, tucked her hair behind her ear and finally noticed Emily in the doorway. "Oh, hi!" She smiled welcomingly. "Sorry, I didn't see you there. Want to help us look for the mysterious secret drawer?"

Ignoring Christopher Maxwell's sudden stiff silence, Emily moved in to get a closer look at the beautiful *secrétaire*. It was made of rich, highly polished mahogany, but it was an intensely feminine piece, with graceful lines and elaborate garlands of inlaid mother-of-pearl.

"Lovely," she said, running her fingertips along the wood, which was cool and smooth, like glass. "But why do you think there's a secret drawer? Who is Lucy?"

Christopher turned toward her. He was extremely good-looking, she realized with a tingle of surprise. Last night, the fog and the fuss and the pain must have kept her from noticing. But he had that rare combination—blond good looks that somehow remained ruggedly masculine. If the blue eyes and honey-colored, wavy hair might have tempted an envious man to label Christopher too pretty, the broad shoulders, strong jaw, weathered bronze skin and no-nonsense gaze made the label ridiculous.

"Lucy Knight was Senator Jack Knight's widow," he said. "The one who hanged herself in the attic back in the 1860s, shortly after Jack was killed. I'm sure you're familiar with that story."

Emily flushed at his rough tone. Of course she knew the story. A chambermaid who'd loved the rich, charismatic senator had stabbed him on his wedding night. When the chambermaid, an illiterate Irish girl, was hanged for her crime, she died protesting her innocence.

Her last words had hung like a miasma around the house ever since. She'd called it an evil house, full of evil people. She'd said that no one would ever be happy here.

Maybe she hadn't meant it as a curse, but the superstitious locals had interpreted it as one. When Jack's widow, Lucy, had miscarried his baby and then been found dead, hanging from the beams in the chambermaid's sad little attic room, the legend had been born.

Locals believed in the curse to this day. Every twenty years—the exact age of the chambermaid when she was hanged—someone must die at the house on Lost Angel Island.

And, whether it was coincidence or not, events seemed to conspire to prove that the curse was real. Twenty years ago, that someone had been Emily's mother.

In fact, her mother's death had forced the inn to close. And many of the locals had actively opposed its reopening now. Why invite trouble? they thought. Why awaken the curse?

"Yes," Emily said, determined to keep her voice steady. "Of course I know the legend. This is Lucy Knight's desk, then?"

"It is," Livvy broke in, giving Christopher a stern look as if to say, *Please don't antagonize the guests.* "Isn't that exciting? A few months ago, we found this key in a hidden compartment in her calling card case, which was the first item we acquired that was original to the house."

She held the key out toward Emily. "We've been hoping to discover what it fits ever since. This *secrétaire*, also original to the house, has so many locked drawers—we were sure it was the answer."

Emily took the key. It was gold, very small and yet extremely ornate, with tiny loops and swirls so intricate it was almost a work of art. She had to agree. If Lucy had hidden such a key, she'd probably had a good reason.

Had this really been the tragic Lucy Knight's own *secrétaire?* Emily looked over at the desk, wondering whether there might be drawers behind drawers. Or underneath. Or perhaps if they looked for suspicious markings on the back…

The intensity of her curiosity surprised her. Emily had come here to solve her own mystery, sort out her own past. Whatever Lucy Knight had locked up with this key a hundred and forty years ago, it had nothing to do with Melissa Carlyle's death.

Unless you believed in the curse…

Just then a pleasant, gray-haired woman in a loud, green-paisley shirtwaist dress stuck her head in through the doorway that led to the courtyard. "Livvy? Any chance Charlie and I could get some more coffee?"

Livvy put her hand to her forehead. "Oh, I'm sorry, Josie—I forgot. Tell Charlie I'll have it out there in two seconds." When the woman smiled and disappeared back into the courtyard, Livvy turned to

Emily. "I'm not being much of a hostess to anyone, am I? I hope you helped yourself to breakfast."

"I grabbed a piece of toast," Emily said. "I thought I might go out and wander a little."

Livvy and Christopher exchanged another of their glances. The two of them seemed so close Emily wondered if they might be lovers. But of course it was none of her business.

"Okay," Livvy said hesitantly. "Just…be careful, won't you?"

"Emily isn't afraid she'll be the next victim of the curse, Livvy," Christopher said coldly. "She's convinced her mother was murdered by a real flesh-and-blood man, not the powers of darkness. And unless she thinks my father was guided by supernatural—"

Livvy frowned. "Chris—"

"It's all right," Emily broke in. "I understand why Christopher is angry. My aunt's accusations were horribly inappropriate. I know we apologized last night, but I'd like to say again that I'm very sorry. The stress of coming back and her emotions—"

"Yes, it was just the stress, Chris," Livvy said, putting her arm on his. "I'm sure you have already forgiven her. I really have to get the coffee for the Farrells, so—"

Christopher smiled, but Emily could see it was an effort. "I'll be good, Livvy. I am capable of being civilized, you know, for your sake."

Livvy smiled back, then hurried off toward the kitchen, her limp slightly more pronounced than it had been last night.

Which left Emily alone with Christopher Maxwell. She had a cowardly urge to bolt after Livvy, to pretend she'd suddenly developed an appetite, but she forced herself to stand firm. She looked back at the *secrétaire,* which gleamed like dark honey in the morning sunlight.

She stooped, then ran her fingers along the underside. She felt nothing unusual—although she was hardly a furniture expert and barely knew what she was looking for.

Still—she just had a feeling…

"Why do you think Lucy Knight might have put in a secret drawer?" She looked up at Christopher, hoping he'd meant his promise to be polite. "What are you actually expecting to find?"

"Who knows? Livvy thinks it might be a diary. Anything of historical value, anything newsworthy, would be good publicity for the inn. Not locally, of course. Too many people around here hate this place. But elsewhere…it makes an exciting story. God knows Livvy could use a break. Her luck so far hasn't been the best. She's got only one couple here this week. Except for you and your aunt, of course."

His tone implied that Emily and Dorothy didn't count.

But Emily knew what he meant. A huge, restored historical home like this would positively gobble money and you would need lots of ordinary tourists to keep it going. Emily had heard about the unfortunate events of the inn's grand re-opening weekend last month. The murder mystery weekend that had attracted a real murderer.

Selfishly, her only reaction had been fear that the owner might close up the inn again and thus deny Emily her chance to revisit her past.

"What about you, Emily Carlyle?" Suddenly she realized that Christopher had moved very close to her, so close he blocked out the sun from the courtyard door.

"What do you mean?"

"I'll ask you the same question. What do you expect to find?"

She wanted to rise, but he was so close he essentially blocked her way. She put out a hand and touched his arm, requesting a little space. To his credit, he backed away immediately, though his dark gaze never left her face.

She stood slowly. She refused to be coy, to pretend she didn't know what he asked.

"I expect to find the truth," she said. "The truth about what happened to my mother."

"How?" He scowled, making his strong bone structure look more rugged than ever. "For God's sake. You look like a rational woman. Do you think you can go stand on the cliff, rub a piece of your mother's clothing, chant a little and the memories will just conveniently come rushing back after twenty years?"

"No, but I..."

"And what if the visions do start flooding back, how would you ever know they were real? What if you were wrong? You imagine you remember something, you tell the police, and suddenly someone's life is ruined."

She shook her head. "That's not what this is all about. I'm not here to ruin anyone's life—"

"Is that so?" He laughed, a short, abrupt sound filled with scorn. "Sorry, but that's generally what happens when you accuse someone of murder, Emily. Or were you just going to say, 'Oh, that's right, I remember now'? 'So-and-so killed my mother, but that's okay.'"

He made her sound so foolish. Why was he being so unkind?

She felt suddenly oppressed by this room, by the heavy, dark furniture and the intense colors of the flocked wallpaper and the Oriental rug. She hated it— and, in that moment, she hated him, too. Hated his cold, handsome face and his mocking voice. Hated him for coming right out and voicing all the doubts that had been tormenting her ever since she'd arrived.

Why couldn't he see how twenty years of guilt and confusion, a lifetime of nightmares and doubt, could make you desperate? Could make you clutch at any straw?

She straightened her back and lifted her chin. "Why are you really being so insulting, Christopher? Are you afraid, deep inside, that it was your father after all?"

Mentally she braced herself, expecting him to explode, but to her surprise, he didn't. He merely gazed at her a long minute, as if she were a problem he couldn't quite figure out how to solve.

"I'm sorry," he said finally. His voice was wry and strangely indifferent. "I didn't intend to be insulting. I actually meant to be helpful."

"Helpful?"

"Yes. You see, if your mother's death wasn't an accident, if there really was a killer, he probably won't much like the idea that you're trying to resurrect your memories. He just might decide that you need to be—"

Christopher paused, and in that pause a chill ran down Emily's back like wet fingers of fog.

"Silenced."

CHAPTER FOUR

AFTER CHECKING ONE MORE time on Dorothy, who said she was still tired and wanted to rest, Emily slowly made her way toward the cliff.

Very slowly. She was suddenly aware that, for all her brave plans, she dreaded seeing again the place where her mother had died.

She wasn't afraid of what Christopher Maxwell had said about the killer wanting to silence her. She knew that his father no longer lived on Lost Angel Island and none of the other guests who had stayed at the inn twenty years ago were around anymore, either. So how could the killer even know she'd come back?

Unless Christopher, himself, was the killer.

But that was absurd. He would have been only fourteen or fifteen the summer her mother died. Why would he have murdered a woman he'd barely known?

No, she wasn't afraid for her physical safety. It was her emotions that were vulnerable today. It was her heart, which over the past twenty years she had slowly and painfully mended. By coming here, she risked breaking it back into a million jagged pieces.

She followed the path beyond the inn's formal grounds, until it became just a scrubby, sandy walkway leading toward the ocean edge. She saw more rocks in the soil, smelled more sea salt in the air. Seagulls circled overhead, their plaintive cries telling her she was getting closer, though she still couldn't see the water.

She perspired a little under the intensity of the cloudless sky. Could she be going in the wrong direction? She hadn't remembered that the cliff edge was actually this far from the inn. For a cowardly moment she thought about turning back, but then she saw the stand of trees up ahead.

A tiny forest, no more than an acre or so of tall oaks and hemlocks. It had been her personal kingdom that summer.

She entered it eagerly now, glad of the shade it offered. She remembered it so well, with its enchanted carpet of moldering leaves, busy ants and exotic beetles.

After a few yards she stopped. Where was the angel? Where was Polly?

She had to look closely, because the curling ferns had advanced, claiming more of the forest floor. But there, between two ancient pines, half hidden, was the little stone angel she remembered so well. Still silently guarding its secret.

She walked over to the small sculpture, a cherub with its hands folded in prayer, kneeling over a square of marble with two words carved on its surface. She had to brush away dead leaves and flakes of slimy mildew, but finally she could see the words.

"Polly," it said. And then, "Fidelis."

To the eight-year-old Emily, the only child staying at the inn that summer, this little angel had become a sort of playmate. She had called her Polly, although Dorothy had told her that was wrong, that instead the angel prayed for someone, or something, named Polly, which had been buried in that spot long, long ago.

A dog, perhaps? A beloved bird? Emily hadn't cared, hadn't felt morbid about the invisible, decaying body just below the surface of the soil. Back then, death had been only a distant concept with no power to touch Emily's life. Her father had died, of course, but that was when she'd been only a baby, and she didn't think of him as real.

So she and "Polly" had shared many a tea party, pretending to drink little lady-slipper cups full of rainwater and making up stories about the fairies who lived in bright-green fern castles and surfed the ocean waves in the moonlight.

Emily had to smile, remembering how her mother had encouraged such fancies. Dorothy, on the other hand, had thought they were a foolish waste of time and had probably led to those nightmares of imagined weeping.

The twenty years of loneliness, with the inn closed and no children playing make-believe in these trees, had changed the little angel. Her soft gray stone body was slick and black with fungus, and one of her wings had been chipped, probably from a falling tree limb. Her eyes were blinded with mildew and ants crawled in the tiny praying fingers.

It was somehow unbearably sad to see. And, in a way, it seemed to echo the loneliness and pain of Emily's own years. Now, for the first time, Emily could see what she hadn't understood as a child—the grief in the angel's posture, the endless sorrow, the life frozen at the moment of great loss. With a heavy heart, Emily bent and began to smudge away the dirt and mold, as if she could erase the damage the past twenty years had done to both of them.

It was silent work. But suddenly, as she reached the angel's eyes, her heart thumped strangely and her skin began to prickle with goose bumps. She tensed, her subconscious mind drumming, *Danger,* a full second before her conscious mind registered that anything was wrong.

Her fingers stilled on the angel's eyes. What was it? A sound? Rustling leaves? She looked up into the tree branches, which were black and restless against the broken nimbus of sunlight.

For the first time she felt the intense solitude of this place, this small, shadowed forest, the halfway point between the warm civilization of the inn and the great gaping violence of the Atlantic.

She was all alone. Except for the sounds that broke the silence. The sound of footsteps, coming through the dead leaves. Coming toward her.

She'd heard them before. She remembered that now. Back when she was only eight years old, when angels were playmates and footsteps were always innocent, she had heard this same sound. Footsteps coming through the trees.

That day, she'd heard them without particularly caring. She had played on, telling Polly about the elves who lived in the morning glories, until she decided she wanted to tell her mother, too. Her mother would like that story—she'd have something new to add, to make the story even better. Emily remembered that she had hoped the footsteps hadn't been Dorrie's, who would not like their stories. She had hoped the footsteps were Mr. Maxwell's, who always played along.

She couldn't remember anything after that. After that, there was only a cold, black lump of dread in her mind where memories should have been. But it was enough. She knew, knew from the shuddering that seemed to have started deep inside her like an internal earthquake, that she really had seen something that day.

She had seen *someone*.

There truly was a memory and someday she would find it again. The certainty nearly buckled her knees. If she knew, perhaps someone else knew, too. Perhaps Christopher Maxwell had been right.

The footsteps came closer, leaves cracking under slow, careful treads.

Instinctively, she picked up a fallen log, even as she wondered if she'd have the courage to use it. She tested its weight, tightened her palm around its rough bark.

"Emily?"

A female figure came cautiously from between two trees. It was just a silhouette, but to Emily's immense relief, it looked like Livvy.

She let the log fall softly to the mulchy ground, feeling foolish. "Livvy?"

"No, it's Beverly," the young woman said. "I'm the maid. Livvy sent me out to get you."

Emily's thoughts immediately shot to Dorrie. "Is it my aunt? Is she all right?"

"She's fine, but she'd like you to go to the store and get her something. A special headache medicine, I think. Livvy has quite a few, but apparently Mrs. Murphy uses only a particular brand."

"Yes, that's true." Emily brushed her palms against each other. "I thought she'd brought plenty. But I'll go right away."

She caught up with the other woman and the two

of them began to walk back toward the inn. As they emerged from the forest into the blazing sunlight, she looked over at the pretty young maid, who did indeed look a little like Livvy with her long brown hair and petite frame.

"I'm sorry you had to come all that way to get me," Emily said.

Beverly smiled. "No problem. It's a beautiful day, and it's good to get out of the house."

Emily had a sudden thought. "But how did you know where I was?" She looked back at the trees. It would be impossible to see anyone through their dense shadows.

Beverly shrugged. "Mr. Maxwell knew," she said. "I guess he watched you go in."

EMILY ENJOYED HER TRIP to the drugstore, which was quite a distance away, down the hill and around the island's big bend to the small downtown area of Cliff's Cove. It felt good to get away from her over-heated imagination and from the oppressive, tragic history of the inn itself.

In fact, as she drove back up the hill and saw Lost Angel Inn above her, dominating the sky with its heavy mustard-colored bulk and its aggressive turrets, she wondered why a woman as gentle as Olivia Hamilton had decided to buy it. Perhaps, given the tragedies the inn seemed to attract, it might be better just to let it stand uninhabited and gradually decay away to dust.

But again, once she was inside, where Olivia's warmth had created such a lovely oasis, she found herself relaxing. There wasn't, she decided, anything intrinsically unhealthy about the house. It was just that the Victorian vision of ideal architecture was a bit overwrought for her twenty-first-century sensibilities.

Emily spent the afternoon in the courtyard, sitting next to the beautiful, crumbling fountain at the back, just reading and drinking in the sunshine. By dinnertime, Dorothy professed herself well and ready to join the party.

The meal was delicious. Livvy had provided rosemary-crusted pork and an avocado-vegetable lasagna for guests who didn't eat meat. By the time Emily had tasted the roasted tomato-and-pepper salad, the delicately seasoned new potatoes and a positively irresistible chocolate-raspberry cake for dessert, she was so full she could hardly move and she was also quite certain that someday Lost Angel Inn would overcome its sad past and be a thriving success.

Emily was pleased to see that her aunt did make an effort. Though Dorothy's personality could never be called bubbly, she was so enthusiastic about the lasagna that, for Dorothy, it practically qualified as raving. She offered several compliments on Livvy's renovations and she even asked Christopher a polite question about his restoration of the ornate staircase finials.

The Farrells were easy company, just a simple Idaho couple celebrating their twenty-fifth anniversary touring the Maine coast. Overall, Emily was pleased, and she could see that Livvy's smile held a clear note of relief.

After dinner, Dorothy went back upstairs. She hadn't ever been a social creature and had probably exhausted her store of small talk. Emily, though, stayed downstairs chatting with the Farrells, who had great stories to tell. Christopher seemed to disappear after dinner, as did Livvy, who obviously was helping the cook in the kitchen.

When the Farrells seemed to want to be alone— it was refreshing to see how in love they still were— Emily politely wandered into the parlor. She had been itching to look over the *secrétaire* one more time. She still felt inexplicably drawn to it and curious about what secrets it might hold.

In the glow of the lamplight, the antique desk looked splendid and mysterious. Emily tested each of the drawers, loving the rich, musky wood smell that floated out of the beautifully constructed pieces. She removed a couple of drawers entirely, feeling around the empty cavities.

What was she looking for? She had no idea. She

knew only that she felt the most peculiar compulsion to explore this piece from every angle.

It was very strange. For the first time, standing here beside the *secrétaire*, she thought she sensed again the vague presence of the chambermaid, the presence that had haunted her every night that summer long ago. She didn't hear any weeping—that seemed to emanate only from the second floor, near the attic and only in the middle of the night—but it was as if the chambermaid had walked into the parlor and was urging her to keep looking.

Emily put the drawer back and tried to shake off the sensation. It was absurd. This luxurious, expensive piece of furniture could only have belonged to a wealthy lady, the senator's wife, not the immigrant Irish servant who lived in their attic. The chambermaid could have no connection to it at all.

"Find anything?"

She looked up guiltily. Christopher stood in the parlor doorway, his face in shadows. She wondered how long he'd been watching.

And she wondered why he'd watched her.

"No," she said sheepishly. "I'm sure if there were anything here you and Livvy would already have found it."

"Maybe," he said. He moved into the room. When the lamplight hit his cheek, sparking off his blond hair like flint, she felt her insides clench. He really was an extraordinarily attractive man. "But there's no harm in taking another look."

He stopped a couple of feet from her. "I actually wanted to apologize," he said. "I came on pretty strong this morning. It's just that…my father isn't well, and this whole thing has already caused him so much pain. I can't bear to think of it being raked up all over again. And of course, Livvy can't afford another scandal."

He looked toward the kitchen area where the sounds of dishes being washed and put away were finally dwindling off. Then he looked back at Emily, shoving his hands into the pockets of his jeans. "Anyhow, none of that is your fault. I just wanted to say I do understand what you're going through, too."

"Thank you," she said, oddly pleased. It was ridiculous to care what he thought of her, and yet she had to accept the obvious truth. For some obscure reason—maybe just because he had known her mother—she did care.

She felt self-conscious, so she turned back to the *secrétaire*.

"It's weird," she said, "but, you know, I just can't shake the feeling that there is something important about this piece."

She rubbed her fingers across the mother-of-pearl garland in front, then pulled open another drawer. "Sounds crazy, doesn't it? But maybe this house has always made me a little crazy. The old legend, the chambermaid part particularly. Did you know I used to think I heard the ghost weeping in the middle of the night?"

"Was that right after your mother died? That would be understandable, I'd think."

"No, actually it was before. I heard it almost every night. My mother said she couldn't hear it, even though we slept in the same bedroom. I guess I was just an overly imaginative child. That's what Dorrie thought, anyhow."

She shrugged and slid the drawer back into place. "Look at me now, obsessing about this thing. I guess I'm *still* overly imaginative."

She risked a glance over at him, ready to see a look of contempt, but to her surprise he was slightly smiling.

"I remember you back then," he said. "You were…what? About seven or eight? You were always laughing and singing. You liked to dress up like a fairy. Once you made wings out of a pair of wire clothes hangers and toilet tissue." He laughed softly. "What a mess that was!"

She laughed, too, but she felt herself flushing. "I rest my case. Overly imaginative may not cover it."

How strange to think that he remembered her. She hadn't been aware of him at all. She'd known that her mother's friend, Mr. Maxwell, had had a son, but fifteen-year-old boys had seemed pretty boring at the time.

He wasn't boring now, though. When he laughed, she felt it move through her, melting little bits of nerve and muscle as it went. Making things move and quiver with new life. Like a thaw.

This wasn't like her. She was twenty-eight, not a teenager. She was a sensible executive assistant for an accounting firm, the same accounting firm from which her staid aunt had retired last year.

People like her didn't have lust-at-first-sight episodes. Besides, Dorothy had always insisted, in her years of strict tutelage, that Emily dress with sober restraint, behave with propriety and reserve, live guardedly, without excess. As Dorothy did herself.

Even as a teenager, Emily hadn't been allowed to fall in and out of love like the other girls. "You mustn't be a flirt," Dorothy would say. Or, "You mustn't make a spectacle of yourself." *Like your mother.* Those were the words that, though they were never spoken out loud, ended every admonition.

"You've changed," he said. It was as if he had read her thoughts. "You don't look as if you wear wings very often anymore."

To her dismay, she felt tears pricking at her eyelids. He was right, wasn't he? Eventually, something alive and buoyant in Emily had been smothered by all that disapproval. To please her demanding aunt, she'd buried that singing, laughing, winged little girl Christopher remembered.

But maybe he wasn't completely right. Yes, she had smothered that part of herself. Buried it. But obviously not killed it entirely. The thing inside her that had quickened under Christopher's smile had wings. She could feel them now, beating faintly at the walls of her heart.

Don't be a fool, she could almost hear Dorrie saying now. *Don't be impetuous, reckless...like your mother. Do you want to end up like your mother?*

But for the first time she heard another question. Did she want to end up like Dorothy?

"Chris?" Livvy's soft voice called from the kitchen. She obviously was looking for him, and it wouldn't be long before she found him here.

"Tell me," Emily said impulsively. "How did you know I'd gone into the little woods today?"

"I was watching you," he said, his gaze dark on her face. "I watch you almost all the time."

She could hear Livvy's footsteps coming toward the foyer, the limp somehow more audible than it had been during the day.

Emily put her hand on Christopher's arm. It was warm and strong. "Why do you watch me?"

He reached up and touched her face with his fingertips.

"Because you're very beautiful," he said. Dropping his hand, he moved toward the door. At the last minute, he turned with an enigmatic smile. "And because you're very dangerous."

CHAPTER FIVE

THE NEXT DAY Emily took Dorothy on a tour of the island. She was still avoiding going to the cliff, she knew, but Dorothy was eager to have lunch at a lobster restaurant in Cliff's Cove and Emily was determined to make her happy at any cost.

Besides, Emily rationalized, there was plenty of time for the trip to the cliff. They would be staying at the inn for a full week.

When they got back around dusk, Christopher's truck wasn't in the parking lot. Emily had to fight a rush of disappointment when Beverly told them, as she set the table, that Mr. Maxwell would be sleeping on the mainland tonight.

Livvy had explained that situation to them earlier. Though Christopher did a lot of work for her and sometimes stayed overnight in a quaint, nineteenth-century workshop cottage on the eastern border of the property, the inn could hardly afford to employ him full-time. He had a carpentry business and a real house on the mainland.

Without him, dinner seemed a dull affair. Everyone went their separate ways as soon as coffee was finished. Dorothy said her headache was coming back and went up early to bed.

Only Emily felt unable to sleep. She grabbed a sweater and walked out to the wraparound porch, thirsty for a long drink of clean sea air. She stayed nearly an hour, finding peace in the beauty of the night. The cloudless sky was as infinite as an ocean itself, with a hundred shining starships cruising along its silent black expanse.

It was very special. But when she realized that a low, tight yearning had begun in the pit of her stomach, a patently female longing for the touch of a man's hand, she stood and went back inside. She knew which man she had been yearning for, and told herself she mustn't be such a fool as to imagine that Christopher Maxwell felt the same longing for her.

If he did, why would he have jumped that ferry and put the distance of the entire Lost Angel Bay between them?

The house was dim, settled in for the night, and she climbed the winding staircase carefully, hoping not to wake anyone with the creaking steps.

But as she reached the top, she suddenly heard a familiar sound, a sound that made the hair on the back of her neck prickle and shift. It was the sound of a woman weeping.

Her knees seemed to have no locks, no muscles—though her hand clutched the staircase railing so hard her fingers ached. Her gaze bored into the shadows at the top of the stairs, which ultimately led to the attic rooms. Was this how the weeping had always sounded? Had it always been so raw, so full of angry pain?

Surely not. If it had sounded like this, the child Emily would have cowered in terror, would have refused to sleep another night in such a house. No, her little ghost had been plaintive, sweetly sad, slightly lost. This sound was cruel. Tormented. The laceration of a soul in too much pain to bear.

She wasn't sure how she found the courage, but she somehow managed to climb the last twelve steps. With every step, the sobbing became clearer, more audible.

More human.

Emboldened by that thought—*human*—Emily moved through the dark corridor toward the chambermaid's room. It wasn't a ghost, it couldn't be. Her skin tingled, but somehow she knew that this misery was real, present, flesh-bound—not the bloodless echo of some old sorrow, some wisp of energy trapped in the space between two worlds.

When she opened the door, the sound stopped instantly, as if someone had turned it off with a switch. It took a minute for her eyes to adjust to the small stream of milky moonlight that came in through the narrow servant's window.

But finally she saw the woman kneeling in front of the window. And recognized her. It was her aunt.

"Dorrie!" Emily rushed to comfort her, taking the older woman's damp hands in her own. "Dorrie! What's the matter?"

At first her aunt didn't answer. Dorothy merely shook her head, and as she did Emily could see that her long-jawed, homely face was streaked with tears, her deep-set eyes swollen from weeping. Her hair, which she normally wore in a long braid when sleeping, had fought its way free and now flew everywhere in coarse, gray wisps that reminded Emily unpleasantly of spider webs.

Emily shifted, kneeling beside her aunt. "Dorrie, please, tell me what's wrong. Why are you up here? Did you hear something? Did you see something?"

"You mean, the ghost?" Her aunt's voice sounded harsh, as if the crying had damaged her vocal cords. "There are no ghosts, Emily. I wish there were. I wish your mother would come. Just once, I'd like to see her. I wish she could tell me—"

Her aunt broke off on another harsh sob.

"Tell you what, Dorrie?" Emily spoke as softly as possible. She thought she understood. She had wished these things herself, so many times. "Do you wish she could tell you who killed her?"

Dorothy shook her head roughly. She seemed more exhausted than Emily had ever seen her, almost too exhausted for caution. "No," she rasped. "I wish she could tell me—" She put her hands over her face. "I wish she could tell me that I've done a good job with you. I wish she knew I've tried to do right by her daughter."

Oh, Dorrie. Emily bent and stroked the tangled gray hair. "Of course she knows that, Dorrie. Of course you've done a good job. You've been a wonderful mother to me."

Dorothy looked at Emily bleakly. "I didn't want to take you away from her," she said without energy. "I never wanted children."

Emily had always suspected that, but somehow the simple admission was painful all the same. Still, she kept her voice and face neutral. "I know," she said. "It must have been very difficult. But you did a wonderful job."

Dorothy closed her eyes, exhaling a long, low sigh that carried a moan on its current. "I did my best. What else could I do? I couldn't bring her back."

Her voice seemed a little slurred and, leaning this close, Emily wondered if she smelled alcohol on her aunt's breath. She'd never known Dorothy to drink, but—

Something was wrong with her. Whether she was drunk from sherry wine or an excess of heartbreak, she needed to get out of this dark, airless room. She needed rest and calm.

"Let me take you back to bed," Emily said. "You're very tired."

"Yes," Dorothy agreed, dragging out the word strangely. She seemed half asleep already. "Tired."

Emily reached over and put her hands under her aunt's arms, ready to pull her to her feet. She hoped she wouldn't have to ask Livvy for help, but Dorothy was a very tall, substantial woman who would not be easy to move.

It took all her strength, but she made it, somehow. Dorothy rose to her feet, though her head lolled against Emily's shoulder.

After a couple of awkward steps, Dorothy seemed to rouse a little. She lifted her head and stared into Emily's eyes with an odd, unfocused gaze.

"You're right," she said in a flat tone.

"About what?" Emily tried to smile, but that gaze was so peculiar...

"I am tired," Dorothy whispered softly. "You've been gone such a very long time."

IN THE MORNING, it was as if it never happened. Dorothy came down to breakfast and seemed, if anything, quite well rested and cheerful. When Emily cautiously brought it up, Dorothy brushed it aside with a simple, "I had one of those sick headaches. I'm sorry I alarmed you."

Emily knew that meant she would discuss it no

further. She let it go, but made a mental note that if her aunt seemed unwell again, they would leave this place immediately.

But right now Dorothy was chatting with the Farrells. Maybe there was something invigorating in the air. The whole house was in a smiling mood.

After breakfast, Christopher, who had returned on the dawn ferry, it seemed, called everyone—including the housekeeper Beverly and even the ordinarily elusive cook—into the little blue parlor.

"I thought you all might like to be a part of the ceremony," he said with a smile. "I found the hidden drawer and Livvy is just about to open it."

Emily caught her breath as she noticed Lucy Knight's beautiful desk, which had been tilted on its side to allow access to the underside. When Emily squinted, she could just barely see the outline of a complex compartment hidden in the joint of one leg. The tiny gold key protruded from it, ready to be turned.

Everyone gathered around the *secrétaire,* coffee cups in hand, eagerly speculating about what might be inside.

Charlie Farrell laughed. "I hope it's not a big, fat, disappointing *nothing*, like what happened on that hyped-up TV show a few years back."

Josie slapped his arm. "Don't be such a killjoy. It's probably a fabulous jewel, like the Hope diamond or something."

Emily smiled at the Farrells, who obviously thought they were getting a good show for their money. Then she turned her attention back to Livvy, whose pale face looked as excited as Emily felt.

Livvy stood beside the *secrétaire*, smiling over at Christopher. "Now?"

He nodded. Livvy bent and carefully twisted the filigreed end of the gold key. It turned and suddenly the bottom edge of the antique seemed to separate, a jigsaw-shaped piece descending toward her hand.

"Oh!" She laughed, and Emily, transfixed, felt a squirm of anticipation in her stomach. Livvy grinned up at Christopher. "There really is a drawer!"

The small, oddly shaped compartment fell completely into her open palm. At first a murmur of disappointment ran across the watching crowd. It appeared to be empty.

"Damn," Charlie Farrell said with gusto.

"No," Livvy said suddenly. "There's something here. It's—" She began to unfold a small piece of ecru-colored stationery. "It seems to be a letter." She flipped it over, scanning to the bottom, and gasped slightly. "It's signed by Lucy Knight."

Charlie Farrell scowled. "Who the devil is that?"

"For God's sake, Charlie, didn't you read a word of the brochures I gave you?" For the first time Josie truly seemed annoyed with her husband. "It's all part of the spooky legend. That's why we're staying here.

A servant killed Lucy Knight's husband, then she miscarried her baby and finally hanged herself in the attic."

He looked stunned. *"That's* why we're staying here?"

During their bickering, Livvy had been silently reading the letter. Emily watched her carefully and saw her pale face turn even paler.

"What?" She couldn't wait for the Farrells to sort things out. She had to know. "Livvy, what does it say?"

"It says—" The hand with which Livvy held the letter was shaking. Christopher put his arm around her shoulders and she leaned back against him, as if grateful for the support. Emily could imagine how strong and safe that arm must feel.

"It says the chambermaid didn't do it."

TWO HOURS LATER, they'd all read the letter, oohed and ahhed and exclaimed over it, analyzed details and phrases, and generally discussed it from every angle.

And what a juicy story it was! The letter was a confession, complete with salacious details. Apparently the elegant, socially prominent Lucy had already been pregnant by a secret lover when she'd married the senator from Maine, Jack Knight. The poor chump had discovered on their wedding night that his wife was a tramp, and had confronted her, vowing to annul the marriage. Unwilling to suffer the public humiliation, Lucy had stabbed him, then framed poor little Nora O'Malley, a young chambermaid who was known to worship Jack. The chambermaid's dying curse had caught up with Lucy, though. Over the next few months Lucy had lost her baby, her friends and finally her mind.

The last lines of the letter had been heartbreakingly simple, a verbal photograph of a woman tormented by guilt and a strange, hopeless anger against her own nature and her self-imposed fate.

"'I am, even now, a coward. I will hide this letter. Perhaps posterity will permit my reputation to go untarnished. But she's strong. She curses this house from the grave, and so perhaps she can guide the authorities to this secret, too. But by then, I'll have made my own gallows and my own peace. Does that amuse you, Nora? We become sisters, now, in death.'"

A couple of the women had tears in their eyes by the time the whole letter had been read. Even Charlie had to clear his throat. "Poor little Irish kid," he said. "I'm Irish, you know. We've always been badly mistreated."

Christopher, too, felt the drama, though he'd never been obsessed with the whole legend nonsense and had never seen or heard a single odd thing in all the hours he'd spent in this house. But he saw that this new revelation was exciting—and would add to the public fascination with the inn.

Finally, though, reality reasserted its claims. After folding the letter carefully and taking it upstairs to the attic rooms, where the inn's safe was kept, Livvy reluctantly went into the kitchen with the cook to get lunch started. Dorothy excused herself, too, saying she wanted to lie down for a few minutes.

For the first time in two days Christopher had a chance to talk to Emily alone.

He found her on the front porch, leaning against the railing, looking out toward the ocean. He stood behind her a long moment, enjoying the way the wind and sun played with her thick, shining hair. For the first time he wished he had his father's artistic talent. He would have liked a picture of this, to look at when winter came.

"You can personally take credit for the whole discovery, you know," he said.

She turned quickly, as though he'd startled her. "I can? Why?"

He joined her at the railing. "You seemed so sure there was something to find. I decided maybe we'd given up too easily. So yesterday I did some research on the craftsman who designed this piece. Talked to some antique dealers up in Portland. Apparently this designer put secret drawers in some of his other pieces, and they gave me an idea where to look."

She smiled. A real smile. If she only knew how much like her mother she looked when she smiled.

"Oh, I'd like very much to think I was a part of solving this mystery! It's funny, I wasn't really surprised to hear the truth, were you? I always thought something in the old story just never made sense. And the weeping I used to imagine I heard… It never sounded evil. Just sad."

"No, I don't think I was particularly surprised," he said. "For one thing, I've seen firsthand how, when a murder investigation is going badly, the police love to pick a scapegoat, preferably one without any social clout, and pin the blame on him."

She nodded. "Your father."

"Yeah." He wondered whether he should get into this and finally decided she needed to hear the other side of the story. "He was just a local artist, not rich or important in any way. And of course he'd committed the sin of falling in love with a woman who wasn't his wife. So, of course, when she died, it wasn't much of a leap from there to label him a murderer."

"But they never found any proof. They never charged him with anything."

"No." Christopher tried not to let his life-long resentment show in his voice. His experience had been difficult, but her loss had been far greater. "But they made his life hell. My mother divorced him, of course. You probably don't even know about this, but a couple of weeks after your mother's death another man went missing. The police chief's brother. He'd also been in love with your mother—she took men that way, you know. She was extraordinary. Anyhow, some people started to say maybe my dad had killed him, too."

"Oh, Christopher. How terrible."

"Yes," he said. "It was. Within the year, he'd had a heart attack and he hasn't been strong since. The police chief had once been my dad's best friend, but even he believed my father was guilty. Finally, Dad just couldn't take it anymore. He quit painting entirely and moved to Portland fifteen years ago."

He wondered if she believed any of this. Obviously her viper of an aunt was convinced that Martin Maxwell was the killer. Which was a hell of a note, because he remembered quite clearly that his dad had been ridiculously nice to the woman that summer twenty years ago. Christopher had thought she was a hideous, mean old bat and had told his father so. Martin had merely replied calmly, "Pretty people aren't the only ones who deserve human kindness, Chris."

But Dorothy Murphy had undoubtedly brought little Emily up on tales of the monster Martin Maxwell. It would probably take a lot more than Christopher's clearly prejudiced statements to change her mind.

Still—she was looking at him with such a gentle expression that he wondered if he might have underestimated her. She had her mother's beauty. Maybe she had inherited her mother's sweetness, as well.

She reached out and touched his arm. She'd done that before. Every time it sent a shock of electricity through his system.

"May I ask you for a favor?" Her wide eyes, with their mottled blues and grays and greens, looked uncertain and a little sad, as if she grieved for his story. He suddenly wanted to pull her into his arms to protect her from everything and everyone. She might be just as beautiful as Melissa Carlyle, but she had a fragility, a vulnerability, that was almost the exact opposite of Melissa's sunny confidence. It was poignant, lovely…and it tugged at men's hearts.

It tugged at Christopher's heart.

"Yes," he said stupidly, not waiting to hear what it was, as if he were a knight who could drive a sword through any dragon's breast just for the asking. "Of course."

She smiled. "Someday soon, when we have a little time alone, will you tell me about my mother?"

He didn't answer that directly. That, he knew, would be a problem. Unless he was ready to lie.

CHAPTER SIX

TIME WAS RUNNING OUT.

The next morning Emily knew she had to act. It was already Friday and she and Dorothy planned to leave Lost Angel Island on Sunday morning. Emily could hardly believe she'd already been here so long without accomplishing her mission. Without even really trying to.

So no more procrastinating. No more excuses. No more getting caught up in a hundred-and-forty-year-old mystery and neglecting her own.

Today she would go to the cliff to see what she could discover.

Luckily, Dorothy wanted to go back into Cliff's Cove to shop, so Emily was on her own. She didn't mention her plans, but she suspected that Dorothy knew. Perhaps that was why the shopping trip had suddenly cropped up so urgently. Dorothy had never approved of Emily's pilgrimage, and she certainly wouldn't want to participate.

Once she had waved Dorothy goodbye, Emily

wasted no time. She threw on jeans and a sweatshirt and at the last minute pulled an umbrella from the mudroom. The forecast was for rain this afternoon and she had no idea how long she'd be out there.

And then, without stopping to tell anyone where she was going, she walked briskly toward the cliff, avoiding sentimental side trips through the little forest.

Finally, just as her thighs were beginning to burn, there she was, standing high in the cold blue wind at the end of the world.

The storm must be closer than she thought. The wind was loud in her ears and the ocean, which stretched out on three sides, was a deep, shifting silver-green. The birds wheeled close to the land, their cries sounding like warnings.

She moved closer, ignoring the Danger sign Livvy had posted. Emily didn't need a sign to tell her about that.

At first she couldn't look down, but, despising her cowardice, she forced herself to lower her eyes.

Oh, God…

She'd forgotten the sheer, merciless, fantasy-movie effect of this cliff. It was a sharp, clean, seventy-foot drop to the water below. She stood at least three feet back from the edge, but even so the first glance of the neatly sliced, sudden *nothingness* almost unbalanced her. Her inner ear rocked, as if the ground beneath her feet wasn't quite trustworthy, as if it might tilt forward at will, spilling her into the ocean without warning.

And not just the ocean. The rocks. The dark, jagged formations that looked like the knuckles of an angry giant, rising from the depths. The rocks clearly made the ocean nervous. Supplicant, the water licked the cruel, pocked surface and then retreated. Then dashed itself against the rock, harder this time, as if maddened with fear, white foam bleeding all over the black.

She shut her eyes. She didn't care if she was a coward. She couldn't look at those rocks. She couldn't imagine her mother lying there, like a sacrifice, with the foamy tongues of water licking at her hair.

She turned instead to the grassy field behind the cliff, where they had so often picnicked. They had been happy here, in the sun, in the innocence of their youth. She realized now how young her mother had really been. Just thirty. Just two years older than Emily was now.

Young, and in love with Martin Maxwell, who had often joined them on their picnics. And with that, another forgotten memory came back to her. Several times her mother and Mr. Maxwell had led her down a little staircase so that she could swim in a tiny, protected cove, where minnows tickled her feet and sometimes birds came right up and took bread out of her hand.

And probably, she realized now, so that they could

stand in the shadow of the cliff and kiss. Suddenly she was glad, so glad, that her mother had found love before she died.

Where was that funny little staircase? She'd always felt happy there—and safe. She remembered thinking that maybe Martin would marry her mother, and liking the idea. Her eight-year-old mind had not understood the real Mrs. Maxwell as an impediment. Martin's wife was nearly a recluse, a pale, worried woman who feared the sun and almost everything else, too.

Emily wandered a couple of minutes, peering carefully over the edges of the cliff, looking for the gentler slope and stairs she remembered.

Finally she found it. A narrow, skeletal wooden structure that looked like temporary scaffolding, attached to the rocky slope, which was probably only about twenty-five-feet high in this spot. The stairs looked rickety, but when she put out a foot to test them, they seemed sound enough. No Danger sign had been posted here, so she assumed they were safe to climb.

Still, she moved gingerly. And she almost made it.

She was just eight feet from the bottom when, with only one loud crack as warning, the staircase collapsed. It simply separated under her hands and suddenly her feet had nothing solid below them. She was walking on air.

There was no time to scream and no one to hear her if she did. She clung to the last inch of railing as long as she could, skinning the palm of her hand, but within seconds it fell, too, and she dropped the last eight feet to the ground.

Luckily, the tide was coming in and the small patch of beach was muddy and soft. Her sore ankle suffered another twisting, but she was pretty sure nothing was broken.

She sat for a long minute, catching her breath. For that minute, it was enough to know she was alive and basically unharmed.

After that, though, she comprehended the real problem. The tide was coming in. The storm was making its way to shore. She was already wet and growing cold.

And she had no way to climb back up the face of this cliff.

She tried, of course. But with her twisted ankle and her torn palms, it was almost impossible. The rocks here weren't large, permanent granite outcroppings. They were small and water-polished, precarious. They shifted under her weight, and time and again they rolled her back to the beach. From a couple of feet that didn't matter much. But what if she got up higher, maybe fifteen or twenty feet, and fell?

At first she waited, her back against the cliff, and tried to think of something clever. But the tiny strip of beach was clearly giving way to the incoming tide. Within an hour, it was no more than a foot from her toes. By late afternoon, when Dorothy was due back and would come looking for her, she'd be swimming up to her waist in freezing seawater.

When the rain started to fall, fat cold drops that drenched her quickly, she decided she had to try climbing again. She took off her shoes, which didn't have enough traction to help. She'd do better if she could feel every inch with her bare toes.

She wrapped her socks around her palms like bandages to protect the raw skin. And then she began to climb.

She fell so often she might have despaired—except that despair was not an option. She thought of Dorrie, who would be so frightened, who had lost so much to this cliff already, and she knew she couldn't give up. She kept climbing, five feet forward, then two feet back, blinking away streams of rain and gritting her teeth against the pain in her hands and ankle.

Finally she reached the point where she no longer needed to look down. She knew she'd come too far now to think about going back.

But at the moment she didn't see how she could go forward, either. She felt around wildly with her less-injured hand, but she couldn't find a rock to hold. Not one that didn't pull free and tumble past her, falling into the water below with an ominous splash.

The wind was loud, and the rain, too, as it pooled in her ears and pelted the rocks. The seabirds were crazed, screaming at each other to head for shelter. Too much noise—it was difficult even to think.

Perhaps, she thought, that was why she imagined she heard someone calling her name.

But then she heard it again.

"Emily!"

She blinked. It sounded like Christopher.

"Can you reach the rope?"

She didn't care if she was imagining it. The sound of his voice gave her an infusion of courage. She blindly groped the rocks, praying it was true. *Nothing here...*

Oh, please...

Suddenly she found it. Her hand stretched, then closed around the scratchy thickness of a huge, wet, knotted rope.

She sobbed once. Just once. There was no time for weakness now. "Yes," she called. She jerked on the rope, in case he couldn't hear her. "I have it."

"Hold tightly. I'm going to pull you up."

It was so unbearably slow, like the most sadistic torture ever devised. She clung to the rope so hard her arm was numb to the shoulder, and clawed at the rocks with her other hand, pretending that, if the rope slipped, the rocks still could hold her up. Her feet bumped and scrambled beneath her in a parody of climbing.

It was surreal, and clumsy, and terrifying, but somehow it worked. The edge of the cliff came into view. She lurched forward onto the grass.

And then, still gasping for breath and clutching the rope in her flayed and bleeding hand, she found herself wrapped in the miraculous bliss of Christopher Maxwell's arms.

CHAPTER SEVEN

CHRISTOPHER WISHED he had cleaned up the cottage this morning. He would have, if he'd known he was going to have to play superhero this afternoon.

After he shoved a bunch of old newspapers into a pile in the corner, he took Emily's soaked blue jeans and sweatshirt and spread them out next to his wet clothes along a handy plank of cherry. The fire blazed nearby, so it was possible they might dry—in a few hours.

He'd pulled on some new jeans and a T-shirt and rubbed his hair with a towel. Through the smoky, dusty windowpanes that led into the storeroom, where Emily was changing into one of his old robes, he could just see the cloudy outline of her body. No details, but the hint of bare shoulder and breast was enough to make his throat go dry.

She was so beautiful. Even bedraggled and frightened, and soaked to the skin, she had the power to make him ache with desire.

God, Maxwell, get a grip. This was hardly the time to think about sex. Emily had damn near died.

If it hadn't been storming, and if she hadn't asked him to stay nearby, he would be out there right now, finding out what the hell had gone wrong with that staircase.

He had repaired it, declared it fit for use only last week.

The door to the storeroom creaked open and he looked up.

"Well," she said sheepishly. "How do I look?"

She held out her arms, looking a little like Dopey of the seven dwarfs, with the old, dingy robe dangling way beyond her fingers. It was about six sizes too big, and about six years past its prime. But if he had hoped it would neutralize her incredible sensuality, he'd been deluding himself big-time.

"Could I maybe add these to the dryer?" She had a small wad of white silk and lace in her hand. She gestured self-consciously toward the cherry plank.

"Sure," he said. He turned his back—more for his sake than for hers—while she arranged the bra and panties. He did not need to imagine how she looked with them on, and he damn sure didn't need to start picturing her as she was now, with them *off*.

Instead he busied himself at the little kitchen sink, preparing the supplies to dress her hands. He'd already called up to the inn and reported to Livvy that both of them were safe, that they'd just wait out the storm in the cottage.

It was pretty tight quarters. The whole cottage was about fifteen by fifteen, and held a twin bed with a rustic, multicolored quilt comforter, an armoire, a small bathroom closet and a kitchenette. It suited him fine when he worked so late he missed the ferry and needed somewhere to crash. But it was hardly a place to entertain company. They could barely walk around without bumping into each other.

"Let's get those hands fixed up, okay?"

He tried to sound friendly and businesslike, but the minute she held out her hands, he had to fight the urge to lean down and kiss the poor torn flesh. Somehow he made himself balance the basin while he poured warm water and then alcohol over her hands. She held them steady, though it must have stung.

"It's not really all that bad," he said, glad that he could be honest. "It looks nasty, but I don't think any of the cuts are very deep."

She was holding her breath, but she nodded and tried to smile.

When he had finished with the ointment and bandages, she let her breath out shakily.

"Thanks," she said. She tossed her head, trying to keep her long, wet hair out of her face. "For this—and for all of it. I don't really know where I'd be right now if you hadn't found me."

He put the scissors and gauze back in his well-stocked medicine cabinet. People who worked with wood and power tools always kept a complete first-aid kit. He'd had his share of nicks and gouges, and his arms had the scars to prove it.

She'd have scars, too. He hoped they were only the physical kind.

"I think you would have done just fine," he said with a hearty smile. "From what I could see, you were almost up to the top before I got there."

She tried to return the smile, but it was a little shaky, too. "*Almost* isn't quite good enough when it comes to scaling a cliff."

He chuckled, glad she still had a sense of humor. She was strong, wasn't she? Strong enough physically to hold on to those rocks, and strong enough emotionally to joke about nearly dying.

She looked out the window, where the rain was still coming down in thick, silver sheets. "I honestly don't know what happened to the staircase. It looked fine. I wouldn't have gone down it if it had seemed rotted or unsafe."

He didn't say anything. He didn't see any reason to alarm her when he hadn't had a chance to check it out. Maybe, during his repairs, he'd missed something. Maybe he'd overlooked a piece of rotten wood…

She touched her fingertips to the pane of glass and traced a zigzag path of raindrops. Her fingers looked small, childlike, emerging from the white gauze he'd wound around her palms.

"I guess," she said, still trying for that joking tone, "that this is one time I should be very glad you were watching me."

"I wasn't," he said. "I had no idea you weren't in the house. This time it was Charlie Farrell who saw you walking along the cliff edge. Apparently he was out on the cliff today, too."

She turned to him, her face registering intense surprise. "He was? I didn't see anyone."

He shrugged. "It's a big cliff," he said.

"So why did you come looking for me?"

He didn't quite know how to answer that one, either. He'd simply had a bad feeling. He'd been in the parlor, making a sketch of the coping that Livvy wanted to replicate in the east wing, when Charlie had come back from his walk, huffing and puffing, pouring himself a big Scotch and water and announcing to the room that he'd seen Emily Carlyle walking all alone on the cliff. Didn't the girl care, Charlie had asked, that a bad storm was predicted to make land by afternoon, not to mention the fact that, according to the curse, some young woman was supposed to die at this creepy house pretty soon?

Christopher had dropped the sketch and headed straight for the cliff, ignoring the rain. He'd wasted precious minutes in the forest, hoping she might have sheltered there, before thinking to look down by the little staircase. Thank God he'd had a strong rope in the cottage. Thank God the cottage was nearby.

So why *had* he bolted out in such a rush, looking for her? He gave up trying to think of some clever answer. What was the point? She might be able to joke, but when he'd imagined being too late, finding her swept to sea or broken on the rocks, he'd nearly gone mad.

Everything he felt was probably showing on his face anyhow. He didn't understand what was happening to him, but for a man who'd spent most of his life "froze up," he certainly was burning hot and fierce now.

"I was worried about you," he said. "I can't help myself, Emily. It doesn't make much sense, but I…care about you. Your safety has begun to matter a great deal to me."

She made a small sound. It wasn't exactly a word and it wasn't exactly a cry, but it sounded lonely, it sounded confused and, above all, it sounded hungry. He knew that sound. It was the sound his own heart had been making ever since he'd met her.

"Emily." He shoved aside the small table that stood between them and went to her. He held out his arms and she sank into them, as if she could no longer stand by herself.

She lifted her face. When he kissed her, she made another little sound. Her lips were full and warm and, tasting their sweet trembling, he was afraid he couldn't be gentle enough, that the fire inside him would drive him to a wildness she wouldn't understand.

But somehow he held back—with care, he stroked warmth into her until he could tell she was on fire, too. She murmured his name as the huge robe slipped from her naked shoulders and he bent to kiss their pale, elegant slopes. He nudged away the oversize lapels with his lips and found her breast. She let her head fall back and her wet hair licked at his fingers.

Time seemed to stretch forever. They were like two lovers in a fairy tale, locked in their quaint stone cottage in the middle of the enchanted woods. They barely noticed the rain beating on the sturdy slate roof and falling down the chimney, making the golden fire pop and sizzle. They thought of nothing but each other, of the pleasure they could find, of the comfort they could give. They had drawn a magic line at the threshold. Pain and fear and danger could not enter here.

He lowered her to the narrow bed, his need so great he marveled at his ability to go slowly. That, too, was part of the magic. Desire that would have overpowered him on another day stayed inside him now like a long, thrilling note of joy. He could have waited forever, if she'd asked it.

But he was a fool—he should have rushed her. He should have pressed the moment. Because suddenly the blissful spell was broken by a rough pounding and an angry voice raised above the wind and rain.

He looked at the door, not immediately comprehending. Who could it be? He'd called the inn. No one needed to worry. Perhaps they would just go away...

But when he looked back at Emily, he saw that the damage was absolute. Her face was as motionless, as fireless, as stone.

"It's my aunt," she said. "She's probably worried sick about me."

"I called," he said stupidly. He knew that wasn't the point. But it was so hard to give up the dream they'd been dreaming. It had been so...so perfect.

"I know, but she's—" Emily sat up, pulling the robe tight and high around her neck. "She's very protective."

He moved away. Begging would be useless, even if he could bring himself to do it. The cottage suddenly felt so cold he wondered if the fire had drowned in its own flames.

"Emily! It's Dorothy. Let me in."

Emily stood, but she didn't move. It was his cottage, his door to answer.

And so, because he had no choice, he had no real magic that could zap Dorothy Murphy straight to hell, where she deserved to be, he answered it. He pulled the door open with a rough jerk—it had a tendency to stick. And there she was, the old viper herself, looking as if she'd like to lynch him from the nearest tree.

"Where's Emily?" Dorothy's hair was flat and

dark from the rain, not a good look for her. It made her face more mannish and spiteful than ever. "What have you done to my niece?"

"I'm here, Dorrie." Emily came up behind him, still holding her robe shut tightly at the throat. "I'm fine. I took a spill, but Christopher came to my rescue."

"Took a spill? What happened? What's wrong with your hands?"

Emily looked uncomfortable, but there was no way for her to hold the robe shut and hide her bandaged hands at the same time. She gave her aunt a placating smile. *Witch,* Christopher thought bitterly. Emily had probably spent the better part of her life placating the bitter old woman.

"It was my own fault, Dorrie. I was stupid—I decided to climb down a little staircase that was obviously not strong enough to hold me. It broke and I fell a little. But I'm fine now, honestly. Thanks to Christopher."

"Thanks to Christopher?" Dorothy turned her venomous dark eyes toward him. He gave her back look for look, but she wasn't intimidated. "He's probably the one responsible, Emily. He was working on those stairs just a few days ago. It's his fault, if you fell. It may even have been deliberate."

Emily made a shocked sound. "Don't say such horrible things, Dorrie. You are letting yourself get upset. Christopher had nothing to do with it. He wasn't even out there."

"He didn't have to be. He'd already set the trap. He's determined that you won't remember what happened the day your mother died, Emily. He'll do anything to stop you from remembering."

"Dorrie, he saved me." Emily gave Christopher a horrified, apologetic look. "You aren't yourself, you don't know what you're saying."

"I know exactly what I'm saying. It's high time someone made him tell what he knows."

Christopher tightened his voice, forced it to be cold. He would not let this woman get what she wanted—he would not let her make him lose control. "What exactly do you think I know, Mrs. Murphy?"

"You know your father did it. Or else you did it yourself." She turned toward Emily. "He probably loved your mother, too. Everyone did. And his adolescent ego couldn't endure her rejection, so he killed her." She glared again at Christopher. "Did you? Did you love Melissa, too?"

He almost lied. He knew it would be better. But, in the end, he couldn't. He wasn't a liar, and this old harpy was not going to turn him into one.

"No, I didn't love Melissa," he said. "In fact, Mrs. Murphy, I hated her."

He felt the sharp intake of shocked breath from Emily, behind him, and the triumphant hiss from Dorothy, in front. He chose to ignore Dorothy and address his explanation to Emily.

"I was fifteen," he said. "All I saw was that Melissa was tearing apart my family. My mother cried all the time, and my father's heart was breaking, torn between them. I hated her for that, but I didn't kill her. You know that, Emily, in your heart. You know I'm not a killer."

"She knows nothing about you," Dorothy said, her voice as sharp as a razor blade slicing the two younger people apart, ripping him out of the picture so that he could be tossed aside.

He saw Emily's gaze falter as she turned toward her aunt.

"She knows nothing except that you're a slick, deceptive son of an adulterer who will stop at nothing to get what you want." Dorothy flicked a contemptuous glance at Emily's tousled hair and rumpled robe. "Apparently, like your father, you don't even draw the line at seduction."

If he had ever felt like killing anyone, this would be the moment. But what he had told Emily was true. He wasn't a killer. He turned to her now with a steady gaze.

"Do you believe what she's saying?"

Emily shook her head. "No." But her voice wasn't one hundred percent certain and they both heard it. That one distant note of doubt was harder to hear than any of Dorothy's vicious insults.

"No," Emily said again, this time putting more force behind it. "But still…I think I'd better go back up to the inn with my aunt now. This afternoon has obviously been very stressful for all of us. I think Dorothy and I need to talk."

He had told himself he wouldn't stoop to begging, but how could he let her do this? "Don't go," he said. "Trust me. Stay here with me."

"I have the car here, Emily. Come as you are."

Dorothy sounded calmer, less strident. She knew she had won. He knew it, too—and he knew that, in every logical way, it made sense. Emily had known him only three days. She'd known her aunt a lifetime.

"Stay," he said again, like a fool.

"I can't," Emily said softly. "I'm sorry."

The rain was slowing. The only sound that remained was a sad, syncopated rhythm of drops from the eaves. He was surprised to see that, beyond the storm clouds, it was still a summer afternoon.

"All right," he said. "Take the robe. I'll bring your things to the inn later, when they're dry."

She nodded and he stepped aside to let her out of the cottage. Dorothy gave him one final gloating glance and began to move through the drizzle toward her car.

At the last second, impulsively he reached out and grabbed Emily by the wrist. She turned, her face somber and burdened with emotions he could only guess at.

"You know what the real tragedy is in all this, Emily?"

She shook her head. "No," she said. "I'm not sure I know anything anymore."

"Well, I do." He hated how angry he sounded, but he couldn't help himself. "The tragedy isn't that you don't trust me. It's that you don't trust yourself."

CHAPTER EIGHT

THEY WOULD LEAVE tomorrow, Emily decided, whether she recovered any memories or not. The past suddenly didn't seem all that important anymore. Emily knew her aunt was cracking under the stress of being back at Lost Angel Inn. Dorothy's future might be at stake.

And what of Emily's close call today? Call it a curse, call it coincidence or clumsiness or just plain bad luck. It didn't matter. It all added up to one thing: they needed to leave this place.

By the time Emily had made her explanations all around—Livvy was horrified to hear that the stairs were unsafe, but had been quick to defend Christopher's workmanship—Dorothy was looking positively ill. She was suffering one of her terrible headaches.

On the surface, Emily might seem to be the injured one, but she knew that a few cuts and bruises were nothing compared to the psychological trauma revisiting the past seemed to have caused Dorothy. She insisted that her aunt go to her room and lie down. They would talk later.

She promised Dorrie she'd try to rest, too, in her own room across the hall. But, alone with her thoughts, she couldn't sleep. She left both doors open just a little, and waited until she heard Dorothy snoring. Then she tiptoed out and went downstairs. She got the telephone number of Christopher's cottage from Livvy, and she called it, letting it ring until finally an answering machine picked up.

"This is Christopher Maxwell. I'm not available to take your call right now—"

Not available? Or not willing?

She hung up. Perhaps it was just as well. What would she have said? She'd seen the look in his eyes when she left him. It had told her, *Stay now or don't come back at all.*

But how could she have stayed? Though Dorothy had clearly been overwrought, approaching hysterical, she'd had a valid point. For Emily to jump into bed with a man she barely knew, a man connected in convoluted, still unresolved, ways to Melissa's death, couldn't be wise. Emily hadn't been thinking clearly.

She'd been attracted to Christopher from the beginning and the attraction grew stronger every time she saw him. Today, it had felt irresistible. Maybe she'd been a little too shaky from her ordeal, a little too grateful for his rescue. Clearly their adrenaline had been running high. The emotions of life and death and survival had blossomed into powerful sexual stirrings.

That didn't mean they had a relationship, or even the hope of one.

In fact, after what he'd said about her mother, and the hatred she'd seen blazing in his eyes toward Dorothy, Emily could be pretty sure they never would.

But knowing that didn't make it any easier to stop thinking about him, about how safe she'd felt in his cottage, in his arms. How alive.

Once she got Dorothy back to the real world, she'd have to do something about that. She was only twenty-eight years old. Surely she should feel *alive* all the time.

Meanwhile, she had to do something to distract herself or she'd go mad.

She found herself prowling the parlor, which reminded her of yesterday's thrilling discovery. Livvy was still deciding what to do with the letter. No one in the judicial system was likely to be eager to admit a century-old mistake, but everyone at Lost Angel Inn desperately wanted to see poor Nora O'Malley vindicated.

Right now, Livvy was leaning toward Christopher's suggestion, which was to send copies of the letter to Maine's governor and to as many New England newspapers as they could think of. The original would be put in a safe-deposit box in town.

One line in Lucy Knight's letter had struck Emily as particularly interesting. "It's hard to believe something so beautiful could become an instrument of death," Lucy had written. It had seemed, at first reading, to be a slightly incoherent raving, the ramblings of a disturbed mind. The guests had discussed that line yesterday and the consensus had been that Lucy had gone around the bend. Only Charlie had disagreed. He'd insisted that Lucy's vanity was showing—she was talking about her own beautiful self.

But Emily didn't think so. Emily knew the legend pretty well, and she knew that the murder weapon had never been found. The courts had chosen to believe that Nora O'Malley had likely used a kitchen knife and then had tossed it into the Atlantic. That was one of the inconsistencies that had always troubled Emily. If Nora had had time to toss the weapon into the ocean, why hadn't she gotten rid of the blood-stained clothes the authorities had found under her little cot in the attic?

Emily prowled the parlor restlessly, frustrated that so many years were gone, so much evidence clearly destroyed, all the principals dead and buried. With Christopher's help, Livvy had worked hard this past year to restore many of the original items to the house, but she could hardly find—or afford—everything.

Livvy was especially proud of a mahogany *vitrine,* a small glass-topped octagonal table, a sort of showcase for miniatures. When she'd bought the inn, she'd found it languishing in the old workman's cottage, the one Christopher now used. Livvy, who apparently was more informed about the inn's history than its previous owners, had immediately recognized this table.

Early descriptions of the newly constructed mansion had included a list of the small, charming odds and ends that were displayed inside it.

Three of those items were still in the *vitrine* when they'd found it: an amazingly intricate miniature piano made of silver so tarnished no one had recognized its value; a small ivory box carved with flowers, and a desk set that, when its plaque was cleaned and polished, turned out to be one given to Senator Jack by the government as thanks for his diplomatic efforts during the war. It had an ink bottle, now dry, a quill pen, now missing, and a letter opener whose sheath was a lovely, etched gold.

A letter opener...

It couldn't be. But Emily felt again that strange prickling she'd come to associate with Nora O'Malley, the same sensation she'd felt when she heard weeping in the night, or when she'd stood beside the *secrétaire* and searched for secret drawers.

Nora was trying to tell her something. Or her own subconscious was. Or her intuition. Whatever she called it, it was compelling her to look.

She took a deep breath and, ignoring the pain in her ankle, hobbled over to the *vitrine*. The letter opener lay there on the green velvet bedding, the gold of the sheath glimmering in the afternoon sunlight. Carefully, aware that her bandaged hands were clumsy, Emily lifted the glass lid of the table and tilted it back on its small hinged chain.

She picked up the sheath, which looked innocent, blunt and unthreatening. But as she slowly slid out the letter opener itself, she made a startled sound.

It was as sharp and lethal as a dagger.

She heard Livvy in the foyer, bringing fresh flowers to the hall table.

"Livvy?" Emily was surprised at how steady her voice sounded. Apparently her excited quivering was all on the inside. "Livvy, I want to show you something."

MAYBE SHE WAS JUST humoring her guest, but Livvy seemed almost as excited as Emily about the possibility that the letter opener had been the murder weapon. The two of them climbed up to the attic and tucked it into the safe with Lucy Knight's letter.

Livvy closed the safe, then moved toward the stairs. When she realized Emily wasn't behind her, she turned.

"Aren't you coming?"

Emily shook her head. "If you don't mind, I think I'll stay up here a little while."

Livvy looked doubtful. "Most people find it terribly sad. This is, of course, where the infamous weeping is supposed to come from. Are you sure you'll be all right alone? Especially after what you went through today—"

Emily smiled. "I'm fine. In fact, Nora O'Malley and I are the best of friends. I know how idiotic it sounds, but I've heard her."

"You have?"

"Yes. Twenty years ago. I heard her weeping frequently. But also—and I know this sounds crazy— right after my mother died I imagined that Nora came into my room and sang me a lullaby to help me get to sleep."

"Well," Livvy said with a slow smile, "she must have liked you. And if she liked you then, she must absolutely love you now. Now that you've helped us find a way to clear her name."

Emily's own smile deepened. "I hope so," she said. "She helped me through a very tough time. I'd love to return the favor."

Livvy departed, obviously content to leave her.

Emily walked around the attic room slowly, her sprained ankle twinging but holding up reasonably well. It was a dark, shadowy room, and proved exactly how little Senator Knight and his trophy wife had valued their servants. It was hard to imagine anyone actually living in such a small space.

But at least the little window had a beautiful view. From here, she could see the flower-lined grounds, the hilly trails that led to the cliffs and even Christopher's picturesque stone cottage, nestled at the edge of the forest.

Emily stood at that window, looking down, wondering why she didn't sense sorrow in this little room anymore. Every other time she'd stood near the staircase that led to the attic she'd felt an overwhelming emotion pulsing down like invisible waves of grief.

Maybe, she thought, it was because Nora O'Malley's restless spirit was free now. Free to leave this unhappy place where she had been so cruelly mistreated. Maybe she had stayed only long enough to see justice done.

Justice. Emily might have helped to bring it to Nora, but she had done nothing to bring it to her own mother. If she left this place tomorrow, she'd never come back. She knew that. And that meant it was over.

She had failed her mother today, just as she had failed her twenty years ago. She felt tears come to her eyes, unbidden. If only she had stuck by her mother's side. If only she hadn't wandered off, daydreaming, building fantasies in her enchanted forest. If only she'd clung to her mother's hand, as a good daughter would have. Who would have dared to kill the mother while the daughter was standing watch?

Dorothy had been right all along. Coming here had been worse than foolish. It had been delusional. You couldn't rewrite the past. Not even the ghost of Nora O'Malley could help Emily Carlyle now.

Just below her, Livvy and Beverly had come out of the kitchen door and begun walking across the grounds toward the far flower bed, where the gardener was weeding. If she hadn't known them, she might not have recognized them. The sun was behind them, so Emily saw their bodies as silhouettes, just long hair and flowing skirts and a hint of something female.

Something female…

Oh, God…

She took the winding, narrow stairs as fast as her ankle would allow. Reaching the second floor, she limped quickly down the corridor and rushed into her bedroom, not even taking time to make sure that Dorothy was still sleeping.

She left her bedroom door open. Dorothy's was ajar, too, but Emily didn't care if her aunt overheard. She would tell Dorrie as soon as she woke up anyhow.

But the most important person to tell right now was Christopher. Emily found the scrap of paper on which she'd written his phone number and dialed it with nervous fingers.

Again she got the answering machine. "This is Christopher Maxwell—"

She waited for the beep impatiently. And then she rushed into speech.

"Christopher, this is Emily. I have remembered something, something important." She stopped to swallow and to try to think how to put this. In the silence, she heard Dorothy's bed creak, though she might just have been shifting in her sleep.

"It's coming back to me, Christopher. Slowly, but a little more every day and—" Oh, she was getting off track, he didn't care about all that. "Anyhow, I wanted to tell you first. You see, I don't remember exactly who I saw with my mother on the cliff that day, but I know it couldn't have been your father."

She took a deep breath. "I know because—it was a woman."

CHAPTER NINE

CHRISTOPHER DIDN'T CALL her back. She jumped every time the telephone rang that evening, but it was always just inn business, once or twice a call for Charlie Farrell, who apparently was a doctor back home.

It was never for Emily.

Her aunt, who had stayed in bed and eaten dinner on a tray, didn't mince words.

"He's not going to call, Emily. Why should he? He wanted only one thing from you, and he can't get that over the telephone."

Emily, who was also eating on a tray to keep her aunt company, tried to respond with only civil, noncommittal comments. But frankly, she was beginning to feel a little nervous about Dorothy's emotional stability.

Dorothy had always been blunt to the point of eccentricity, but over the past couple of days she had seemed to tip into a coarseness that shocked Emily more than she dared reveal.

Though she knew it meant she'd probably never

see Christopher Maxwell again, Emily couldn't help being glad they were leaving this island tomorrow. Maybe, when they got home, she could persuade Dorothy to get some emotional help. Grief bottled up for twenty years apparently had an extremely corrosive effect.

"There's another reason he won't call," Dorothy said. "You know what that is, don't you?"

Emily looked up from her beef stew, a delicious entrée that she'd been almost unable to eat. Emotions had tied her stomach into a hopeless knot. She'd spent the whole meal sipping at a large mug of hot, honeyed tea.

"Well," Dorothy repeated. "Do you?"

Emily looked away. "No," she said wearily. "I don't. Why?"

"Because he's still afraid. It may not have been his father you saw—though I'm not sure these memories of yours are entirely to be trusted. But who is to say it wasn't his mother? Jean Maxwell probably hated your mother more than anyone else on the island."

Emily put down her fork. She was getting a headache. She took another sip of tea to give herself a chance to calm down before she answered.

"Dorothy, why are you so insistent on blaming the Maxwell family? It wasn't Mrs. Maxwell."

Dorothy glared at her, as if she were being willfully stubborn. "How can you possibly know that? You said you can't remember the details yet."

"I can't," Emily admitted. "In my mind, I can see only a black shape, like a silhouette. But you remember Mrs. Maxwell, don't you? She was terrified of the sun. She always wore a huge sunhat. Always. The woman I saw wasn't wearing a hat."

Dorothy didn't have an answer for that. She stared at Emily a moment and then she put down her fork, too, quite suddenly. She pressed her hand to her chest.

"I shouldn't have eaten that stew," she said. "I'll be sick tonight."

Emily rose and went to the side of the bed.

"No, you won't," she said gently. She was suddenly very tired and she just wanted to get the trays back to the kitchen and go to sleep herself.

"You'll feel better in the morning," she told Dorothy. "Don't worry about a thing. I'll get up a little early and pack for you."

Dorothy nodded slowly. She watched Emily carefully, as if she were wondering if she'd gone too far, antagonized her too much. Some of the vitriol seemed to have leaked out of her and she seemed smaller, like a deflated balloon, lying there propped against the soft white pillows.

"I'm sorry," Dorothy said suddenly. "I'm—"

She broke off. She had turned her head, as if transfixed by something out the window, though it was fully dark. Emily looked, too. But there was nothing to see.

"It's okay," Emily said. "I promise, sleep will help. We'll feel better tomorrow."

She hoped that was true. She pressed the heel of her hand against her forehead, wondering if she might be getting a fever. She felt…strange.

"It'll be cold tonight," Dorothy said softly, as if this were logical, though Emily was puzzled. Hadn't they been talking about tomorrow? She realized she was having trouble holding on to the thread of the conversation.

"Yes. Very cold," Dorothy said again, and the monotone calm of her voice sent chills down Emily's spine. "It always is after a storm."

Emily picked up the tray. But she got it only a couple of inches off the bed. Suddenly the room started to spin. The strangest fog seemed to have begun to fill her mind.

Frowning, she dropped the tray. She felt her legs soften, as if she had overcooked spaghetti for bones. She knew she was going to hit the floor, but somewhere on the way down the bed, the room, the whole entire world, simply blinked out.

And disappeared.

NORA WAS WEEPING again.

Emily heard the sound from inside a very dark place. It broke her heart. It was the saddest sound she'd ever heard.

I'm sorry, Nora. The words didn't come out as sounds, but maybe Nora understood. Emily had tried to set her free. She had tried to remember what happened, who the real murderer was, but it was so many years ago, and everything was so dark inside her head.

So full of fog and clouds and rain.

And she was so cold. Probably she was in Nora's little attic room, and there was no heat. It was cold tonight. It always was, after a storm.

Nora must be cold, too. She was here, right beside Emily. Her tears were falling on Emily's cheeks and they, too, were cold. It was terrible to be so cold and not be able to move or to speak or to tell anyone your heart was breaking.

The most she could do was moan. It sounded no bigger than a whisper.

But Nora must have heard. The crying stopped.

"Don't move," Dorothy said, her voice coming out of the darkness like sudden thunder. "You're very close to the edge."

The edge of what? Small flashes of cold fear exploded across Emily's mind. *The edge of what?*

"I thought it would already be over by now," Dorothy said, her tone strangely distant, faintly apologetic. "But when we got here, I realized I wanted to explain everything to you. I've kept it inside for twenty years. I need to tell someone. And after you're gone, there won't be anyone to tell."

After she was gone?

Emily's head was finally clearing a little, the fog parting to let in a cold, black fear. She realized she was outside. The tears she'd imagined falling on her face were actually drops of rain. She wiggled carefully and learned that she was lying on her side, curled into an uncomfortable ball-like position, with her cheek and ear pressed against rocky ground.

She opened her eyes and saw only a dark void, empty and yet subtly swirling as if she were looking into the black depths of a crystal ball. She knew what it was—nothing else was that big and nothing else quite sounded the same. It was the Atlantic, lunging and growling seventy feet below her, impatiently lapping at the foot of the cliff.

Her heart began to race inside her chest, as if it could force her limp limbs to run, run fast, run away from her aunt. Away from this monster, whom she now knew was not just eccentric, not just grief-stricken, but mad.

Completely, cruelly insane.

But she felt the warmth of Dorothy's body at her back, and she knew that her aunt blocked any path of escape. The only path open to Emily now was down.

She began to pray. *Please. Don't let this happen.*

In the books, in the movies, they always said, "Keep them talking." So she swallowed, although her head hurt and her mouth tasted strange.

"Tell me, Dorrie. I want to hear."

"No, you don't." Dorothy still sounded oddly distant, as if she were only half connected to her own body, her own voice. "You just don't want me to push you over yet. You just want to live a little longer."

Emily struggled against the urge to sob. Of course she wanted to live. Everyone wanted to live.

"Yes," she said. "I do. But I also want to understand. You did it, didn't you? You killed my mother. But I don't understand why."

Dorothy chuckled, a terrible sound. "Of course you don't understand. How could you? You're beautiful, too, just like she was. You also drive men crazy without even trying. You have no idea what it is like to be invisible. To be ugly."

Emily opened her mouth, made half a sound, but suddenly she felt a sharp, pointed pain in her back as something pierced the wool of her sweater.

Dorothy was pressing a knife into her flesh. She turned it, just a little, and the pain flared white and blinding.

"No, Emily. Do not try to tell me I'm not ugly. Don't you dare, at a moment like this, condescend to me. I know what I am. I've had to live with it all my life."

Emily bit her lower lip and arched her back, but she couldn't risk pulling away from the pain. She wasn't sure how many inches she had before the black cliff stopped and the black void began.

"I think I could have stood it," Dorothy went on, "if Melissa, my own sister, hadn't been so beautiful. Can you appreciate how unfair that is? Can you imagine watching her, day after day? The constant reminder of how my life could have been?"

"Yes," Emily said. The terrible thing was, she could imagine it. She did, finally, catch a glimpse of the hell of envy Dorothy must have endured.

"And the men. She had so many men. Fools, most of them. Just slobbering half-wits who wanted to make love to her. I didn't care about them. I didn't want any of them. But Martin—"

Dorothy moved restlessly. She seemed to have forgotten she held the knife, because it shoved harder into Emily's back. Emily managed not to cry out, though she felt a warm trickle of blood move sideways down her shoulder blade.

"Martin was different." Dorothy's voice had changed. It sounded softer, almost wistful. "I wasn't invisible to him. He saw me. He talked to me. He thought I was smart. Sometimes, around him, I was funny."

Emily moved the fingers of her right hand slightly, inching them forward, trying to feel for the edge of the cliff. If she had any hope of escaping, she had to orient herself somehow.

"Martin was handsome, like his son, like Christopher. You think Christopher is handsome, don't you? You are already half in love with him, after only a week. So you can see how it was for me. I loved him."

Dorothy breathed in a sob that was so harsh it sounded as if it tore her vocal cords. "I loved him," she said, her voice rising. "And he could have cared about me, too. If Melissa hadn't taken him away."

"Dorrie—"

Dorothy suddenly grabbed Emily's shoulders and shook them violently, as if venting twenty years of repressed resentment. Emily's heart lurched toward her throat, and she suddenly thought she might vomit. She felt the bitter aftertaste of too much hot tea.

That's how Dorothy had done it, of course. She'd put something in the tea. Her headache medicine, perhaps? Or had she, on her trip into town, bought something more sinister?

"Why? Why?" Dorothy was keening now, out of control. "She could have had anyone! Why did she have to take the one man who could ever have cared for someone like me?"

She began to cry. But Dorothy wasn't used to crying. As if ashamed, she put both hands up to her face, smothering the sound of tears.

The knife left Emily's back.

It was now or never.

Though she didn't know if her legs were steady enough to hold her, though she couldn't really be sure they wouldn't pitch her into the long, fatal fall, Emily scrambled to her feet.

Cursing, practically growling, Dorothy tried to stop her. She tried to hold her down. The knife pressed into Emily's thigh.

But it was too late. Emily was already standing.

Hope surged briefly. But it wasn't, in the end, much of a victory. Emily's back was to the cliff edge and her head swam with a poisoned vertigo. Dorothy might not even have to push her. She might simply lose her balance and her life in one helpless stumble.

Dorothy still held the knife in her hand and Emily was now close enough to see the golden hilt. Not a knife, after all. Lucy Knight's letter opener. An instrument schooled in the art of murder more than a hundred years ago. And newly darkened at the tip with Emily's own blood.

How had she managed to steal it from the safe? But Emily remembered that the safe had been in the attic rooms. She remembered, too, the night she'd found Dorothy up there, nearly incoherent with distress. Could she have been planning this even then?

Both of them were breathing hard. Dorothy's eyes glimmered in the moonlight, her features contorted with rage. Rain ran in ugly runnels down her long, sloping jaw. Her hair was plastered in dark hanks against her cheeks.

Emily knew that she, too, must look strange, wild, primitive. The fight for life was not a pretty sight.

"Dorothy," she said, trying to meet her aunt's eyes, trying to find something in them she could reason with. "You don't want to do this."

"I have to. You were going to remember." Dorothy laughed again, that harsh, chilling sound. "You already *had* remembered. You just didn't understand. You didn't *want* to understand."

Emily still didn't understand. How could this be happening? Her aunt…a murderer? This was the woman who had taken care of her for twenty years. Tended colds, hemmed skirts, checked homework, cooked casseroles. The ground might still be steady under Emily's feet in physical reality, but her emotions felt as if they were spinning in an alien space.

Suddenly, just behind Dorothy, Emily saw something move. It had been moving for several seconds, but she had thought it was the wind, the trees, the night fog.

Instead, like the answer to a prayer, it was a person.

It was Christopher.

He was drenched, as they all were, his hair darkened by the rain. And he was holding a gun. It was trained on the back of Dorothy's head. He caught her gaze. He gestured once with the gun. *Move away*, the gesture told her. *Get out of the line of fire.*

"No," Emily cried. She knew better than to look

at him for long, but she hoped he understood. He mustn't shoot. Not yet. Not while there was still hope.

Dorothy thought Emily was talking to her. "Yes," she said. "I'm sorry. But it has to be done."

"It doesn't," Emily said. "Dorrie. You don't have to."

Dorothy waved the little dagger airily. "Don't beg, Emily. Make it easy on yourself. Just step back. One step. That's all it will take. And then it will be over."

Tears were streaming down Emily's face now, mixing with the rain. She felt the taste of salt water on her lips. It reminded her of the seawater. Oh, God, she did not want to die.

But she didn't want Dorothy to die, either. Not out here, on the edge of the world, with anger and sins on her conscience. She needed help, not a bullet through her brain.

"Dorrie, please," she said, holding out her bandaged hands. The rain had soaked them, too, and the soil had muddied the once-white gauze. "Don't do this. You've spent so many years being a good mother to me. Don't let all that be in vain."

Christopher was moving closer. The gun never wavered. His intent was clear. If Dorothy moved a single inch forward, he would shoot her.

"Do you remember when you used to drive me to school in the morning?" Emily tried to smile. "And made my lunches? And listened to my endless knock-knock jokes?"

"Of course I remember. I—" Dorothy looked suddenly confused, as if she were being split between two worlds—the present world of rage and pain, and the yesterday world of laughter.

"Yes," she said, her voice low. "I remember."

"You were beautiful then, Dorrie. When you were showering all that love on a little girl who had no one else to love her. You were beautiful then."

"That's a lie," Dorothy said harshly. "That's the lie everyone tells. That beauty is more than skin deep." She inhaled harshly. "But it isn't true." Though she sounded fierce, she seemed to let the knife falter just a little. She was suddenly sobbing, and she used the back of her knife hand to wipe the rain and tears out of her eyes. "It isn't true."

"I love you, Dorrie," Emily said softly. "That part is true. And that's the part that matters in the end."

Dorothy stared at Emily a long, terrible moment. Crazily, she began to shake her head. She shook it, rhythmically, nonsensically, over and over.

And then she simply crumpled. She fell to her knees, the letter opener dropping with a wet thud into the ground beside her.

She was boneless, gone—she might as well have been dead. The crumbling was so complete it was as if something had possessed her and then had flown out of her, abandoning her body like an empty shell.

The wind whistled in Emily's ears and cold rain stung at her skin.

Christopher lowered his gun. He walked slowly toward them and picked up the letter opener, tucking it into his belt. In the distance, Emily suddenly saw lights flashing against the trees. First blue, then red, then blue again.

Christopher must have called the police. She heard voices shouting. She heard footsteps running across sodden ground.

Ignoring all that, she fell to her knees in the mud. She took her aunt's limp body into her arms and held it carefully, brushing away the wet dirt and tangled hair from her closed eyes.

"It really is true, Dorrie," Emily whispered, looking up at Christopher's face as she rocked her aunt back and forth in the rain. "The love is all that matters in the end."

CHAPTER TEN

BY THE TIME the police were finished interviewing Emily at the Cliff's Cove emergency room, it was almost dawn.

She'd had her hands redressed, her ankle X-rayed and two stitches taken in her back. Everything checked out fine, but still the doctor decided to admit her to the small hospital, just for a day, just to be sure the drugs Dorothy had given her weren't going to have any negative effects.

They'd found an empty bottle of sleeping pills in Dorothy's suitcase, but they weren't sure whether that was all Dorothy had slipped into the tea, or exactly how many. Even Dorothy herself, who had been taken to a larger hospital on the mainland, didn't seem to remember exactly anymore.

They hadn't let Emily talk to Dorothy at all—but the kind policeman who interviewed Emily had assured her that Dorothy would get psychiatric help before she had to endure a trial. In fact, there would be no trial, not until Dorothy recovered enough to understand what was happening—which everyone could tell wouldn't be any time soon.

Livvy, who had arrived on the cliff with the police, had been Emily's constant companion. It was from Livvy that Emily learned that Dorothy had carried her down the back stairway, out through the courtyard and into the car. Charlie and Josie Farrell had spent the evening at a show on the mainland, so the inn was almost empty. No one had witnessed anything strange.

Livvy had assumed that both aunt and niece were sleeping, resting from the ordeal at the cliff, and was cloistered in her room, going over accounts, hoping to keep the inn soothingly quiet.

She clearly blamed herself for not being more vigilant, though Emily tried to reassure her. No innkeeper could be expected to watch the doors constantly, just in case one of her guests suddenly turned—

Even now Emily couldn't say it, not out loud. *Turned homicidal.* Even in her head, the word sounded like treason. She couldn't speak of Dorothy in those terms. Not yet.

But God only knew what would have happened if it hadn't been for Christopher. Apparently he'd been away for several hours, playing cards with some friends in Cliff's Cove. But when he'd returned to the cottage, he had listened to her message. Apparently that was all he'd needed. He'd come barreling into the inn, Livvy said, and had dashed up the stairs without even asking her permission.

He'd kicked open Emily's door, which Dorothy apparently had locked. And then he'd kicked open Dorothy's. Good thing he was a carpenter, Livvy said, obviously hoping to lighten the tone a little. He was definitely going to owe her two new doors.

After that, it was pure chaos. He'd seen that Dorothy's car was gone and, cursing viciously, he'd obviously understood what that had meant. Ordering Livvy to call the police and have them meet him on the cliff, he'd raced out without another word.

Emily knew the rest.

But she couldn't think about that now.

The little white hospital room was comforting in a way. After the dirt and darkness, the insanity and confusion of the cliff, this sterile, orderly cell felt safe. People moved around just outside her door with a low, professional hum, constantly gliding in to monitor her charts and machines and vital signs. She was glad of them. Livvy would have to go home to get some sleep soon—she looked exhausted, and a full day's work at the inn surely awaited her—and Emily did not want to be alone.

Though she was exhausted, too, she knew she wouldn't sleep.

"You'd better get back to the inn, Livvy," she said

bravely. She couldn't impose on this gentle, empathetic woman any longer. She'd already brought chaos and horror into Livvy's life, which wasn't fair. Even though it looked as if the chambermaid's name would ultimately be cleared, another attempted murder at the inn would leave Livvy with terrible publicity and unhappy memories.

"Yes," Livvy said apologetically. "I'll need to start breakfast for the Farrells. And the man's coming about the fountain. I'm so sorry to—"

"I'm fine," Emily said with the best smile she could muster. "Really, I am."

Livvy's gaze darkened. "But I hate to leave you alone right—"

"She won't be alone," a low voice said from the doorway.

Emily and Livvy both looked over, startled. It was Christopher.

It was strange. Ridiculous, even. But, Emily, who had not shed a single tear since they'd led her away from the cliff in the police car, suddenly felt a stinging warmth behind her eyes. He was rumpled and dark-eyed and somber, but she thought he was the most beautiful sight she'd ever seen.

Coming into the little room, he put his hand on Livvy's shoulder. "Go home, Liv," he said. "Get some sleep."

Livvy frowned gently. "But, Chris," she said.

"Don't you have work? Appointments? She needs—
I mean, I doubt that Emily will sleep."

He nodded. "I know."

"I can't get back until after dinner. Can you really
stay all day?"

Emily held her breath. Tears were seeping down
the sides of her face. She felt foolish, but she was so
relieved to see him. He was like sunlight after darkness, heat after bone-chilling cold.

He looked over at her with a smile that made her
heart thump in her chest. The monitors zigzagged,
telling everyone.

"All day," Livvy reiterated, suddenly grinning.

"Longer than that," he said. "If Emily will have me."

The monitor beeped her fervent answer and even
Livvy had to laugh. A nurse poked her head in the
door. "Are you all right, Miss Carlyle?"

Emily took a deep breath. "I will be now," she said.

* * * * *

*Watch for Kathleen O'Brien's exciting new
Superromance trilogy, The Heroes of Heyday*

*October 2004: THE SAINT. Superromance #1231
Janurary 2005: THE SINNER. Superromance #1249
April 2005: THE STRANGER. Superromance #1266*

Because it's worth holding out for a hero.

SHADOWS OF THE PAST

Debra Webb

CHAPTER ONE

MURDER.

Livvy Hamilton slid down the wall onto the polished hardwood floor.

This couldn't be happening.

A young woman was dead.

Emotion knotted in her throat, churned in her stomach.

Poor Beverly.

Livvy wiped her face with the back of her hand and closed her eyes to block the gruesome images. Why had she sent Beverly to do what she should have done herself? She should have been the one to check that all the doors leading to the courtyard were locked for the night. She always took care of locking up. What had made her change her routine last night?

A call from the chairman of the Christmas Tree organization had distracted her. An important call. One that could make or break her planned Christmas event. Though it was only September, plans had to be made now to ensure a successful winter season. If she got the support of that organization, her decision to reopen Lost Angel Inn might just pay off. Being added to the annual charity fund raising activities, specifically as one of the stopping places on the widely publicized holiday parade of historical homes, was essential.

Most of the numerous villages that dotted Maine's rugged coastline had winter events to entice tourists. Camden and Rockport held a mini-Olympics. Around here it was the Christmas Village. Every shop owner in Cliff's Cove participated, ultimately turning the small, quaint island town into a sort of winter wonderland, and depended upon that tourist draw almost as much as they did the beachcombers, fishermen and sailors in the summer. A decent showing around Christmas would get Livvy through the year. It wasn't much to ask.

She leaned her head back against the wall. How could she think about finances now? Beverly Bellamy was dead.

This was no publicity stunt to promote business, no illusion to tease guests. It was real.

Too damn real.

She refused to believe in ghosts or legends…but she had to admit that this turn of events carried with it a ghastly link with the past.

Every twenty years someone died, a sacrifice to a centuries-old legend—no, not legend, curse.

But surely that old curse was over. After all, Nora O'Malley's name had been cleared.

So why had this happened? Beverly hadn't harmed anyone. She'd been kind and hardworking. Of course, Beverly probably hadn't been the target. She'd simply been doing Livvy's chores. But who'd want to kill Livvy? Hadn't she been through enough?

Her arms went around her bent legs, hugging them to her chest. She grimaced at the ache the move generated. Almost three years and the pain still haunted her. She blinked. Tried to put the past out of her mind, but it wasn't going anywhere. A whole jumble of new images tumbled into her mind. The man she'd married screaming at her. Pushing her. Then she was falling...falling...until she lay in a battered, crumpled heap at the bottom of the stairs.

Livvy rubbed at the nagging ache in her thigh. It had taken several surgeries and three long months in rehab for her to mend and to learn to walk once more. Even now she limped, especially when she pushed her physical limitations, as she had done lately in an effort to get everything organized before the cold weather descended.

He had marked her that way, ensuring that even after his death she would remember him.

She looked around the lovely entry hall she'd worked so hard to bring back to its original splendor. Her eyes came to rest on the painting she'd rescued from the attic. She'd been so excited when she'd found it. It was original to the house. She'd read about the precious painting in stories written by visitors to the mansion prior to the death of the man who'd built it. The senator had purchased the celestial depiction to hang in this very entry hall...to watch over his bride whenever he had to be away.

Fat lot of good it had done him or his bride.

The angels pictured there seemed to mock Livvy now.

Other angels had become a part of the decor, as well. There was the large bronze statue beneath the portico and the one topping the fountain in the courtyard. But those hadn't been a part of the house originally. They had come along later in remembrance of a small child who had been searching for her father and presumably drowned in the ocean that battered the cliffs outside. A kind of obsessive homage to the loss.

Livvy rested her chin on her knees. She could only imagine how devastating it must be to lose a child. She'd always wanted children. But God had certainly done her a favor by not allowing a child to come of the doomed union with her monster of a husband. Bringing a child into that terrifying situation would have been a travesty.

So here she was. Three years later. Finally free of one evil and now being tormented by another.

She'd sunk every penny she'd had into this place and its restoration. Failure was not an option. This old house with its numerous painful memories had felt like a fitting place for her to begin her new life.

She and the grand old structure could heal their wounds together. Every moment she'd spent restoring the house, she'd felt herself becoming stronger. The labor was a kind of pilgrimage back to wholeness. But strange things had been happening at the inn ever since the opening weekend.

Livvy suddenly felt cold...alone. She would not believe in ghosts. Or foolish legends. There had to be an explanation for every incident that had occurred in this house. Somehow she had to find the truth. Not that anything she could do would bring back Beverly. Even if Livvy could prove what had really happened, Beverly's life was over.

Every instinct warned Livvy that she'd been the intended target though she had no idea who might want her dead. The idea made no more sense than the maid's murder.

With her cruel, obsessive husband dead, Livvy had no enemies. A tiny voice echoed an adamant denial of that statement, sending a shiver through her. Her imagination was running away with her, she concluded, nothing more.

She scrambled to her feet, never an easy accomplishment from a seated position on the floor. As she straightened her skirt she considered the idea of enemies once more. Could she really say she had none?

Despite some local opposition to her reopening the inn, most folks around town had welcomed her.

For the first time in a very long time she'd had a family...in a way. Her parents had died soon after she'd graduated high school, leaving her with no blood relatives. But she'd had a few close friends from her childhood days in Santa Barbara, so she hadn't felt alone. However, after she'd married Dr. James Hamilton, the friends had gone away. He'd seen to it.

At first his sweet, albeit relentless, pursuit of her had been kind of romantic, but she'd soon learned that his desire to have her all to himself went far deeper than the usual newlywed selfishness.

James had been a sick, devious man whose sole purpose on earth had been to control and to demean those within his dominion. Livvy had learned that though his patients and associates had loved and respected him, the people who knew him best feared him. No one more so than his wife.

"Enough," she muttered. A walk down memory lane was the last thing she needed at the moment.

She had to call Beverly's parents to convey her condolences. The body had been moved to the mainland for an autopsy early this morning, after the forensics technicians had completed their work. Livvy shuddered. The thought of the ruthless procedure made her stomach churn. But she knew they had to be certain...though the letter opener buried to the hilt in Beverly's back was clearly the cause of death.

Livvy pushed the memory from her mind. Whoever had done this terrible thing had used the same letter opener the senator's bride had used on her husband all those years ago. Even more recently, a crazed guest at the inn had tried to use it on her niece.

This morning the chief of police had explained that someone had stolen it yesterday from the historian in town who'd hoped to start a collection on the inn's history at his small museum. He'd authenticated the beautiful but deadly blade with its jeweled sheath. Another shiver went through Livvy at the idea of something so beautiful being used to accomplish such an ugly, cruel act.

Smoothing her hair back from her face, Livvy strode into the kitchen. Coffee would help. She'd given Clara, the cook, a few weeks off to visit her family in Massachusetts. Ralph, the gardener and general handyman, was busy removing the summer's potted flowers and replacing them with lovely fall chrysanthemums and pansies. The year-round housekeeper, Edna, wouldn't be back until tomorrow.

Though it was only September, Livvy could already smell winter in the air. It was coming, Ralph had promised sagely. Last year the first snow had fallen by the beginning of October. A part of her yearned to see that fluttery white stuff now. Maybe it would somehow cover up the evil that had touched her new home…her new life. This time last year one of the villagers had told her that snow was like God's gift in the winter. Its pure, white beauty brightening the long, gray cold season. But Livvy knew that not even a pure white blanket could mask murder.

Nothing could make this right. Whether she chose to believe the legend or not, the coincidence of another violent death at the inn twenty years after the last was chilling. Even some of the geriatric locals had murmured that Livvy had tested fate by holding that murder mystery weekend as her grand opening at the beginning of the summer season.

But she hadn't believed.

She'd lived with the devil himself and he had been flesh and blood. There were no such things as ghosts.

A ghost wouldn't have to steal a letter opener with which to commit a murder.

This horrendous act had been committed by a human. One who had invaded her home and killed an innocent young woman as she'd completed a task Livvy herself usually attended to.

With the instinct she'd honed so sharply after years as James's abused wife, she sensed that this was not a random killing. She was the one who should be lying in that morgue today.

But who would want to kill her just because she'd reopened the inn?

That couldn't be. The few locals who didn't like her business venture surely wouldn't want to see her dead. Of course, the chief had warned her that a number of citizens were quite upset with what she'd done. In fact, she recalled as she dumped coffee grounds into the drip basket then poured water into the coffeemaker, the chief had seemed to take pleasure in informing her about the opposition to her renovations as well as her grand opening. She got the distinct impression that Chief Fraley would like nothing better than to shut her down.

She crossed her arms over her chest and sighed in disgust. The chief had never liked her. Not that she didn't understand why he'd put a stop to her exterior renovations until the investigation was concluded, it was more what he didn't say than what he said. He seemed to enjoy causing her angst.

But why?

She'd never been in trouble with the law. She felt certain he'd checked her out thoroughly when she'd first come to town. Her hands moved up and down her arms in a futile attempt to warm her skin against the sudden chill she felt. Her history was clouded by only one thing: the untimely death of her husband.

Livvy went still inside. Surely the chief wouldn't attempt to blame this murder on her by trying to connect her past to the present. Not possible. She hadn't even been there when her husband had died. The detective who'd witnessed his death had been Livvy's friend, that much was true, but he hadn't caused her husband to take that ironic tumble to his death. Ironic in that he'd died in the same way that he'd very nearly killed her.

She brought her palms down on the counter with a loud thwack. No more. She couldn't keep turning this over and over in her head. There was no way to make sense of this awful tragedy. No way to connect any part of it to her or to the inn…not yet anyway. She refused to believe any of the townsfolk capable of murder. These were good, caring people. It had to have been someone from the mainland.

Maybe someone had been looking to rob the inn or maybe someone had held a grudge against Beverly's family. The chief claimed he was looking into both possibilities, but Livvy had her doubts.

She shook off that line of thinking. The chief had no reason to harm her. He didn't appear to like her but that was his prerogative. Her misgivings about him had no real basis at this point. Maybe she was feeling a little sorry for herself.

After pouring a fresh cup of coffee, she forced herself to drink slowly, cooling the steamy brew with her breath.

She thought of the happiness she'd felt since coming here. She loved the island. Loved the inn. Loved every single piece of period furniture she and Christopher Maxwell had found. She relaxed a bit as the coffee did its work, chasing away the cold, soothing her frayed nerves. The beautiful pieces they'd discovered that were original to the first owners of the house were true treasures. No amount of thanks would ever be enough for Christopher.

Livvy smiled. She was so happy that Christopher and Emily had found each other and were planning their wedding day here at the inn. She was also relieved that the mystery shrouding the death of Emily's mother had been cleared up, effectively exonerating Christopher's father of any involvement once and for all. In addition it had proved that the last tragedy connected to this inn had had nothing to do with that damn legend.

Christopher's happy ending hadn't been the only one of the summer season. There was Jeff Cunningham, aka the mystery writer Denton Drake, and Ellie Gresham. Those two were perfect for each other, as well.

Livvy's smile faded. There would be no happy ending for her in the romance department. She'd learned that lesson the hard way. Men were off-limits. At least for a while longer, maybe forever. Three years hadn't been nearly long enough to recover from the emotional injuries, not to mention the permanent limp, she'd had to learn to live with.

An explosion of quick, firm knocks thundered down the entry hall. Livvy jumped, almost dropping her cup.

Taking in a steadying breath, she set her coffee aside and headed toward the unexpected cacophony. She had to pull herself together. There was so much to do. She had that call to make, had to see to Beverly's things. Another task she dreaded.

Livvy hesitated, bracing herself for another wave of grief. The whole incident felt so impossible. Murder…right here in her own home.

The door shook with a second onslaught of banging. She frowned. What the—?

She'd scarcely pulled the door open when Chief Fraley railed at her, "I don't like to be kept waiting, Ms. Hamilton."

Just when she'd thought the day couldn't get any worse. He'd been here until dawn as it was. What else did he want from her? She didn't need any more of his accusations. Every muscle stiffened with anticipation of more of his improbable scenarios regarding what had happened last night. Don't let him get to you, she ordered. He's upset, too. No one wanted to believe this could happen in their town. Livvy summoned her calmest tone, "Sorry, Chief, I was in the kitchen."

"It's all right, ma'am," Deputy Chief Chase Fraley, the only other man on the island who represented law enforcement, offered kindly.

Livvy relaxed marginally. Chase was the exact opposite of his rude, overbearing uncle. He was polite and kind. And quite good-looking. Sandy-blond hair, like the beaches in California. And eyes every bit as blue as the ocean pounding the rocks of the cliffs outside. A sincerely nice man.

Something deep inside her closed down. Every time she ran into Chase, her reaction was the same.

She'd feel the beginnings of an attraction...a little sizzle. But then a warning voice deep inside would remind her of old hurts, and the sizzle would disappear. She understood the response for what it was. A self-defense mechanism. A caution not to trust a man on that level again. No matter how kind or how handsome.

Like walking, trusting was something she would need to relearn. But unlike walking, it wouldn't be a simple matter of mind over body...of grit and determination. The truth was, she really had no idea how to let herself trust again...wasn't even sure if she wanted to.

"I need to take another look around the crime scene," Chief Fraley snapped. "I don't need your permission but since this is your private residence as well as a place of business, I'm giving you notice as a common courtesy."

How thoughtful, she mused, but she forced herself to be polite. "Of course, Chief, come in." She pulled the door open wider and stepped back. She had nothing to hide and she had no intention of getting in the way of his investigation.

"Chase, you keep Ms. Hamilton company," Fraley barked as he strode past. He didn't look back or even slow down until he'd reached the double doors that led out into the sun-washed courtyard.

Livvy sighed. What had she done to get on that man's bad side?

"Don't mind the chief, ma'am," Chase said quietly. "He's a tad unsettled by this…case."

This *murder.*

He didn't have to say the word. The whole island would be disconcerted by this horrible tragedy. Many would hold Livvy responsible.

Another of those shivers raced over her skin, settling like a damp winter storm in her bones. Murder. Dear God. How could she go on knowing that if she hadn't come to Lost Angel Inn, Beverly would still be alive? If Livvy had picked some other place instead of stirring up this big old house's murky past, none of this would have happened.

She looked around the enormous hall, the staircase that flowed up to the second floor cutting a circular path that was at once inviting and architecturally pleasing to the eye. Maybe she should have believed in ghosts.

Though a few of her guests had claimed to, she'd never heard any weeping…never experienced any of the strange sights and sounds that legend associated with this beautiful old place.

Like her, Lost Angel Inn had its secrets. Maybe too many. Maybe that's what had drawn her here. She'd always loved history and literature. And love stories—even those that ended in tragedy—always captured her imagination. Oddly, at that moment, standing in that big hall with Chase Fraley, she felt once more as if she and this house truly belonged together. Two entities of this planet whose time for love and prosperity had come and gone.

But she refused to accept such a cruel fate. God had not allowed her to survive an almost-fatal fall down that staircase in Santa Barbara for nothing. She had a future. And so did this house.

"I suppose you're right," she said to Chase. "This case has all of us upset."

He nodded, a hint of a smile on his lips. She hadn't ever really looked at his lips. Now that she did, she couldn't help noticing that they were very nicely formed. Not thin, but not too full. The slight crinkling around his mouth told her he smiled a lot. Another likable trait.

"Ms. Hamilton!"

The chief's bellow made her tremble, as much from impatience as from fear.

"It's all right," Chase offered again as he touched her arm reassuringly. "He probably has a question for you."

A pleasant jolt went through her at his touch. She tried not to react, to focus on his words, but the sensation was so unexpected she couldn't stop the blush from spreading to her cheeks.

He pulled his strong hand away instantly as if sensing her unease. "Let's go see what's got him riled."

Livvy nodded, not certain she trusted her voice.

She led the way to the courtyard, struggling to regain her composure.

"Ms. Hamilton, I thought I made it clear that no one was to touch anything in this area." The chief stood in the center of the courtyard, near the big old tree whose leaves would soon be flaming with those gorgeous New England fall colors. His hands were planted on his broad hips, framing his bulging belly and screaming loudly of his irritation.

"I haven't touched a thing." She looked around the courtyard. It looked just as it had this morning. Yellow crime-scene tape cordoned off the area around the fountain and the doorway leading to the east wing where Beverly had been found. One end of the tape flapped in the wind like the tail of a downed kite.

Closer to the house, everything also looked normal. Tables and chairs sat around the big tree. The angel atop the fountain stood like a sentry. Mature shrubbery lined the stone pathways, lending a softness to the hard surfaces. Beyond that, the flagstones had been removed, making room for the digging necessary to repair the fountain. The master stonemason Christopher had contacted to restore it had ordered new water and electrical lines to be run from the house, not to mention some additional foundation work beneath the massive structure. Once the work was finished, the courtyard would again be the magnificent outdoor entertainment area intended by the original builder. It was imperative that the masonry work be completed before the first freeze.

"I can assure you, Chief," she insisted, "that no

one has even been out here." The stonemason hadn't appreciated being ordered to stop his work before he finished, but all involved understood the importance of this investigation.

"Is that so?" He pointed to several intricately detailed clay and concrete pots. "Then why are there new flowers in those pots?"

Livvy winced. Ralph. She hadn't considered that he would change the flowers in the courtyard, as well. Obviously she should have.

"I apologize, Chief. I'm sure Ralph didn't think it would be a problem since he didn't venture into the cordoned-off area." In spite of last night's tragedy, work had to go on. It was necessary as well as therapeutic. Livvy had thought it best as the morning dragged on that she and Ralph go about their routine. She'd scarcely slowed and when she had, gloom and depression had all but overtaken her.

The chief pointed to the fountain. "I don't want anybody going near that, do you hear?"

Livvy nodded. "I'll make sure it doesn't happen again."

"I've got more forensics techs coming out to inspect the area."

Maybe it was the way Chase looked at his uncle when he made that last statement, but for an instant Livvy had the distinct impression that the chief wasn't telling her everything.

Could he already know who had committed this

heinous act? His investigation had barely gotten under way. Did he believe it was Livvy? One thing was certain, if she was accused and convicted of murder, she sure wouldn't be reopening the inn.

And just maybe that was the whole point.

CHAPTER TWO

IT WAS ONLY A DREAM.

Livvy told herself again and again not to be afraid. But the fear wrapped around her throat like long bony fingers prepared to drain the life from her. Night had come to Lost Angel Inn and she had walked the floors for hours in an attempt to exhaust herself physically. She desperately needed a good night's sleep. Sleep had come…but it was far from good. The dream had descended, dragging her into the cold, relentless embrace of fear.

In the dream she ran along the edge of the cliffs, her bare feet slipping and sliding as she frantically fought for purchase in the loose soil near the hazardous precipice. Her lungs burned with the need to take in more oxygen. Her heart pounded savagely against her sternum. Still he gained on her. Grew closer with every thump of her flailing heart.

Please, God, don't let him catch me.

Powerful arms suddenly wrapped around her, flung her to the ground. The heavy weight of a big male body slammed down on top of her.

She was dead. She didn't have to see the method of execution. Deep inside where no one else could see...no one else could touch, she knew she was dead. This time he was going to kill her.

Those dark, menacing eyes stared deeply into hers. "You must learn your lessons, Liv," he whispered roughly. "Why do you insist on trying my patience?"

Then she was inside her Santa Barbara home tumbling down the stairs...pain searing through her as a rib punctured the tissue of her left lung, making it difficult to breathe. She felt the femur in her thigh shatter. Her last thought before the black of unconsciousness took her was that she would surely die before help arrived.

Livvy bolted upright in bed.

The sound of air sawing in and out of her lungs filled the heavy silence of her dark room.

A dream. Just a dream.

Her nightgown clung to her damp skin. Her thigh throbbed as if the injury she'd dreamed of had taken place only moments ago.

"Just a dream," she murmured out loud, trying hard to reassure herself. "Not real."

She slumped back onto the pillows and struggled to calm herself. She was safe now. James was dead. Would never hurt her again. A slightly hysterical laugh choked out of her. The most bizarre part of that whole night was the fact that she would surely have died if her husband, the beloved doctor, had not called 9-1-1 and provided emergency medical care. A broken femur could be fatal, extreme blood loss the primary threat. He could have let her die and claimed he'd done all he could. Her own clumsiness had caused her to fall, he would say. Dear Liv was always falling or running into things. Livvy felt sure his associates had felt sympathy for his plight. He'd married a mousy nobody and couldn't train her to be an appropriate doctor's wife. She couldn't even descend a staircase properly.

Livvy never looked good enough at the country club, never said the right things. Didn't keep the house in proper order. Everything she did was wrong, stupidly wrong.

But he'd let her live that night. Because he couldn't bear to let her go…she provided far too much of a challenge for his psychopathic ego. He didn't love her…he loved controlling her…making her obey his every wish. Toying with her life.

And she'd known with complete certainty that next time she would die. It was the final warning. *I can kill you anytime. Fail me once more and you die.* He'd recognized her mounting desperation. Had known she entertained ideas of divorce. He would sooner see her dead than allow that. The humiliation would have been far too big a blow to his ego. Besides, a widower looking for a new wife to use as a puppet was much more palatable than a divorced man. Livvy'd had no choice but to take drastic measures.

The doctor in charge of her care after the fall, a woman who sensed Livvy's predicament, had insisted that she stay a full three months in rehab where she was watched night and day. Dr. James Hamilton had been furious. During that time Livvy and two of her old friends who'd sought her out after the accident, with the help of her doctor and a sympathetic detective, had formed an escape plan.

They should never have underestimated James Hamilton. He'd known they were up to something. All that had saved Livvy from facing his final wrath was the detective's interference. He'd waited in the hospital for James to arrive and discover that his wife was gone. The ensuing fight had ended at the bottom of a stairwell.

At the inquiry, the detective said he'd told Hamilton to back off and had tried to walk away, but the good doctor was having none of that. He wanted to know his wife's whereabouts. He'd followed the detective into the stairwell and attacked him. Livvy had never asked any questions. It was over. The official inquiry had cleared the detective of any wrongdoing.

Livvy rubbed her hands over her face. She'd thought the nightmares were over. But Beverly's murder had awakened all the old demons.

Livvy shivered, dragged the covers up close around her. For the first time since she'd bought the inn she felt lonely. It was ridiculous. During the off-season, like now, she was alone most every night. Ralph and Edna went to their own homes each evening. In fact by October, Edna would cut down to only three days per week. Ralph, however, would come every day if for nothing more than to clear the snow from the steps and walk. But there would be no need for round-the-clock, full-time help unless the inn was filled with guests. The month of December would be the only exception to that winter schedule.

Being alone hadn't bothered Livvy before. It felt good to know she had no one to answer to but herself.

But that satisfying feeling had deserted her in light of recent events. Along with the peace of mind Lost Angel Inn had given her the moment she'd set eyes on the vivid images in that online real estate ad.

Evil had visited her once more.

She froze…a sound brushing across her auditory senses.

Had she left a window open? Allowing the breeze to waft through the downstairs hall?

The sound came again.

Her heart thumped hard.

She listened intently…afraid to move…scared to death of what her brain recognized as the source of the sound.

Weeping.

Soft and forlorn.

Remote and aching like the sound of the foghorn

she'd grown accustomed to, scarcely noticing its presence anymore.

But this was no foghorn.

Livvy threw back the covers and rushed to the door. Not stopping long enough to think, she eased it open, holding her breath as the click of the old mechanism echoed loudly down the hall.

She eased into the pitch-black corridor. Vaguely, she wondered what time it was. Hours before dawn…three or four o'clock maybe.

Her bare feet stilled on the carpeted floor. The sobs grew fractionally louder…more desperate.

Downstairs somewhere.

She moved quickly to the stairs, tamping down the fear rising in her throat. She had to know…had to see where this was coming from. Others had insisted they'd heard it but this was a first for her.

Descending the staircase with a caution born of necessity, she focused on the sound, attempting to determine where it was coming from.

She frowned as she reached the entry hall. The sounds seemed farther away now.

Her pulse fluttering like a butterfly trapped in a wind tunnel, she padded along the wood floor, trying to avoid the areas that squeaked.

The weeping drew her toward the first-floor portion of the east wing. The elegant hardwood gave way to tattered carpet. The smells of lemon oil furniture polish and the fragrant bouquet of flowers gracing the hall table surrendered to mustiness and neglect.

Her heart still thundering, Livvy stopped in front of the final door on the left…one of the rooms facing the courtyard. Yellow tape guarded the locked room.

The weeping abruptly halted, leaving utter silence in the air.

Beverly Bellamy had died in this room. Someone had lain in wait for her as she'd checked door after door. Then, when she'd arrived at this room, flipped the switch to find the overhead light out of commission, she'd taken her final steps into the dark room.

When Livvy had gotten off the phone that night and gone in search of Beverly, she had come upon the gruesome scene.

Beverly was dead.

Livvy stood stock-still…waiting for the weeping to resume.

Others, most recently Emily Carlyle, had heard the weeping. Emily had been certain the sounds had come from the maid's chamber…the same maid who had been put to death for a murder she hadn't committed. A woman who had lost her life in the place of another. Just as Beverly had died when it should have been Livvy entering that dark room where death waited.

Fury at the senseless loss of life prompted Livvy to rip away the yellow crime-scene tape and open the door. A blast of cool air hit her in the face and fear speared through her once more.

Her fingers groped along the wall until she felt the switch. Too late she remembered that it wasn't working. She flipped it upward, and the room was flooded with light. She blinked more in surprise than to adjust her vision. Then it took a full five seconds for her brain to assimilate what her eyes saw.

The doors to the courtyard stood wide open.

LATER THAT MORNING Livvy waited until Ralph and Edna had arrived to begin their daily chores. Saying nothing about the predawn incident, she made her excuses and headed to town. She opted for walking, knowing the exercise and fresh air would do her good. Her leg ached a little, not a sharp pain, just that same old nagging reminder that her body, like her psyche, was damaged. However, if that was her only problem today, she could deal with it. Unfortunately that wasn't the case.

She thought again of this morning's decidedly creepy episode. She'd found the room empty, the courtyard, as well. But someone had obviously opened the doors. The chief had insisted that the room remain locked and undisturbed until further notice.

Livvy had skirted the chalk outline of where Beverly's body had been found and had closed and re-locked the doors. By the time she'd made it back into the hall, shutting off the room from the rest of the house once more, she had been gasping for breath.

She was sure the chief had also told her that the light switch had been tampered with. Had he repaired it? The light had worked fine for her. Why would he do that when he'd insisted that nothing be touched? The forensics technicians from the mainland had checked for fingerprints and other evidence. She'd heard them vacuuming for trace evidence. She'd watched enough crime dramas on television to have a vague idea of what they'd been doing. Had one of them repaired the light switch?

She shook off the confusing thoughts. What difference did it make? Someone had left the door open. It wasn't her—so that left only the chief or an intruder. She had to know which, but she did not relish the idea of facing the chief.

For the next few minutes she distracted herself with the picturesque landscape as she made her way into Cliff's Cove. The blue of the sky and the ever-moving liquid sapphire of the sea made the perfect backdrop for the quaint village. The clean, salty smell of ocean air combined with the occasional whiff of a chimney's smoke relaxed her as nothing else could. The cool September mornings had already prodded her into contacting the chimney sweep to prepare the fireplaces at the inn.

Preparations last year had included a good deal more than a simple cleaning. There had been mortar repairs and the like. But the roar of a fire had definitely helped to ward off the harsh, cold Maine winter.

At a few minutes past ten in the morning, the shops of Cliff's Cove were already alive with activity. Livvy smiled and greeted several of the owners as well as early morning shoppers. Thankfully only one pair of eyes gazed at her with suspicion. Most were filled with empathy, and she greatly appreciated the gestures.

As she'd anticipated, the walk had done her good, helped to clear her head. But now anxiety mounted again as she approached city hall. Somehow Chief Fraley would turn this around, make it her fault.

Much like the rest of the businesses lining the village's main street, city hall dated back to the island's first settlers. Though the long, low building that also housed a couple of additional shops had been renovated numerous times in the last century or so, the original facade remained, maintaining the historic look of the area. Livvy liked that. So many towns and cities tore down the past to make way for the future. The whole island, residents and business owners alike, had worked hard to keep the past a viable part of the present.

She exhaled loudly, reminded herself she couldn't dally out here admiring the lovely architecture forever. Bracing herself for the worst, she entered the small reception area. Like the exterior, the interior was very much in keeping with the Victorian era. Lots of lavish moldings, rich, paneled walls, even the carpeting wasn't the usual commercial-grade stuff.

Period furnishings and a couple of nice pieces of art—both landscapes—completed the decor.

This town was not the kind of place where murders happened.

The secretary's greeting tugged Livvy's attention back to the business at hand. She pasted on her best smile for the blue-haired lady who had worked in this office for forty years, through the comings and goings of three chiefs of police. The current one had managed to be re-elected each term for the past twenty odd years. Livvy told herself that fact alone had to mean the man was basically good. The entire town surely couldn't have been fooled for two decades.

"Good morning, Mrs. Whitman, is the chief in?" Livvy held her breath in an effort to slow her racing heart. *Calm, stay calm.* She was only here to report what she'd discovered this morning.

CHASE FRALEY PAUSED in his review of the forensics report on the Bellamy murder. His brow furrowed as he canted his head to listen more intently. Someone had come into reception. He could hear Ms. Shirley speaking in her loud, firm tone. He chuckled. Shirley Whitman could fend off an invasion of the staunchest enemy.

Then the softer, quieter female voice he would recognize anywhere filtered into his office.

Olivia Hamilton.

He was out of his chair and striding toward reception before good sense could slow him down long enough to analyze his intentions. The chief had told him in no uncertain terms to keep his nose out of this case. He wouldn't like it at all if he knew Chase had taken the preliminary forensics reports from his office. But he needed to know the details. Not just because he liked Olivia Hamilton, but because he had a personal connection to that damn inn. He had a right to look into what had happened in this latest incident.

"Well…I'll…call the chief later," Olivia offered, glancing his way and looking nervous. Chase wondered if she'd been nervous when she'd arrived or if his sudden intrusion had rattled her.

"Good morning, Ms. Hamilton," he interjected before Ms. Shirley could respond to her suggestion. "Is there something I can do for you?" Chase hoped like hell the offer wasn't as transparent as it felt. He'd been attracted to Olivia Hamilton from the moment he'd first met her the day she'd arrived on the island. But he'd kept his distance, mainly because she hadn't encouraged him. She seemed to keep everyone at a distance. Even now, her withdrawal on an emotional level was as plain as day.

She moistened her lips, calling his attention to their fullness. He didn't understand why a woman as attractive as Olivia would avoid any sort of social life. Not that she didn't have events at the inn, but those were always for guests and she always played the perfect host. But she never got personally involved with anyone or anything—except Lost Angel Inn. As if she'd decided being the mistress of that old place was enough.

Chase doubted it would keep her warm at night.

"Something has happened…" She looked anxiously from Chase to Ms. Shirley and back. "I need to talk to the chief." Her big brown eyes brimmed with uncertainty.

Chase looked to the secretary. "Ms. Shirley, hold my calls, please." He gestured to his office. "Come in, Ms. Hamilton, and we'll talk."

For a second or two Chase wondered if she would bolt. He couldn't help noticing she was behaving more skittishly than usual. But she relented and moved in the direction he'd indicated.

He followed her inside and closed the door. "Have a seat."

She looked around the room before taking one of the two chairs in front of his desk. He wondered again what made her so guarded. What had happened to make her so cautious of people, men in particular? He'd noticed her slight limp. An accident of some sort? Maybe she'd lost someone she'd loved and wasn't ready to risk that kind of emotional hurt again. Though he'd had several relationships, he hadn't fallen in love yet. At thirty-three he wondered if maybe it wasn't going to happen. Yet each time he saw Olivia, he couldn't help contemplating the possibility.

He settled into his chair. "Why don't you tell me what happened, Ms. Hamilton? I'll be happy to help any way I can."

She pressed her hand to her throat, drawing his eyes there. As always, she was dressed conservatively. The lightweight sweater had a high neckline, not quite a turtleneck, but almost. The long skirt practically reached her ankles. Sturdy shoes covered her feet. Nothing frilly or frou-frou.

"This morning I thought I heard something…" She licked those lush lips again. "In the…room where Beverly was…killed."

Chase snapped to full attention. "What did you hear?"

She shifted in her chair, clearly reluctant to continue.

"It's all right, Ms. Hamilton," he urged gently, "you can tell me anything." He hoped she understood that he meant what he said. Chase didn't quite understand his uncle's obvious dislike of Olivia. The chief had been unfriendly to her from day one, way before the murder.

But then, giving the man grace, he had a personal tie to that old inn, as well. Chase's father and the chief's only brother had died investigating the last murder that had occurred there twenty years ago. The difference between Chase and the chief was that Chase didn't hold Olivia responsible. The chief apparently considered her decision to renovate and re-

open the place an outright attack against him personally…against the whole island.

Livvy shrugged, calling his focus back to her once
more. "It sounds foolish I know, but…" Her gaze settled on his. "I swear I heard someone crying. But
when I got to the room it was empty."

Chase nodded. Lots of folks had insisted they had
heard the infamous weeping. Personally, he'd
chalked it up to vivid imaginations. However, Olivia
didn't strike him as the sort to let hers run away with
her.

"The sound woke me up," she went on, her dis-
comfort visibly growing. "It's not impossible that I
imagined it." Her gaze found his once more, this
time hers flashed determination. "The part that con-
cerns me is that the doors to the courtyard were
standing wide open."

Chase hadn't seen that one coming. "Open?" he
echoed, surprised.

She jerked her head up and down. "The room was
empty, but I'm sure someone had been in there."

"Was anything disturbed?" Chase didn't like the
sound of this. He and the chief had been there yesterday. The doors, interior as well as exterior, had
been closed and locked then.

"Not that I could see."

"Who else has a key?"

She thought about that a moment. "Just me, Ralph
and Edna." She hesitated. "And the chief, of course.

I gave him a key so he and the forensics people could come and go as they pleased."

"You're sure it wasn't Ralph or Edna?" Chase had known both for most of his life. No way either of them would carelessly leave a door open, especially under these circumstances.

"The doors were all locked last night. I checked myself after Ralph had gone home. Edna had the day off. I woke up and found them open before dawn."

She eased forward in her chair, wringing her hands in her lap. "I know how this sounds, Deputy Fraley, but it's true. Is it possible whoever hurt Beverly came back for something he thought he'd left behind? Some sort of evidence?"

Chase could see by the fear that abruptly widened her eyes that she'd only just thought of that prospect.

"Well, Ms. Hamilton, I can't say for sure, but it certainly sounds plausible." No wonder she was nervous. The idea that someone had been in her house last night tied knots in his gut.

She stood. Chase did the same. "I should get going," she declared. "I just wanted to let somebody know about the doors."

"Why don't I walk you back?" As usual, whenever he was around Olivia, the offer was out of his mouth before he'd had time to think about what he was going to say. "I can take a look around. Write up a report."

She managed a faint smile. "That would be best, I suppose."

Despite his completely selfish reasons for making the suggestion, it was, in fact, the proper procedure. A report should be made. Whether she'd opened the doors in her sleep and simply didn't recall or an intruder had entered for the very purpose she'd suggested, protocol required that he look into it.

In the lobby he said, "Ms. Shirley, I'm going to walk Ms. Hamilton home."

"I'll hold down the fort," Shirley Whitman responded with an inquiring look.

Maybe he should warn Olivia Hamilton that being seen with him, even doing something as innocent as walking home, might put her in the rumor mill. Several townsfolk were apparently laying odds on when Chase would settle down and take a wife. It wasn't acceptable for the future chief of police to be single despite the fact that the current one was. After the death of his father, his uncle had taken Chase under his wing. Now everyone had decided Chase would be the son and heir the revered Chief Fraley had never had.

He held the door for Olivia and wondered where the hell that line of thinking had come from. This was just a walk.

On the sidewalk, she hesitated and looked up at him. "Thank you."

Chase settled his hat into place and gave her a smile. It was easy to smile around her. "For doing my job?"

She shook her head. "For making this—" she looked away "—a little less unpleasant."

He resisted the urge to reach out to her. "This whole thing will go away eventually," he promised, feeling the need to reassure her. "We'll find out what really happened and then life can get back to normal."

She laughed. The sound warmed him. He liked the way she laughed. It reminded him of the tinkling notes of a sweet melody. Easy on the ears.

"Normal would definitely be a change for me," she murmured, almost to herself.

Chase didn't question the comment because she caught herself and withdrew in the same breath. But the idea that she'd had that one slip in his presence gave him hope. Just maybe he could discover what made this mysterious woman tick.

As they walked, the breeze lifted her hair, allowing it to fall down around her shoulders in a kind of dance that made him long to touch the silky tresses. She didn't speak as they strolled toward the inn, so he kept quiet himself. Looking at her was enough. If he was lucky, she wouldn't catch him staring. He didn't want to make her uncomfortable again. He liked when she relaxed around him.

The two ominous turrets of the inn caught his eye as they approached the stately old place. He would be the first to admit that the old mansion looked like something from a Hitchcock film. Spooky in a classic way. But he didn't believe in ghosts or legends. Whoever had taken his father's life had had something to do with the murder Wayne Fraley had been investigating. Though Dorothy Carlyle had not admitted to killing his father as well as her own sister, the woman might not remember all that she'd done. Clearly she'd gone over some mental edge when she'd murdered her own sister.

Chase might never know exactly what had happened to his father that night, only two weeks after Melissa Carlyle's murder. But—he surveyed the inn and its gothic landscape—the fact remained that his father had died here…at Lost Angel Inn.

Maybe he was wrong not to believe in the legend. His gaze swung back to the stoic woman at his side. Maybe she should believe it, as well. Call it cop instincts, call it ESP, but Chase had the sudden, overwhelming feeling that her life depended upon how this investigation turned out.

CHAPTER THREE

LIVVY HAD BARELY opened the door when Edna rushed from the kitchen to meet her.

"Thank God! Livvy, I've been calling all over town trying to find you!" Her miss-nothing gaze slid from Livvy to Chase and back. "I called the chief. I'm sure glad to see Deputy Fraley found you."

"No, we—" Livvy started to explain.

"The chief is as mad as an old wet hen!" Edna interrupted, her petite frame literally vibrating with excitement. "I've never seen him so worked up."

"The chief is here?" Chase asked the agitated woman.

Edna rubbed her palms against her apron, nodded, then pointed toward the east wing. "It's awful...just awful."

"I didn't see his car," Chase went on, ignoring Edna's tirade.

"He parked around by the carpenter's cottage," she hastened to explain, her tone still pressed with urgency. "He called for Mr. Maxwell as well as that stonemason who started the courtyard renovations."

She shook her head, the bun of long gray hair wagging uncharacteristically loose as if it, too, had been affected by the frenzy.

Livvy prayed no one else had gotten hurt. "Where's Ralph?" she demanded on the heels of that thought. Dear God, let him be safe. She couldn't bear the idea of anything happening to the kind old man.

Edna glanced in the same direction she'd pointed. "Chief's questioning him, too."

Deputy Fraley ushered Livvy in the direction of the crime scene before she could ask anything else. Her heart hammered so hard in her chest, she wondered whether a heart attack was imminent. Wouldn't that just tickle James? She could see him in hell right now laughing at her. She couldn't do anything right. She was just as stupid and inept as he'd always told her she was.

Chief Fraley's booming voice left no question as to his location and frame of mind. But something else nudged Livvy's senses even before she heard his voice. The smell of fresh paint. Had Ralph started painting in this wing again? Was that why the chief was so upset?

She stumbled when she realized which door was open…would have lost her balance completely if Chase hadn't caught her.

Even the little surge of electricity his touch caused couldn't detract from what she knew was coming as they continued down the hall.

Oh, no.

The scene inside the room where Beverly had

been murdered forced Livvy to an abrupt halt. Her breath caught in her throat.

The deep cranberry paint she had purchased for one of the guest rooms in this wing had been poured over the chalk outline, mixing with the ugly bloodstain Beverly's violent death had left behind.

But that wasn't all. Other splashes of color—the rich forest-green and bold royal-blue—were on the walls…the floor…everywhere. The smell of fresh paint was stifling.

Who would do this?

Livvy heard the heavy exhale of the man beside her. Even better than her, he knew what this meant. The crime scene had been thoroughly contaminated. Any hope of finding additional evidence was likely now lost.

"You!"

Livvy lifted her gaze to the chief's furious gray one. The heart that had been pounding in her chest suddenly paused awkwardly at the accusation she saw in his eyes.

"I told you to keep this room secure!"

"Hold on now, Chief," Chase said, stepping slightly in front of her in a protective move. "Ms. Hamilton came to the office to report that she'd found the doors leading to the courtyard open when she got up this morning."

Livvy appreciated his not mentioning the weeping she'd heard. For the first time since this insanity started, she felt as if someone was on her side.

"What?" The chief pushed his nephew aside. "What the devil do you mean, the doors were open? I ensured that they were locked myself when I was here yesterday."

Livvy managed a nod. She cleared her throat and summoned a steady voice. "Yes, sir, I know. That's what startled me so. When I found the doors open, I knew you would want to be informed." She looked around the room, utterly shaken by the ghastly vandalism. "But it wasn't like this." She shook her head in renewed disbelief. "I've only been gone for a little while. Ralph and Edna were here when I left. Surely one of them would have heard—"

Before she could finish, the chief swung his analyzing gaze toward Ralph. "Can you explain this, *Mr. Cook*?"

He spoke to Ralph with the same kind of suspicion in his tone that he'd directed at Livvy. She winced at the sound of it and at the look of confusion on the poor gardener's face.

"I—I've been outside all morning," Ralph stammered.

"I don't know what your problem is, Chief," Christopher Maxwell put in, reminding Livvy of his presence, "but throwing around accusations is not going to give us any answers. You've known Ralph

Cook for years, you know he didn't do this any more than I did." He chucked his thumb toward the stonemason. "Or Mr. Dotson here. This entire charade is ridiculous."

Livvy wanted to pat Christopher on the back and thank him for expressing all that she felt. "Surely you don't believe one of these men did this?" she repeated Christopher's sentiment, allowing her disbelief to weigh heavily in her voice. She met the chief's glare with lead in her own.

Chief Fraley studied each man in turn before shifting his full attention back to Livvy. "Your gardener has paint on his hands," he said flatly, as if nothing any of them had said had filtered through his skull. "Look for yourself, it's the same as what's on the floor."

Livvy controlled her expression, refusing to glance in Ralph's direction. She would not give the chief the satisfaction of allowing him to see that for just one second she'd wondered.

"So what?" she snapped. "Ralph has painted many of the rooms in this inn. It's quite likely that he walks around with paint on his hands most of the time. There's always something to be patched up."

"I touched it, ma'am."

All eyes turned to the tall, thin man who still worked hard despite his age. Before Livvy could ask what he meant, the chief said wearily, "He claims he touched the paint on the floor just to make sure it was paint." Fraley shook his head and heaved a sigh. "Not a single one of you is making my job easy here."

Livvy stared at the large, crimson puddle on the floor. It did look like blood, and in spite of the paint cans, she couldn't say she wouldn't have done the same thing Ralph had done.

"Whoever did this," Chase cut in again, "it won't make any real difference now."

He had the attention of everyone in the room with that statement.

"The forensics technicians didn't find anything useful to the investigation. Not even a stray hair that didn't belong to the victim or to you, Ms. Hamilton," he added, his gaze lingering on her for a time.

The chief's face flushed. "Why don't you take out an ad in the *Foghorn Press*?"

Something passed between the two officers. Whatever it was, it wasn't pleasant. Again Livvy thought of the way Chase had looked at the chief when he'd mentioned the subject of forensics yesterday. The two were clearly at odds on this case.

But why?

She thought of the kind way Chase treated her. Maybe the chief didn't want him being nice to the prime suspect.

"Since you're so adamant about your hired help's innocence and since you claim no one else has access to the inn's keys," the chief said to Livvy, "that only leaves you. Did you do this, Ms. Hamilton?"

"I don't believe this!" Christopher huffed.

"Livvy wouldn't hurt anyone," Edna scoffed. Ralph seconded her conclusion, his voice gruff in defense of his employer.

"What about someone in Beverly's past?" Livvy reminded him. "I thought you were checking into that possibility."

"Already did," Chief said. "There is absolutely no one who would have wanted to hurt Beverly or anyone in her family. Can you say the same, *Ms. Hamilton*?"

His words had the intended effect. He had looked into her past. Knew about her husband.

Anger charged through her, obliterating her common sense. "Yes, Chief, I can safely say that there is no one in my past who would want to do this to me."

"Really?" He baited her. "No one?"

She knew what he wanted. "No one," she returned. "The only person who ever wanted to hurt me is dead."

Chief Fraley didn't stop there. "Tell us, how did your late husband die, Ms. Hamilton?"

All attention was suddenly on her. Fear and humiliation coalesced into one overwhelming emotion twisting inside her. She had told no one about her past...about what she'd been through. "He fell down a flight of stairs." She managed to get the words out.

"Where were you when this fatal accident occurred?"

"That's enough."

Chase Fraley's harsh command startled her, pulling her gaze to his rigid stance. The look of contempt on his face startled her.

The chief directed his next statement to his deputy. "Her two friends testified that she was with them."

"I was," Livvy protested. For God's sake, she'd scarcely been able to walk at that point. Had only just been released from the rehab center.

"We've done all we can here," Chase growled before storming out of the room.

The chief maintained his position for another thirty or so seconds, his presence keeping everyone in the room paralyzed in anticipation of his next move. "Whatever is going on here—" he thrust an accusing finger at Livvy "—I will get to the bottom of it."

With that ominous threat, he stalked from the room.

For several moments nobody moved or spoke. Livvy imagined each person was as stunned as she was. She could also just imagine what they were thinking about her now. None of them had known about James Hamilton.

It was official now. The chief thought Beverly's murder had something to do with Livvy. She didn't doubt that he fully suspected she was the killer. Chase's words suddenly echoed inside her skull. *Not even a stray hair that didn't belong to the victim or to you, Ms. Hamilton.*

"Are you all right?"

Livvy shook off the haunting words. "Yes," she said to Christopher. "I'm okay."

Her assurance didn't change his worried expression. "I don't know what's up with the chief but I think he's losing it. Maybe this murder has dredged up the memory of losing his brother and not being able to pin it on my father."

Livvy knew a little about the story. Maybe she needed to know more. "He just disappeared, right?"

Christopher nodded. "Into thin air."

Edna made a harrumphing sound. "Went over those cliffs is my guess. Lots of folks over the years disappeared that way. Unless you land on the rocks, it's impossible to find the body."

"Whatever the chief's problem," Christopher, her loyal friend and the man who'd helped her restore so many of the inn's intricate details, said to Livvy, "he needs to stop harassing you like this. Maybe you should contact an attorney."

Fear trickled through her. She'd been through that kind of nightmare already. "I'm all right, really. The chief is only trying to do his job." She hadn't done anything wrong. There was no reason for her to worry. Was there?

"Will someone please tell me when I can get back to this project?" Mr. Dotson demanded. "I don't want to be attempting to reset all those stones once freezing temperatures hit."

"I understand." Livvy let go a troubling breath. "I'll see what I can do. Surely if they were going to find any evidence in the courtyard they would have already."

Heads bobbed in agreement. Livvy noticed that Ralph remained oddly silent.

Christopher patted her shoulder. Concern still clouded his face. "Livvy, let me know if you need anything. Emily and I are here for you."

She produced a shaky smile. "Thank you. I appreciate your kindness."

His expression relaxed fractionally. "I'll keep you posted on the new bedroom suite I spotted on the mainland."

"Do that."

She had hoped to have the east wing renovated and furnished by Thanksgiving, but that might not happen now. As much as she hated to think about that reality, she worried that the investigation was going to hurt her chances of a decent winter season. It wasn't fair to think about that, not with Beverly lying on a slab in the morgue. But reality wouldn't let her keep those worries at bay. Especially not after that heart-wrenching call to the young woman's folks yesterday.

Christopher and Mr. Dotson left, with Edna urging both to come by for lunch tomorrow, she planned to try her hand at making Clara's famous chicken salad. Now there was something Livvy could definitely count on, the mere mention of Clara's chicken salad could change the worst of moods.

She hesitated in the long corridor that led back to the entry hall. "Are you all right, Ralph?"

He still hadn't said a word. It was one thing for the

chief to give her a hard time, but it was not right for him to pick on Ralph. A kinder man couldn't be found.

He hunched his shoulders in a halfhearted shrug. "I don't know, Ms. Livvy. Maybe this old place should have been left alone."

Livvy stilled. He didn't have to explain. She understood perfectly what he meant. "If I hadn't reopened the inn, Beverly would still be alive." It was that simple and yet immensely complicated.

His face a solemn mask, he moved his head up and down in silent agreement.

The weight of guilt settled even more heavily upon Livvy. He was right. There was no denying the charge. She was guilty of setting the stage, but she hadn't killed Beverly any more than Ralph or Edna had. Of course evidence that she had been in the room would be found. Her fingerprints and various forms of DNA were all over every room in this house. She'd scrubbed, vacuumed, measured, painted, leaving behind the occasional broken nail, trace of blood from a skinned knuckle and no doubt plenty of shed hairs. This was her home, who would expect otherwise?

None of that made her a murderer.

She could only hope that the chief would soon see that and actually start looking for the real murderer.

Another realization struck her with the intensity of a train exploding from a dark tunnel. What if the murderer wasn't finished? Why else would he have come back here? Assuming the unlocked doors and spilled paint were his work? And who else would have done such a thing? What if he didn't plan to stop until he'd killed everyone involved with the continued operation of the inn? Edna, Ralph, Clara as well as Livvy might all be his targets.

She hated herself for it but she had to consider all the possibilities. She glanced at Ralph's hands as they moved toward the entry hall and thought of another scenario. What if the unlocked doors and the paint had nothing to do with Beverly's death? What if someone was trying to get her to close the inn for good? Someone who saw Beverly's death as a sign or omen of some sort. *I don't know, Ms. Livvy. Maybe this old place should have been left alone.*

And maybe he was right.

It wouldn't be the first mistake of a deadly magnitude she had made.

But she couldn't admit defeat...not yet.

"WHAT THE HELL are you trying to prove?"

Chase's demand echoed over the cliffs surrounding Lost Angel Inn. He didn't especially care who heard him. This had gone too far. This case wasn't any more personal to his uncle than it was to him, and he certainly wasn't going around making unsubstantiated accusations.

"I will not discuss this with you now, son."

Son. That was the way it had been between them for the past twenty years. Chase's father had gone missing, presumed dead, and Benton Fraley had taken over as both father and mother. Chase's mother had died when he was just a baby. His father and his uncle were all he'd ever had. But the changes he'd noticed in the man in the past year just didn't add up. From the moment Olivia Hamilton had come to the island, his dislike for her had been expanding.

"I know the opening of the inn has resurrected the past. It's been tough for both of us," Chase offered as he matched his pace to the chief's deliberate one. They'd crossed the lawn and started around toward the rear of the property. Maybe it was the uncharacteristically warm day or maybe it was his annoyance at his uncle's obsessive insistence on treating Olivia like a suspect, but Chase could barely keep his own temper in check. Olivia Hamilton was not responsible for what happened twenty years ago any more than she was for the murder of Beverly Bellamy. The chief had to see that.

Chief Fraley stopped abruptly and glared at Chase. "Do you really understand what's going on here?"

There was something wholly unnerving about his manic expression, as if he was about to explode.

"That woman—" he stabbed a finger toward the inn "—is desperate. You know as well as I do that a desperate person is capable of most anything. I checked her out. The last time her life got out of control, someone died. Do you see a pattern forming here?"

Chase shook his head in disbelief. "You can't really suspect that she murdered Beverly Bellamy. Good God, Chief, Beverly was killed doing Livvy's job. Doesn't that put her in danger rather than make her a suspect?" Just another reason why Chase intended to keep a close watch on Livvy. Apparently he was the only one who considered that she might have been the intended victim.

The chief shook that accusing finger at Chase now. "I see what's happening here. You're falling for her...making the same mistake your daddy—" He stopped abruptly, his eyes bulging with surprise at his own words.

"What about my father?" Chase demanded, his fury building again. "What mistake did he make that has any relevance here?"

The tense silence thickened for three beats before his uncle spoke again. "He made the mistake of becoming obsessed with a woman, and it cost him his life. I see how you look at Ms. Hamilton."

The words were like a blow to Chase's gut. "What're you talking about?"

Conviction that he was right burned in Benton Fraley's eyes. "Suffice to say that Martin Maxwell might not have killed the woman but who's to say he didn't kill the competition? There are times when a man's desire for a woman can get him killed."

Speechless, Chase watched his uncle march in the direction of his parked car. Why the hell had

Chase never heard anything about this before? Why now? Out of the blue?

So what if Chase liked Olivia Hamilton, felt protective of her? What did that have to do with the murder of his father? If Chase's father had been connected to Melissa Carlyle in any way, why would Chase not have heard rumors around town?

He knew he wouldn't get the answers he wanted from his uncle. But there was one person he could ask who would know all about those days. And Chase intended to find out the truth.

He followed the path his uncle had taken and climbed into the cruiser's passenger seat. He didn't say anything else to the man, there was no point. His uncle had his reasons for feeling the way he did, and Chase would learn what they were, but from a more rational voice. Then maybe he would understand what made a levelheaded man like Chief Benton Fraley go around making groundless accusations.

Chase frowned as his uncle shoved the vehicle into gear and rocketed forward onto the washed-out back road that led toward town, eventually intersecting with the more commonly used thoroughfare. There was a hell of a lot that didn't add up here. Since his uncle apparently couldn't look at this case with any objectivity, Chase would have to solve it himself. Otherwise a murderer might just get away.

And a woman's peace of mind, as well as her livelihood, might be shattered.

He couldn't let that happen.

Maybe he was obsessed, but he couldn't turn his back on Olivia Hamilton.

CHAPTER FOUR

CHASE RUMMAGED IN the archives until he found the box that contained the files on the Carlyle case. He wiped away the film of dust and sat at the table to review the contents of the box.

For more than two hours he read through statements and investigation reports. The newspaper clippings were the most troubling. There was plenty of speculation about his father and the primary suspect, Martin Maxwell, but there had been no evidence. Of course, now they all knew why. Melissa Carlyle's sister had killed her. But there had been no revelation about Chase's father. His death still remained a mystery.

Chase carefully placed the files back into the box and returned it to the designated slot on the appropriate shelf. There was only one other source of information he could trust with complete certainty.

He headed to the lobby. Ms. Shirley would be returning from her lunch break about now. Chase needed to get pertinent questions out of the way before his uncle returned. The chief was already furious that Chase had read the forensics report. Not once in their ten years of working together had his uncle behaved so possessively over a case.

Chase closed the files room door behind him at the same time Shirley Whitman settled into the comfortable chair behind her desk. She shifted, adjusting the decorative needlepoint pillow her granddaughter had made for her, and glanced up at him.

"Anything exciting happen while I was out?"

Chase sat in an upholstered chair flanking her desk. "Not really. Jeb Kendrick called about that community dinner coming up Friday night."

Shirley's eyes brightened. "That so?"

Chase grinned. Obviously, Shirley had herself a new suitor. "I told him I'd give you the message."

"I'll have to give him a call back…later." She looked pleased with herself. "After he's had time to sweat awhile."

Chase managed a chuckle. Poor Jeb. The man would definitely need to be on his toes if Shirley was his romantic interest.

Chase let the silence go on longer than he'd intended in an attempt to find just the right words.

Shirley's expression turned knowing. "If you want to ask me something, Chase, you should just go ahead. No use beating around the bush."

That was just one of the things he liked about her. She was not only efficient; she was direct. Well, at least in all things not related to romance.

"I heard something about my father this morning that I didn't know."

One gray eyebrow lifted speculatively. "Your father was a fine man. Could have been chief but he knew how badly Benton wanted it so he stepped aside."

Chase had known that. His uncle had always been open about who had been the better politician. In a small town like Cliff's Cove the position of police chief was more about politics than cop skills. Benton Fraley had even gone on to say that his brother had passed on the position because he had a son to take care of, unlike Benton who'd never married. It had made sense at the time to the two brothers. Benton would serve as chief since he had no outside responsibilities and Wayne, Chase's father, would serve as his deputy. The perfect plan.

Taking care with his words, Chase ventured into the sensitive territory. "Did you ever hear that my father was involved in any way with Melissa Carlyle?"

Shirley looked surprised by the question but swiftly recovered. "They were friends. Most of the men in town wanted to be Melissa's friend," she added frankly.

Chase frowned. "What exactly do you mean by that?"

She heaved a sigh before she responded. "Melissa Carlyle was an extraordinarily beautiful woman. Everyone loved her. Couldn't help themselves. Personally, I believe your daddy was quite taken with her, but I'm fairly certain he kept it to himself. He wouldn't have trespassed on another man's territory."

"Martin Maxwell?"

Shirley nodded. "Wayne knew how Maxwell felt, so he kept his own feelings to himself. He simply loved her from afar, so to speak."

The news only served to further bewilder Chase. "You think that could have gotten him killed?"

Shirley pursed her lips and regarded his question for a bit. "Benton would like to think so. You have to understand," she explained, "Martin Maxwell, your daddy and your uncle had always been the best of friends. But Melissa somehow changed the dynamics of their relationship. I'm certain it wasn't intentional, it just happened."

Chase nodded, understanding coming to him slowly. "Do you think it's possible the chief still considers Maxwell the prime suspect in my father's disappearance?"

"I believe that's exactly how he feels, though he has never been able to prove it." Shirley inclined her head, her expression taking on a faraway look. "I also believe that's why your uncle has been so troubled by the opening of the inn. To him it's a constant reminder of his own failure."

Now Chase was confused again. "Failure at what?"

Shirley leveled her gaze on his once more. "To find the truth, what else? Until just recently the entire case was a complete mystery. Now, since the inn opened, a major portion of what actually happened has been revealed—none of which is as a result of the chief's superior investigating skills."

Chase followed her reasoning. He hadn't considered that his uncle might feel humiliated that someone else had solved the Carlyle murder. But there was still one very large unanswered question. What had happened to Wayne Fraley? If neither Dorothy Carlyle nor Martin Maxwell had had anything to do with his murder, who had?

A thought plowed into Chase's brain...one he dared not speak out loud.

What if his father had killed himself? What if he couldn't bear the idea that Melissa was dead? Would a man really feel that strongly about a woman with whom he hadn't even had a physical relationship? Could he have loved her from afar more than he did his own son?

The bottom dropped out of Chase's stomach. Maybe that's why the chief had said those things to him this morning. Maybe he knew.

Disappointment and dread pooled in Chase's gut.

He wouldn't allow himself to think that. Couldn't bring himself to believe that his own father could have deserted him in such a way. But was it any easier to believe that he'd been murdered and that his murderer was walking around free to this day?

"Give your uncle time," Shirley went on, dragging

Chase back to the present. "The chief will get past the fresh hurt in time. Once he finds who murdered the Bellamy girl, he'll even get over the reopening of the inn."

Chase nodded. He knew how heavily this case weighed on his uncle. It troubled Chase, as well. He hadn't realized until now how badly his uncle had wanted to keep that old place in the past. Maybe Chase hadn't taken the time to consider how much dragging that past into the present might hurt the man who'd raised him when he'd had no one else.

Pushing to his feet, Chase said, "Thanks for your insight, Ms. Shirley. I think I'll take a look at the chief's file on the Bellamy murder and see if there's anything we may have missed."

Shirley made an agreeable sound. "That might not be a bad idea. The chief's being awfully possessive on this one." She raised a skeptical eyebrow. "We both understand why, but that doesn't make for the most objective investigating."

Exactly the conclusion Chase had come to. As much as the chief wanted to keep him out of this, he couldn't. Chase was involved. His father's murder had something to do with that inn and its past. There was nothing Chief Benton Fraley could do to protect Chase from that fact. And now someone else had been killed. The possibility that a local had resorted to murder merely to prevent the inn from succeeding seemed unlikely. Unless he or she had something else to hide.

His mind working, sorting through the possibilities, Chase ventured into the chief's office and shuffled through the files on his desk. The one on the Bellamy murder was surprisingly light. Chase opened it to find the chief's report consisted of a single typed page and a list of names of Beverly Bellamy's family and friends.

What startled Chase was the missing forensics report. He sifted through the papers on the chief's desk, carefully checked each drawer and file cabinet, but found nothing.

He didn't like the idea gnawing at him. This wasn't right. Then again, maybe the chief had the report with him. Perhaps he had met with a person from the forensics lab on the mainland. He had said that one of the technicians was coming to take a second look, though Chase had heard nothing about it. Only one way to find out.

Chase took the file and closed himself up in his own office. He sat behind his desk, picked up the phone and entered the number he already knew by heart. Anticipation surged through his veins as he waited. His hopes were dashed when the voice that answered after the second ring was not Olivia's.

He shook his head at his foolishness. "Edna, this is Deputy Fraley. Is the chief there by any chance?"

"No, sir. Haven't seen him since he left with you this morning."

For one beat Chase considered asking to speak

with Olivia. Just to see if she was all right, of course. But he thought better of it. "Thanks, Edna."

Chase hung up. Cursed himself for the idiot he was. He'd let all that the chief said this morning get to him. He wasn't obsessed with Olivia. He simply liked her, wanted to know her better. What was wrong with that? Nothing. His uncle's suspicions were unfounded. Olivia had nothing to do with this murder. She certainly had nothing to do with the inn's past problems.

Somehow Chase had to find out what had happened to Beverly Bellamy. Maybe then Olivia, as well as the inn and the town, would be free of this curse once and for all.

"I'M GOING HOME before the storm hits."

Chase looked up at Shirley, who stood in the door of his office. He hadn't even been aware she'd opened the door. If she'd knocked, he definitely hadn't heard her.

He blinked, looked down at the papers spread on his desk then back up at her. "I guess I lost track of the time."

"Past five," she said, shouldering into her coat. "Weatherman says it's gonna be a mean one."

Chase glanced out the window for the first time since he'd sat down. The sky was dark. The branches of the trees lining the street whipping in the wind left no doubt of what was to come. Rain, thunder and lightning. Maybe even a little hail.

"You'd better get home," he said to Shirley. "I'll hang around a little longer to see if the chief's coming back."

"Don't forget to switch the phones over."

"Will do."

He heard the door close behind her as she exited the suite of offices that made up city hall. The phones were switched to the 9-1-1 dispatch operator on the mainland after business hours. If an emergency came up, dispatch would contact the chief or Chase. Between the two of them there was always a representative of the badge on the island. And most folks knew to call him or the chief directly after hours.

Chase dropped his gaze to the pages in front of him. He'd spent the past few hours calling every relative and friend of Beverly's. Her parents had already answered the chief's questions and didn't understand why they had to do so again. Chase hated putting them through the pain, but instinct pressed him to do just that. He'd asked the routine questions first, then tossed in a couple about whether Beverly had mentioned seeing or hearing anything out of the ordinary at the inn. He'd gotten exactly what the chief had said: nothing.

He had almost let it go at that, but then he'd called the next name on the list, then the one after that, until he'd called every friend and relative on the chief's list. Chase's confusion grew as he did so. No one else on the list had been contacted. The chief hadn't questioned a single friend or relative other than the parents.

Admittedly, Chase had learned nothing new, but that wasn't the point. The chief should have made those calls. That he hadn't was bad enough; that he'd lied about making them was far worse.

Chase flipped through the Rolodex and punched in another number. This one for the forensics lab. He recognized the voice of the technician who answered. "Hey, this is Deputy Fraley over in Cliff's Cove," he said by way of greeting. "I know it's late, but I just have a quick question. Were any of your techs planning to come back out to Lost Angel Inn for a second sweep of the crime scene?"

The answer wasn't the one he wanted to hear. Several seconds elapsed before Chase found his voice. "Thank you." He hung up the receiver, his instincts humming a warning now.

Why would the chief lie? Why had he told Olivia to hold off on her renovations because forensics was coming back to do a second sweep?

The body had been released today. The funeral was the day after tomorrow. It didn't make sense to keep the crime scene off-limits if there was nothing else to find.

Chase mulled over this morning's vandalism. If there hadn't been a murder, he could picture some local vandalizing the place in an attempt to thwart the inn's continued operation. Some folks just didn't think it was right to disturb the ghosts of the past who surely lived there. But Chase knew everyone in this community. There wasn't a soul he could point to who would kill anyone.

Beverly Bellamy's friends and family had checked out. There was no apparent motivation among the small, close-knit group. Not one knew of anyone with a grudge against her.

None of it made sense.

And there was the fact that Olivia was the one who generally did the locking up. Was she really the intended target? Who would have known her routine? Probably Ralph, Clara and Edna. Chase couldn't see any of them wanting to harm Olivia or Beverly.

He gathered the contents of the file and strode back to the chief's office, pausing long enough to switch the phones as Shirley had reminded him. Chase might as well call it a day. There was nothing more he could do here. All he wanted to do right now was to find his uncle and have a nice, long talk. Get past all this subterfuge. Get all the cards out on the table. They had a murder to solve. This was no time to be keeping secrets. And Olivia might very well need police protection.

As he turned away from the chief's desk, something snagged his attention. Frowning, Chase moved closer to the massive mahogany desk. The corner of a manila folder peeked out from beneath the blotter pad.

He lifted the pad with its weeks of scrawled notes and pulled the unmarked folder from under it. Dread buzzing in his ears, he opened it to view the contents.

The name Olivia Hamilton jumped off the very first page.

CHAPTER FIVE

THE RAIN had started.

Livvy poured herself a brandy and moved to the parlor's front window. When a storm blew in off the sea, it was a sight to behold.

The kind of storm coming in on the tail of a hurricane wasn't so romantic, but this kind, the plain old storm that built up as a result of the changing season or maybe simply as heaven's way of showing off, tugged at Livvy's senses. She felt oddly alive as the thunder rolled and the flash of light in the distance followed at its own leisurely pace. The surface of the water grew restless, reacting to the brewing natural phenomenon.

Though she was completely alone in the inn on this jagged thrust of earth where the land met the sea, she didn't feel lonely just now. The atmosphere felt charged with energy. The house stood tall and strong against the wind. Livvy felt protected within these massive walls.

"Now there's an ironic thought," she mused out loud.

Two days ago she'd been certain she would never feel safe here again. Maybe the old inn was trying to comfort her. After all, she'd spent her life savings to restore it. And now she had nowhere else to go.

If whoever killed Beverly intended Livvy harm, what could she do? Run? Leave behind all she'd invested in the inn? She'd had to walk away from one life, she wasn't doing that again. Fear was not going to send her running...not ever again. *Not ever again*. She had to be strong...couldn't let the terror get a grip on her.

An ache sliced through her. There was no way she could leave this inn. She was a part of it now. She felt as if she'd always been here.

No matter what the chief or anyone else thought, Livvy had recently concluded that fate had brought her here to rescue this grand old place. To rescue this place as her doctor, that detective and two loyal friends had rescued her three years ago.

She downed her brandy and poured another, wincing at the liquor's burn, then surveyed the room, proud of how well it had turned out. All summer long her guests had been awed by the renovations she had done. Of course, she couldn't take credit for the more intricate work, that had been Christopher's doing. Cleaning and painting had been the extent of her contributions. But she wasn't ashamed of her part. Those things had been every bit as necessary.

She thought of Ralph's reaction to this morning's vandalism, and her chest squeezed painfully. It was difficult not to understand how he must feel. Part of her wanted to be angry that his comment had sounded so disloyal, but the other, more rational side recognized that he was only human. Who wouldn't think just exactly what he had?

She'd considered the same herself. Maybe reopening the inn had been a mistake.

But it was done. There was no undoing it. Closing up now wouldn't bring Beverly back.

The brandy went down a little more smoothly this time. Knowing she shouldn't, Livvy poured another and decided to take a nice, long soak in the tub.

She turned out the lights and checked the front door, then slowly, sipping the brandy perhaps more for courage than she would have liked to admit, she checked the rest of the exterior doors downstairs. Except for one. That room was still cordoned off with the yellow tape, and the chief had reaffirmed his orders that very morning that no one was to go inside.

Holding her breath, Livvy did ensure that the door leading from the corridor into that room was secured. She breathed easy once more when she found it locked tight.

Taking her time, she climbed the stairs, noting that with the help of the brandy her old injury scarcely ached as she made the arduous journey.

Turning her thoughts to more pleasant subjects, she hoped she would be able to proceed with the painting and carpeting of the east wing soon. With that behind her as well as the courtyard renovations, the property would be fully restored. From that point forward she would only have to worry about normal maintenance. If her busy seasons went well, perhaps she could start to put a little something away for a rainy day.

She laughed at the pun. It was a rainy day and outside the money she'd set aside for the new carpeting and fountain restoration as well as minimal operating expenses until the Christmas season arrived, she was pretty much broke.

Livvy filled the deep, claw-footed tub with steaming water. Her bathroom was the largest in the house and romantically decorated, except for the safety bar she'd had installed for helping herself out of the tub. She tried not to use it, however there were times when it was essential. But she wasn't going to feel sorry for herself.

She was alive. In celebration of that wondrous fact she lit the candles that sat here and there in the room. Some scented, some not, but all providing the desired cozy illumination.

With a couple of big fluffy towels nearby, she eased into the tub. The hot, steamy water closed in around her, immediately relaxing weary muscles. Once she'd settled back to soak, she finished off her brandy and set the little glass next to her shampoo on the antique table she'd chosen as a kind of tub-side service center. Steam wafted up around her, wound around the soft glow of the candles.

With that peaceful image on her mind, she shut her eyes and told herself to close out all other thought. Just relax. Let go of the worries. The sounds of the storm rumbled outside. The rain splattering relentlessly. Wind whining and moaning, punctuated from time to time by the grumble of thunder. Once in a while a stark bolt of lightning would brighten the dimly lit room, a vivid contrast to the faint glow of the candles.

The brandy had calmed her so thoroughly that she might have a tough time staying awake through the bath. The sweet aroma of roses and lilacs scented the air. This serene place out on a cliff's serrated edge was what she'd sought…what she'd longed for when she'd been searching for a place to start fresh. Solitude broken only by the interesting and diverse guests of her summer and Christmas seasons. Being her own boss, forging her own destiny.

A new beginning in something as close to paradise as she could find. This remote New England spot had been it. Far away from the hustle and bustle of the rest of the world. A place deeply infused with the past. And the inn. She smiled. God, it had been everything she'd wanted. Beautiful in a rugged sort of way. Brimming with mystique and history.

The only thing she hadn't found was true love.

Livvy's eyes popped open on that thought. She

hadn't been looking for love. How could she possibly ever trust herself or anyone else to recognize the real thing?

She couldn't.

Her mind immediately conjured Chase Fraley's handsome face, defying her conclusion.

She sighed softly, her body instantly heating on the inside at the mere thought of him.

Knowing full well she shouldn't, she allowed her eyes to close once more and the finer details of Chase to invade her senses. The nice fit of his uniform. He was tall, broad-shouldered. Strong. The sandy color of his hair gave him the all-American-boy look, as did the vivid blue of his eyes.

But that strength and that beauty could morph into something else, something evil, she knew firsthand.

Chase Fraley wasn't James Hamilton, a part of her protested. He'd been protecting her from the chief's wrath the last couple of days. Had put himself directly in line for the full brunt of that wrath.

That spoke highly of him.

Made her want to know him better.

Could she let herself feel that way? Really feel that way? The attraction was there, but she was so afraid to trust herself.

But she had needs.

For the first time in too many years to remember, she recognized those needs. She wanted to be touched.

She allowed, just for a moment, her mind to float…permitted the powerful feelings of desire that Chase elicited to take over.

She remembered the feel of his strong fingers when he'd touched her…the sound of his deep voice. The caring way he looked at her.

She wasn't blind, she'd seen the longing in his eyes. He had feelings for her that went beyond professional concern.

A new reality invaded the soft thoughts. Livvy blinked, her glorious state of relaxation shifting into tension.

What she'd seen in Chase's eyes couldn't have been desire for her, she argued. She was ugly, plain. Hadn't James told her that often enough? She jerked at the rush of memories that spilled into her mind. His ranting that he couldn't even remember why he'd noticed her. And now there were the hideous scars left from the numerous surgeries after that plunge down the stairs.

Her hand drifted down to her thigh. No man would want a woman so grossly marked. She traced the thick ridges of healed flesh. Chase surely had noticed the limp. Her inability to walk long distances or to jog had forced her to attempt to stay in good physical condition by other means, but she hadn't been very successful. Her body had lost its look of youth and firmness.

Chase was muscular. His body was no doubt perfect. A startling jolt shook her at the thought of him naked. Her breath caught sharply at the intensity of it. Her hand went to her throat, trailed down to her breasts, which were stinging with their own urgent need.

Perhaps her breasts were her one saving grace. Fairly large and still reasonably firm. She pulled her hand away. Why did she even bother worrying about such nonsense? She could never let him get close. She knew that with absolute certainty. To torture herself with such foolish notions was ridiculous.

Abruptly, Livvy sat up and listened.

Goose bumps rushed over her skin in spite of the warm water.

What the hell…?

Music. She could hear music.

She pushed herself out of the water, using the safety bar for assistance.

Quickly dabbing off her wet skin, she tried to make out where the sound was coming from…what the melody was. She hadn't turned on the light in the bathroom since she'd lit the candles. Had the power blinked off and then on? Sometimes the television came on of its own accord when that happened. A radio maybe?

She slipped on her robe, cinched the belt tight at her waist and padded into her bedroom. The music was a little louder now.

She opened the door and eased out into the upstairs hall.

Classical music.

Mozart.

Fear froze in Livvy's veins.

She recognized the piece.

James's favorite.

Livvy didn't know how long she stood there, paralyzed with terror. She had to move. Had to determine the source of the music.

Had to run, another part of her brain urged.

She hurried to the staircase. Hesitated there, staring through the consuming darkness below. She flipped the wall switch. The entry hall flooded with light.

The music seemed to be coming from the parlor.

"Just a coincidence," she murmured. The radio probably came on from the power surge. Just happened to be playing that song.

Couldn't be anything else.

She choked out a sound that was supposed to be a laugh.

Any second now the deejay would break into the music and announce the current time or an update on the weather.

Calm down.

Calm down and go to the parlor.

Turn off the radio.

Everything is fine.

Livvy descended the stairs cautiously. With each step she reminded herself that it had to be a coincidence. A joke played by fate to shake her.

She reached the parlor doorway. Felt along the wall for the switch. Table lamps around the room lit instantly, chasing away the darkness. Air she hadn't even realized she'd been holding rushed past her lips in a surge of relief.

Okay, it's okay.

The crescendo of the music rose higher and higher as she moved determinedly toward the built-in bookcases where her CD player/radio combination sat on one of the many shelves.

She licked her lips and reached toward the power button.

Her hand halted midway to her destination. A frown wrinkled her brow.

It wasn't the radio.

The CD player.

Her entire body went numb with renewed fear as she pressed the stop button, then eject. The tray holding the CD slid outward. Her fingers closed around the shiny disc and lifted it out of the tray.

A collection of Mozart.

The disc fell to the floor.

Livvy stared down at it.

Not possible.

She'd given away all of his belongings. She'd kept nothing. Not even a single photograph.

A blast of cold air whipped down the entry hall. The sound of breaking glass jerked her from terror's grip long enough to prod her in that direction.

The flowers lay on the floor. The elegant vase she kept on the side table shattered, pieces lying around like glittering slivers of ice. She must have overfilled it with the long-stemmed arrangement. Left it off balance, she reasoned.

The wind lifted the hem of her robe, making her shiver.

As if time had lapsed into slow motion, Livvy turned toward the front door. It stood wide open. Wind and rain blasted into the house.

Another sound rose above that of the wind.

Livvy's gaze swung toward the corridor waiting to be renovated. Weeping. Loud…forlorn. Her heart launched into her throat.

"No." The single word squeezed out of her on a sob of anguish.

Livvy bolted for the door. She grabbed her keys from the hook on the wall as she passed and ran out of the house.

The wind pushed against her. The rain blinded her but she didn't stop. Kept going. Had to reach her car. A stab of pain pierced her thigh. She cried out and her legs buckled and she went down in a tangled heap in the damp grass.

Get up! Get up!

She struggled to her feet. Scrambled forward. Not far now, she told herself.

Reaching her car, her fingers curled on the driver's side door latch…jerked. Nothing. It was locked.

She swore…fumbled…finally succeeded in pressing the unlock button on the remote in her hand.

She flung the door open and lunged behind the steering wheel. She shoved the key into the ignition. *Hurry!* A voice deep in her brain kept screaming at her to hurry. Her heart pounded so hard she could hardly breathe. Her fingers trembled so violently she had to squeeze them together a moment before she could summon the strength to turn the ignition.

The engine started on the first try. *Thank God! Thank God!* She threw the car into reverse and stomped on the accelerator. The sudden backward motion propelled her forward, almost slamming her forehead against the steering wheel.

Struggling for control, she moved the gearshift into drive and took off in the direction of town. "Get hold of yourself," she muttered. She would be in town in no time. All she had to do was to calm down and keep the vehicle out of the ditch.

The engine stalled. She pounded the steering wheel with the heel of her hand. "No!" She patted the accelerator but the engine died. "Damn it." She twisted the ignition over and over but it wouldn't start.

"What the—?"

Her gaze settled on the fuel gauge.

Empty.

But she'd filled it up just two days ago. Hadn't driven anywhere since. She remembered distinctly…

The grit and determination she'd used to force her

damaged body to relearn how to walk suddenly so-
lidified. The terror twisting inside her abruptly vanished, fury took its place.

Livvy shoved the car door open and climbed out
into the driving rain. She stared back at the inn with
its ominous turrets jutting skyward.

This was her home. By God, no one was going to
drive her out of it. And that was exactly what was
happening here.

She marched back to the house, each step ratch-
eting up her outrage another notch. Whoever was
doing this wasn't going to get away with it. He—or
she—had to be a coward to do this kind of thing
without showing his face.

She was not a coward. She refused to be a victim
again. Not ever again.

Livvy stalked into the entry hall and slammed the
door behind her.

She leaned against it for a moment and listened.
The storm outside still howled, the rain pelted down
insistently. But inside, it was as quiet as a tomb.

The idea that some coward had done this to her
and then scampered away to hide only made her
more furious.

She skirted the broken glass and went in search
of the necessary implements to clean up the mess.

With the glass and flowers in the trash and the
water mopped up, she went through every single
room in the house, upstairs and down.

She even opened the off-limits room. She didn't go inside, but she did scrutinize the exterior doors from her position across the room. They were locked. With that room secured once more, she headed back to the parlor. She retrieved the CD and studied it a moment.

She didn't use the CD player often. Couldn't even remember when she had played it last. One of her guests over the summer could have left this CD in the player. If the electricity blinked as she'd suspected, the CD player could have turned on as a result of the ensuing power surge.

Livvy laughed wryly, stared down at her damp robe. She was an idiot. Had let her imagination get the better of her.

This house was old. It wasn't impossible that she'd believed she'd closed and locked the front door securely, but actually hadn't pushed it into place quite hard enough. The wind could have done the rest. As far as the weeping went, she didn't know quite what to make of that, but *if* it was a ghost, she wasn't afraid of ghosts. It was people who killed people.

She trudged into the kitchen, tossed the CD into the trash and put the kettle on. She could definitely use a cup of hot tea to soothe her seriously frayed nerves. More brandy was out of the question. The liquor may very well have fueled her imagination.

While the water heated she would dry off again

and drag on some soft flannel pajamas. She intended to relax tonight, one way or another.

She started for the door but hesitated. Damn. She hadn't gone shopping this week with all the excitement—if one could call murder exciting. Was she out of tea? This morning she hadn't seen anything but coffee in the cupboard. When there were no guests at the inn, she didn't bother with inventory and stocking so meticulously.

No point in heating the water if she didn't have any tea. Annoyed that she might not be able to savor her favorite blend, she tromped over to the cupboard.

She swung open the doors and her breath evaporated in her lungs.

A large tin of imported tea stared back at her.

Livvy swallowed hard. Assam Indian tea.

Had Edna decided to take the shopping upon herself since Livvy hadn't gotten around to it?

But Livvy hated Assam tea. It wouldn't have been on her list. She didn't even stock it for her guests. It had to be special ordered…had Edna or Clara ordered it?

No…no…that couldn't be right.

Her hand shaking, she reached for the canister. She lifted it from the cupboard and her heart bucked mercilessly. Another can sat behind that one. Then another.

This wasn't right. She *hated* Assam tea.

James had loved it. He had insisted that Americans didn't know good tea. Livvy remembered the first time she'd placed his special order and gotten the wrong blend…she flinched at the recollection of the explosion of rage he'd showered on her.

This just couldn't be…

No one else knew about before…about what she'd been through. Who would order James's tea?

Livvy stood in the middle of her kitchen…suddenly afraid to move. Afraid to scream.

Impossible. No one knew. No one.

It had to be him…

CHAPTER SIX

CHASE WAITED in the darkness.

Eight p.m.

Benton Fraley entered the office, switching on the light as he closed the door behind him.

He blinked, seemingly startled when he noticed Chase sitting there.

"What the hell are you doing sitting in the dark, son?" he asked cautiously. Suspicion narrowed his keen gaze.

Chase tapped the two folders lying on the edge of Shirley's desk. "Tell me what's going on. *Now.*" He wanted to shake his uncle until he told him everything. A new wave of anguish washed over Chase when he thought of what Olivia Hamilton had lived through with her demented husband. He'd wondered about her slight limp...had speculated on her skittishness in his presence.

Now he knew. She'd been abused in the strongest sense of the word. Dear God. The medical reports indicated numerous past fractures that had healed without treatment. The plunge down a staircase had

almost taken her life. She'd finally admitted to her
doctor and friends that her husband had pushed her.
But the psychological report had been the most hor-
rifying of all. Repeated mental abuse to the point she
now feared anything that reminded her of that life.

She'd come here, no doubt seeking a fresh start
far away from her past, and look at what she'd
inadvertently stumbled into. The unfairness of it
made his chest constrict all over again. No one
should have to suffer the way Olivia had.

The chief glanced at the files. "There are things
you don't know, Chase."

Fury obliterated all other emotion in a flash. "Like
what? That you didn't even bother interviewing Beverly Bellamy's friends and family, other than the parents? Or that forensics wasn't scheduled to come
back like you said?" He surged to his feet. "Why all
the lies? I don't understand."

His uncle met his gaze, his blue eyes, the mark of
the Fraleys, incredibly calm in light of Chase's accusations. "Sit down and I'll tell you everything."

"You'll tell me everything anyway," Chase snapped,
his hands at his waist, impatience pounding through his
veins. Someone had murdered Beverly Bellamy. Olivia
could be in danger, as well. He would have the truth.

"I've just spent the last two hours interviewing
Edna Bradley."

The statement took Chase aback. Olivia's housekeeper? "For what purpose?"

The chief sighed wearily and dropped into a chair as if too exhausted to stand a moment longer. "I've been watching the inn. I knew something wasn't right." His gaze bore determinedly into Chase's. "As soon as I had spoken to Beverly's parents and ensured there were no skeletons rattling around in the girl's closet, I felt certain the motivation revolved around the inn. So I've been doing a good bit of surveillance. Ralph Cook appeared to be coming and going at rather odd hours, not his usual eight-to-five shift."

Chase shook his head. "I can't believe you're trying to lay this at Ralph Cook's door. He wouldn't—"

"You're wrong, Chase," his uncle interrupted. "Edna told me she'd noticed Olivia as well as Ralph behaving oddly, in particular after I openly accused him of the vandalism. So, I followed him home this evening at five-thirty."

A new kind of anxiety mushroomed inside Chase. "Then why didn't you bring him in?"

The chief shook his head. "Because he gave me the slip. That's why I went to Edna, to see if she had noticed anything. She was my only other hope of getting to the truth."

Chase flung his arms outward in disbelief. "You really think that Ralph killed Beverly?"

The chief reached into his interior coat pocket and withdrew a plastic bag. He placed it on the desk.

Chase didn't have to pick it up to know what it contained. The jeweled sheath that belonged with the letter opener…the murder weapon in the Bellamy case.

"Oddly enough," the chief went on, "when I got to Edna's, she was just about to call me. When she did the laundry at the inn this afternoon she changed some linens and found this—" he tapped the plastic bag "—in Olivia Hamilton's bedroom, hidden beneath the mattress."

The reality of what he was suggesting slammed into Chase like water breaking on the rocks. "You can't be serious."

The chief nodded. "Edna also told me that she'd seen Ralph and Ms. Hamilton engaged in what looked like intense conversations or confrontations—always out of her earshot. She got the impression Ralph was questioning the orders he'd been given. Don't get me wrong here," his uncle asserted, "Edna thinks highly of Olivia, but when I pushed, she admitted that she was afraid the woman might be bordering on a breakdown of some sort. Real jumpy, acting kind of funny about everything, and too quiet…withdrawn."

Stunned, Chase could scarcely voice what he knew his uncle to be saying. "You think Olivia either orchestrated or carried out this murder? For what purpose? To torture herself?" The ferocity of the emotions soaring through him now tilted his equilibrium, making him feel unsteady on his feet. This was insane.

"I believe she's mentally unstable. That perhaps she even killed her husband." He shrugged. "Maybe it was self-defense, who knows? She came all the way out here for a fresh start and things started to go wrong. The only thing she knew to do was to take desperate measures. I told you, Chase, that she was a desperate woman. Desperate people do desperate things. Who's to say she isn't as crazy as a loon?"

He tapped one of the files Chase held. "Didn't you read that research I did on serial killers? Most of them were abused in one way or another as children. I think Olivia Hamilton's abusive husband may have pushed her over the edge."

Chase had read the research all right and it didn't add up to anything in his opinion. His uncle was clearly grasping at straws. Chase wasn't listening to any more of this. He grabbed his keys. "If you think you can prove it," he challenged, "arrest her. Personally, I think she might be the one in danger. Whoever did this may not be finished yet."

The chief lunged to his feet. "Are you implying that someone on this island would be capable of murder just to shut that place down?" His own fury roared in every word.

"You accused Ralph Cook. Why not?"

The chief stabbed a finger at Chase's chest. "I accused him of being caught up in the woman's spell. I didn't say anything about him committing the murder."

"You're wrong," Chase growled.

"No," his uncle snapped. "You are. You're allowing your obsession with the woman to color your judgment, just like your daddy did."

Chase put his face close to his uncle's. "Maybe I am, but I'll take my chances. What you're suggesting is crazy. She'd be stupid to do something like this even if she were capable. That inn is her livelihood, why would she jeopardize that?"

"Maybe for the publicity," Chief Fraley offered unrepentantly, then shrugged. "Maybe because she just can't help herself. Whatever the case, I'm putting out an APB on Cook," he went on. "And then I'm going for a search warrant on the inn. Fair warning—after that, I plan to arrest her."

"You do what you have to do." Chase hurled the words back at him. "And I'll do what I have to." With that said he walked out, slamming the door behind him.

Chase strode to his vehicle, ignoring the pouring rain. He'd warn Olivia that she needed to find an attorney. He would help her. Find a way to prove his uncle wrong.

He swore hotly, repeatedly, as he started the engine, then fastened his seat belt. This whole thing was completely out of control. He didn't doubt that his uncle felt he was doing the right thing, but he'd clearly had it in for Olivia from the moment she'd arrived on the island—which meant he wasn't being objective. Maybe dredging up the past had pushed *him* over some edge.

Chase's cell phone rang, dragging him from the troubling thoughts. He pulled it from the carrier at his waist and flipped it open. "Chase Fraley."

"Deputy Fraley, this is dispatch."

Chase's senses moved to a higher state of alert. "What's up?"

"Got a call a couple minutes ago from a woman who sounded more than a little hysterical. She asked for you, but as soon as she realized she'd gotten 9-1-1 instead of your office she hung up. I attempted to call back but didn't get an answer. She was on line long enough for the system to pinpoint the location."

Uneasiness slid through Chase. "What's the address?"

The dispatcher rattled off the island address that turned Chase's blood to ice.

"Got it," he said and ended the call. He tossed the cell phone into the seat and rocketed away from the curb flanking city hall.

The hysterical woman had been Olivia. The address, her inn. Chase imagined every sort of horror in the few precious minutes it took him to reach the long winding drive that led to the inn. About fifty yards from the house he skidded to a stop when he came upon Olivia's car sitting in the middle of the drive.

He jumped from his SUV without even bothering

to close the door. She was in the car. Sitting up. Alive. Relief gushed in his chest.

She stared up at him through the trails of water sliding down the glass of the driver's side window. He tried to open the door but it was locked.

"Unlock the car, Olivia," he called loudly enough for her to hear over the still raging storm. Lightning flashed and he got his first good glimpse of her starkly pale face. Absolute terror glinted in her brown eyes.

Her movements robotic, she depressed the unlock button.

He opened the door and crouched down to put himself at eye level with her. "Are you all right?" he asked softly, his eyes visually examining what he could see of her body.

"I can't go back in the house."

Her voice was so small he almost didn't hear her. "Tell me what happened," he urged, afraid to touch her but wanting to so badly he could hardly restrain himself.

She looked back at the inn. "I think…something is in there."

It took Chase several minutes, but finally he talked her into getting into his SUV. The robe she wore was soaked. She shook so brutally her teeth chattered. The cool night air combined with the rain had no doubt chilled her to the bone, but he imagined her physical condition was more a result of the fear he'd seen in her eyes than the cold.

But she needed to get out of those wet clothes. With that in mind, he drove up to the inn. The front door stood wide open.

Chase shut off the engine and turned to her. "Is someone in there?"

She struggled with her answer. "I—I'm not sure."

"I'm going inside to check it out. I'll lock the doors. You'll be safe in here."

Livvy shook her head. "Please," she pleaded. "Don't leave me alone."

The concern on Chase's face gave her such relief. Thank God he'd come. She'd known she could count on him.

"All right. Let's check it out."

Once they were inside and Chase had secured the front door, Livvy gathered her scattered wits and told him everything that had happened. She led him through each room, finally coming to the kitchen where the cupboard still stood open, the tins of tea staring out at her, taunting her.

Chase stood silent a moment. Her hopes fell. He thought she was crazy. She should have seen that coming. Even she had to admit that the whole thing sounded completely nuts.

"Okay," he said finally. "Let's consider what we've got here."

Hope glimmered once more.

"The house is empty and secure. But the music was real. We have to assume the weeping was, as well." He indicated the cupboard. "It's possible Edna could have taken it upon herself to order a different blend of tea." He looked down at Livvy. "That's something we can confirm tomorrow morning."

She nodded. This was good. A plan. She needed a plan. But a part of her couldn't believe that with all the blends of tea on the market that Edna would have ordered that particular one. And so much of it…

"Let's see if we can find where that weeping was coming from," he suggested.

Livvy blinked back the tears that had crested. He believed her. Thank God. She'd been so afraid that no one would.

They started upstairs where she'd first heard the sound. From there they searched every room, every closet, every single nook and cranny. Chase Fraley didn't miss a thing.

But they found nothing.

Until they reached the downstairs laundry room. In the storage closet where the vacuum cleaners and miscellaneous mops were kept, high on a shelf above Edna's line of vision, was a cassette player. Wires ran from the player to the ceiling above it.

From his position on a step stool, Chase counted four different wires. "They probably lead to speakers located in various places in the house." He studied the cassette player again. "It can be set like an alarm clock, allowing the playing of the tape to start at specified times." He depressed the rewind button, then the play button and within seconds the distant, forlorn sound of weeping could be heard upstairs.

He shut the machine off. "Let's leave it where it is so we don't do any more damage to any prints that might be here."

Livvy nodded. "What do we do now?" She shivered. Her robe had started to dry but it was still a little damp and she felt as cold as a Sub-Zero freezer.

Chase stepped down off the stool. "We get you warmed up."

His clothes were wet, as well. "What about you?"

He smiled, not his usual high-voltage charmer, but one brimming with warmth. "I'll be fine."

Livvy led the way up to her bedroom. No way was she going anywhere alone. She was glad she hadn't had to ask him to accompany her.

She rounded up a towel for him and retreated back into her bathroom. She blew out the candles she'd forgotten all about. Thank God a fire hadn't started. Working quickly, she peeled off her robe, swabbed her body with a dry towel and slipped on a flannel gown. It fell all the way to her ankles and fit like a tent, but it was warm. She'd worry about panties later.

She tugged a comb through her damp hair and hurried to rejoin Chase in her bedroom.

He'd removed his shirt and was in the process of scrubbing the towel over his sculpted chest. Livvy paused in the open doorway, her gaze riveted to his movements. She had known his body would be beautiful. Heat slid through her, warming her as nothing else could. A throb of need followed the path of the heat, reminding her of just how long it had been since she'd wanted...

He looked up, apparently noted her wide-eyed gaze. "Sorry." He gestured to the shirt he'd draped over the back of a chair. "I thought I'd take it down and put it in the dryer for a few minutes. If that's okay."

She nodded jerkily.

His gaze roved over her granny gown. "You look comfortable."

Definitely not a compliment, but he was right. She hugged her arms around her chest. "I feel...comfortable." And she did...oddly. She felt no need to withdraw. It felt right being alone in her bedroom with him.

Good Lord. What was she thinking?

Her cheeks flushed. "Would you like some coffee?"

"That'd be nice."

She started across the room, a spear of unexpected pain bringing her to an abrupt halt. She winced. Rubbed at her leg.

"You okay?" He was at her side so fast she swayed.

"I'm okay." She remembered falling outside. All the fear and excitement had kept her from noticing the nagging pain, she supposed. She rubbed her thigh a little harder and considered that her worn-out body only added to the granny picture. How romantic. She shook herself. What man would want damaged goods? And she was damaged, inside and out.

"Olivia," he said softly.

Meeting his gaze proved the most difficult task. She didn't want to see pity in his eyes and she was certain that's what she would find.

"I know what happened to you," he went on when her gaze at last came to rest on his.

Her heart bumped hard against her sternum as she recognized what she saw in that sea-blue gaze. Not sympathy, not pity. Desire…need, almost as strong as the need strumming through her soul.

She twisted her fingers together, unsure how to react. "It's not such a pretty story." She had to look away, couldn't bear the intensity any longer. So much had happened. Everything was out of balance…out of control.

"I would never hurt you, Olivia," he murmured. "I want you to know that. I'll do everything in my power to protect you."

She lifted her face up to his, desperate to believe he could mean such sweet words. "I don't know what's happening," she admitted. "I…" She shook her head. "Beverly's murder. The tape." She shivered. "The tea. Who's doing this?"

He caressed her cheek so gently that she whimpered with longing. No one had touched her that way in so long.

"I promise I will get to the bottom of this. I won't let anyone else hurt you."

The feel of his warm hand, the strength emanating from his touch…made her want to lean into him.

"Thank you." She worked up the courage to say the words. "Thank you for believing in me."

She saw him lean toward her. Her body instantly went rigid with trepidation.

"I have to do this," he whispered as his lips brushed the same cheek he'd caressed.

Livvy's eyes closed, her heart fluttered like a caged bird.

"I'm not taking any chances…I'm staying with you tonight." She felt his words against her cheek, those full lips moving with infinite softness and restraint.

For the first time in nearly half a decade she followed her heart, reached out to another human being. Her arms went around his lean waist and she wilted against that powerful chest.

"Hold me."

She vaguely recognized the desperate plea as her own voice…her own aching need.

"All night long," he promised.

CHAPTER SEVEN

AT 2:00 A.M. Livvy awoke. The digital clock on her bedside table glared insistently through the darkness.

For several seconds she held very still, grappling to get her bearings.

The feel of a big, strong male body next to her sent a barb of terror ripping through her before she remembered who that body belonged to. Chase. That knowledge rose above the other frightening scenes from the night before that flashed one after the other across her mind's eye.

She was safe.

He would protect her.

She exhaled a heavy breath. He would find out who was doing this to her...who had murdered Beverly.

She tried to think if a dream had awakened her. Chase had held her close to him for a long while. After he'd dried his clothes, he'd settled her onto her bed, then lain beside her. He'd held her close in that same way all night, not once taking things further than that chaste embrace. She gave in to the urge now to glide her palm over his chest. She was glad he hadn't slipped his shirt back on before lying down with her.

The sensations of pleasure that flooded her made her pulse pound and her heart race. His skin felt so soft and smooth, the muscles beneath so powerful and hard. The contrast intrigued her. She licked her lips, held her breath and kissed that soft skin, tasted him. Couldn't help herself.

He groaned, tightened his arms around her. "I thought you were asleep," he whispered.

Her face heated with embarrassment. She was glad he couldn't see. "I thought you were." No telling what he thought of her now.

Chase rolled to his side, peered down at her through the darkness. "I should move to the chair," he suggested huskily.

Livvy shook her head. "Stay with me." She splayed her fingers over his chest again, relishing the wondrous feelings that mere touch evoked.

He took her hand in his and brought it to his lips, pressed a tender kiss there. "We should be careful."

He was right. She wasn't ready for this to go any further. Deep down she knew that, but a part of her had yearned for this kind of intimacy for so long.

He tensed. Sat up.

"What is it?" She hadn't heard anything.

He moved up from the bed and across the room

to look out the window. She hurried to his side, unable to wait on a response.

The storm had passed, taking with it the cold rain. But in its wake had come the fog, thick and swirling, ghostly. She shivered as she watched it curl around a lamppost in the courtyard. Chase had suggested they leave the exterior lights on. Now she was glad she had, though she still couldn't see a thing except the wispy snakelike path of the ever-moving mist.

Chase grabbed his shirt and tugged it on. "I'm going to take a look around outside."

"What?" He had heard something.

He pulled on his utility belt next. She didn't need any light to see what that meant. His weapon was among the items on that belt.

"You think someone's out there."

It wasn't a question.

"I just want to be sure," he offered, his voice devoid of any telltale emotion, unlike hers. He'd surely heard the fear in hers.

"I'm going with you."

He took her by the shoulders and held her still. Though she couldn't make out the features of his face, her eyes had adjusted enough to know that he looked directly at her.

"You stay here. Lock the door behind me. Call 9-1-1 if you hear anything suspicious."

A new rush of fear detonated in her chest. "Call someone now, Chase. Don't go out there alone."

"I'll be fine. You just do as I say."

She didn't want to stay put, but he was right. He had a gun. He had the training. He knew how to handle this sort of thing. "Okay."

Reluctantly she followed him to the door.

"Lock it," he ordered. "Don't let anyone in but me, not even the chief. Call 9-1-1 if I don't come back."

Before she could demand to know why he'd specifically mentioned the chief, he was gone. She closed the door and locked it. She hurried to the bedside table, fumbled for the phone, then went back to the window and strained to see anything in the eerie mist.

She sent a quick prayer heavenward for God to keep Chase safe.

The reality that whoever was behind these incidents was no mere ghost set in all over again. James Hamilton was dead, but whoever had committed these acts knew what he had done to her. Knew how to use her past against her. Maybe the whole point was for her to look crazy. A crazy woman might very well murder her employee and not even remember it.

Had Chase's warning meant that the chief believed she was guilty? Or had his warning carried a more ominous message?

She pressed her shaking fingers to her mouth, the phone clutched to her chest. God, what did all this mean?

A crashing sound echoed up from the courtyard. She peered through the fog. Had Chase bumped into something in the murky mist? Could she take the chance? No. She had to call for help. Now. He shouldn't have gone out there alone.

She pressed the talk button and then the three necessary numbers. She frowned. Nothing. She tried again. No dial tone.

Livvy threw the phone aside. Where was her cell phone? Downstairs in her purse.

Without hesitating, Livvy unlocked the door and rushed down the stairs, ignoring the insistent throb in her leg. She moved through the darkness, alert to every sound, afraid to turn on a light. She found her purse. Made the call. Refused to stay on the line…she had to find Chase.

She listened.

Nothing.

She couldn't let that stop her.

Cold air wafted in from the doors leading to the courtyard. She didn't need any light to know they stood wide open beyond the stairs. He'd gone out there.

Before good sense could dissuade her, she padded quietly to the open doors and strained to see through the thick gloom. She couldn't see a thing.

Her heart hammering, she carefully eased out onto the courtyard. The cold, wet flagstone sent another fizz of adrenaline upward from the soles of her bare feet. She opened her mouth to call out to Chase but quickly snapped it closed. Not smart. If someone else was out here, she would give her location away.

She moved cautiously forward, listening, trying hard to make out any moving form in the creepy fog.

Her foot struck something solid. She stumbled but caught herself. Barely.

A body.

Anticipation bursting in her veins, she squatted, her head starting to spin. As if on cue, a sliver of moonlight cut through the darkness just enough for her to see that it was Chase and then it went dark again.

A scream died in her throat. She quickly ran her hands over him, searching for injury. Leaned her face close to his to see if he was breathing. He was. Thank God.

Her breath coming in ragged spurts, she forced her brain to analyze the situation. She felt no sign of injury, then her fingers encountered something warm and thick in his hair. Her heart climbed into her throat. She forced herself to pay attention…to think. A lump and gash. But his breathing was steady. Help was on its way. He would be all right. He had to be all right.

Then she smelled it.

Smoke.

Her gaze shifted across the courtyard. Her chest seized with terror when she saw a flame lick upward through the darkness.

The garden shed was on fire.

Oh, God!

Livvy shot to her feet and ran as best she could over the stone courtyard's slick surface. She carefully avoided the obstacles she knew to be present. She had no idea what she would do when she got there but she had to do something. The shed was very close to the house. Would the dampness from the rain slow the flames? If a spark were to fly onto the roof of the inn…

She skidded to a stop at the gardener's shed. The fire appeared to have started on the inside. The exterior walls looked unharmed as of yet but the flames were quickly devouring their way through the wooden shingle roof. The door stood ajar.

Her first thought was to look inside, at the same time a self-protective instinct warned her to stay clear. But she couldn't. She had to be sure no one was inside. She couldn't risk allowing anyone else to die at Lost Angel Inn.

She shrugged off the hesitation and rushed to the door, the pain in her thigh shooting sharply up to her hip, sending its own kind of warning. She'd pushed too far tonight.

When the door banged against the far wall and her eyes surveyed the interior, a new terror ballooned in her chest.

Ralph lay facedown on the floor.

She dashed inside and tried to rouse him.

"Ralph!" She shook him hard, but he didn't respond.

The crackle of the fire, the falling embers, alerted her that she didn't have much time.

Using all her strength, she grabbed him under the arms and dragged him toward the door. She grunted with effort, coughed as the smoke seared her lungs.

Hurry!

She tugged hard, falling backward as she pulled him into the cold night air.

Scrambling for purchase, she dragged him a little further away. She felt for a pulse, put her face close to his. He was still breathing, but it was shallow and weak. She needed help.

She stood and hurried toward the house, as fast as her lame gait would allow. She needed an ambulance. Help should be coming but she couldn't be sure if EMTs would automatically be sent.

In her haste she completely forgot the wet flagstone...the fountain...the digging...

Her feet hit the mud, flew out from under her and she landed in a heap in the wide, shallow ditch that had been excavated near the fountain.

She disregarded the pain arcing up her leg, fought to get back on her feet. The slippery mud made it difficult.

Her fingers dug into the sodden earth in an attempt to brace herself for some upward momentum.

She stilled.

The fingers of her right hand had encountered something long and hard…slim and smooth.

She plopped back down on her knees, pulled her hand and the object upward. The fingers of her left hand traced the length and form as her mind assimilated the clues her senses provided.

Long…cylinder-shaped…

Moonlight peeked from between the clouds once more, highlighting the slender white object in her hand.

Bone.

Human.

The angel hovering over the fountain peering down at her seemed to cry out in agony.

She heard the scream echoing off the walls of the inn, only then recognizing that it had come from her.

The bone dropped into the muddy water with a splash.

Punishing fingers gripped her from behind, dragged her upward. A brutal hand covered her mouth before she could scream again.

She was suddenly moving backward, being hauled by some force that she couldn't see. Human. Male.

For what seemed like an eternity, she couldn't move. Couldn't fight back. But when they rounded the corner of the west wing, survival instinct kicked in once more. She tried to jerk free, pounded with her fists, dug her feet into the wet ground.

Her assailant's grip turned even more brutal. Her

efforts didn't slow his forward movement in the least. When they passed between the far corner of the house and the blazing garden shed, she tried to twist around to see her captor's face in the light of the flames.

He wrenched her back, almost snapping her neck. Fear surged anew inside her. Livvy relaxed in his hold. Her heart flopped helplessly in her rib cage. She had to do something. Had to get free.

The terrain under her feet changed...the grass gave way to gravel...then back to grass.

The cliffs.

He was moving her toward the cliffs.

She struggled again. Fought to free herself. Her elbow collided with an object at his waist, sending a shattering vibration up her arm.

And then she knew.

Chief Fraley.

The weapon on his belt was just like the one on Chase's. Her elbow had collided with the unmistakable butt.

He flung her to the ground. She landed so close to the jutting land's edge, the sudden downward drop of the landscape made her head spin as if she were still falling.

"Stand up!"

She looked up at him, the gruff order echoing over the restless sea. His frame vaguely visible in the veiled moonlight.

"Why are you doing this?"

"Because you wouldn't leave it alone," he snarled. "I didn't want to hurt anyone, but you wouldn't give up and go away."

She shook her head, confused. "I don't understand."

"I didn't mind so much that you reopened the inn but the renovations had to stop. I couldn't let you do that. But you screwed up everything, causing the death of an innocent woman, then there was no turning back. I had to stop you at all cost."

He was the one who'd killed Beverly.

The revelation shocked her, rumbled through her like an earthquake. Nausea roiled in her stomach.

"That's right," he said. "I killed her. I thought she was you."

Livvy hadn't realized she'd said the words out loud. But his admission, spoken with such indifference, sent rage rocketing through her.

"What did you care about the renovations?" she demanded. She carefully got to her feet, conscious of her closeness to that lethal precipice.

A bout of déjà vu struck her…just like before…she would fall…only this time she wouldn't survive.

"All I wanted was to keep the past where it belonged," he said, sounding unexpectedly weary, "but you wouldn't let it go."

Everything…all of it…coalesced at once. "You buried that body in my courtyard. That's why you didn't want me digging." The chief hadn't complained so much as the interior renovations had taken place, but the very day the digging around the fountain had occurred, Beverly had been murdered.

"It was an accident. I loved him…"

Livvy couldn't make out the details of the chief's face but she heard the regret in his voice and she knew then and there whose body had been buried.

"You killed Chase's father."

The words rang in the air, a death toll for her since she would never be allowed to live with the knowledge.

"I should have moved the remains a long time ago, but I never figured on anyone like you coming along. Now it's too late. More lives will be lost because of you."

"Ralph?" Her heart surged into her throat. He needed immediate medical assistance. And Chase…God…Chase was hurt, too.

"That's right. The two of you did this. Edna took all the bait I'd laid. Went along with my every theory. She'll be my material witness."

Livvy clenched her fists into determined balls. "Chase will never believe you." He had to be all right. Help had to get here in time. She had to keep the chief talking until then so he wouldn't have time to go back to finish what he'd started with Chase or Ralph. Though she doubted it would do her any good. Even without any real assistance from the moon she knew he had drawn his weapon.

"Eventually he'll believe me. He always does. I've got enough documentation on your background and what can happen to a person suffering from post traumatic stress syndrome to convince any jury. You couldn't help yourself." He made a sound that wasn't quite a laugh.

"I'll make everyone believe that you killed Ralph to try to blame this on him. But I caught you…you struggled to get away and well…" He gestured to the cliffs. "The rest will just be another tale for folks to pass along to the tourists. I'll clean up my own mess and call in the mainland authorities. Poor Chase will have been unconscious through the whole thing. You even fooled him."

That's why she'd found that bone in the mud, the chief had been getting rid of the evidence. Had likely just finished digging up the remains.

"You're throwing Wayne's remains over the cliff."

"That's where everyone thinks he is anyway."

His words were empty, emotionless.

"Why did you kill your own brother?"

The chief charged her. She couldn't back up, barely kept her balance as she stood on the very edge, held herself so very still. He wrapped his fingers in her hair and snapped her face upward, nearer to his.

"Because he was obsessed," he snarled. "I had Melissa's murderer. It was Maxwell, I knew it. But Wayne wouldn't believe it. He kept coming out here and pining over her like a fool, trying to find the answer. He'd had a beautiful wife once, had a good, strong son. It wasn't right. I should have been the one grieving over Melissa's death. People should have been comforting me. But he always got the best. I had to make due with his castoffs. Just like this job. I was never as good as him…never."

Livvy couldn't believe what she was hearing. The man had obviously lived in his brother's shadow for years. "You were in love with Melissa Carlyle, too," she murmured.

"That's right," he growled. "Even I had feelings back then. But she paid me no mind, was too busy flirting with my brother and screwing my best friend. I wasn't good enough for her. But I would never have hurt her." His grip on Livvy relaxed. "I loved her." A bark of cruel laughter issued from his throat. "It wasn't right for him to grieve for her…she should have been mine. He'd already had a wife…had the son I'd always wanted. Had it all. The whole town loved him. With his help, I could have nailed Maxwell even without real evidence, but he wouldn't go along, so the bastard walked."

And there it was. Jealousy…obsession.

"So you killed your own brother to stop him," Livvy reiterated. God, how sad. Chase would be devastated.

"I didn't mean to kill him." The chief released her entirely now, so abruptly she almost toppled over that treacherous edge. "But I couldn't take it anymore. I found him back at the inn, pining around like a fool. Looking for clues that didn't exist. I told him how I felt. How he was being selfish. We fought. He hit his head on the fountain…it was an accident."

"Why did you bury him there?" Livvy asked, surprised at his lack of foresight. It would have been so much simpler to have thrown him over the cliffs. *Like he is about to do with you,* a voice cautioned.

"I couldn't risk his body falling on the rocks," the chief murmured more to himself than to Livvy. "Too much time had passed to get away with blaming it on Melissa's murderer. I couldn't be sure Maxwell wouldn't have an alibi. So I buried Wayne next to the fountain."

The chief moved toward her. "You caused this," he accused.

"Don't move!"

Chase.

Livvy's heart jolted with equal measures relief and fear.

The chief spun away from her, focusing his attention on the new threat. As the two men argued, she tried to ease away from the edge.

"Don't make me shoot," Chase warned.

Livvy froze. This couldn't be happening again. No! Her mind reeled. History was about to repeat itself…

For long moments nobody budged. Then just as she moved to throw herself to the ground, the chief dropped his gun.

"It was an accident," he said, the hollow words directed at Chase. "I tried to protect you from it."

And then he jumped.

Livvy screamed.

Chase was suddenly at her side.

"It's all right now," he murmured against her temple as he held her close.

She sagged against his strength. Let the tears flow.

Abruptly she remembered, pulled back. "Ralph!"

"Shh." He rocked her in his arms. "Help is here."

Everything happened at once then. She was dimly aware of the mainland police hurrying toward them.

An EMT from a local emergency clinic followed immediately. He assured her that Ralph was alive.

Chase's face was covered in blood but he was not seriously injured.

Livvy was bruised and battered but she had survived worse.

She was alive. Chase was alive.

For now that was enough.

He stayed close as the EMT checked her over.

His presence gave her the courage to get through the night.

The night the final mystery of Lost Angel Inn was laid to rest.

EPILOGUE

SNOW FELL SILENTLY outside Lost Angel Inn.

Livvy peered out at the delightful, thickening blanket of white. The weatherman had forecast another six inches on top of the ten they'd gotten three days ago.

"Are you going to take this tray or daydream?" Clara scolded.

Livvy jerked to attention. "Sorry."

The inn was filled to capacity, both wings. Christmas was only one week away, and she was booked for the entire season.

Smiling, she took the tray laden with lovely biscuits and muffins and backed out of the kitchen. The guests would be stirring soon and no one wanted to wait for Clara's famous breakfast treats, including a new, special blend of coffee available no other place on the planet. Clara's own secret recipe.

Ralph and Edna were scurrying about, as well. Both had been cruelly used by the chief but were putting the past behind them. The chief had been the one to special order the Assam tea and place it in the kitchen cupboard that fateful night. He'd prepared the CD to play that haunting music as well as set up the weeping sounds.

But all that was over now. Livvy settled the tray on the buffet and began to arrange the baked goods on the various platters. Hmm. They smelled heavenly as always.

Footsteps echoed behind her. Before she could turn around strong arms had enveloped her.

"And how is my Livvy this morning?" Chase stole a kiss before she could answer.

She couldn't possibly resist, even if Clara had a stroke in the kitchen waiting for her. Livvy melted in his arms, loving the feel of him...the taste of his lips.

"Aren't you supposed to be at the office?" she inquired between his attentive little teasing nips.

Chase had intended to walk away from law enforcement but the whole town had come out in support of his staying. A proper funeral and burial for his father had been conducted. A separate, quiet service had been conducted for the chief, a man consumed by jealousy and obsession.

Any lingering tarnish to Martin Maxwell's reputation was cleared once and for all. In fact, Christopher and Emily were busily planning a Valentine's Day wedding at Lost Angel Inn.

"Well," Chase mused, those beautiful blue eyes staring with adoration down at her, "I decided to take the morning off and come back home to make love to my wife."

Livvy grinned, her body quivering in response to his words. Lovemaking with Chase was everything it should be and more. It had taken time and he'd been patient, but she'd come around, giving him her full trust. He'd proposed long before that, but she'd put him off until she could be the kind of wife he deserved. One free of the past.

They'd married the weekend before Thanksgiving. Most everyone in town had filed into the inn, taking up every square foot of space to hear their favorite son exchange vows with the woman he loved on the second-story landing of the spectacular staircase.

"Clara might not like my taking a break," Livvy countered, her fingers walking down his shirtfront toward dangerous territory.

"She'll get over it," he said silkily as he swept Livvy into his arms.

She gasped. "Are you sure you're up to this?" she teased as he strode determinedly toward the staircase.

He lifted a skeptical eyebrow. "You're kidding, right?"

She smiled and relaxed against his broad shoulder. "Right," she relented.

He mounted the stairs with no visible effort. He kicked their bedroom door closed behind him and lowered her onto the fluffy down-filled comforter.

"In a few months I doubt you'll be able to do that," she teased as she nestled into the mound of equally fluffy pillows. "Pregnant women put on weight, you know."

He pushed up the hem of her sweater and leaned down to place a gentle kiss on her still flat belly. "I'll just keep you in bed then."

She pulled his face up to hers. "I love you, Chase." She searched his eyes and wondered how on earth she'd gotten so lucky. He'd made her life everything she had ever dreamed it could be. He would be an amazing father, already was the best husband in the world. He'd taken her to a level of happiness that transcended the shadows of her painful past.

"Olivia Fraley, I love you," he echoed.

As if nothing else existed outside that room, he unhurriedly undressed her, then himself. Slowly, thoroughly, he made love to her the way a man should make love to a woman.

Minute by minute, day by day, they would make a new history in this lovely old inn, hopefully filling it with at least four or five sweet little real-life angels of their own.

* * * * *

Look for two new installments of Debra Webb's bestselling series, Colby Agency, coming from Harlequin Intrigue.

October 2004: SITUATION: OUT OF CONTROL.
November 2004: PRIORITY: FULL EXPOSURE.

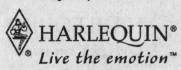

A special bond, a special family...

Logan's Legacy

Because birthright has its privileges and family ties run deep.

FOR LOVE AND FAMILY

by

VICTORIA PADE

When widower Hunter Coltrane's adopted son needed an exact match to his rare blood type, he turned to the Children's Connection and the boy's biological family. Luckily Terese Warwick, a shy beauty with a heart of gold, answered his prayers and breathed new life into his shattered soul.

Available in September 2004.

Where love comes alive™